Life's a Beach

Life's a

ALSO BY
Claire Cook

Summer Blowout

Multiple Choice

Must Love Dogs

Ready to Fall

"Claire Cook has an original voice, a sparkling style, and a window into family life that will make you laugh and cry. *Life's a Beach* is filled with hilarity, sister love and sister hate, juicy arguments and hard-won reconciliations, but most of all, heart."

—ADRIANA TRIGIANI,
BESTSELLING AUTHOR OF
Home to Big Stone Gap

"If I had a sister, I'd want her to be Claire Cook. If I had a summer, I'd want it to be the summer that two sisters stropped their tongues and sparred over everything from fertility to photography to family. And if I could follow up the wry, wacky poignancy of *Must Love Dogs* with any book, it would be *Life's a Beach*. Claire Cook is wicked good."

—JACQUELYN MITCHARD,
BESTSELLING AUTHOR OF
The Deep End of the Ocean AND *Still Summer*

"*Life's a Beach* is a delicious coming-of-age novel—about two forty-something sisters who don't quite manage that feat until it's almost too late. I devoured this slice of family life served up in Claire Cook's inimitably warm and witty style. Tender, touching, and terribly, terribly, funny!"

—MARY KAY ANDREWS,
AUTHOR OF *Savannah Breeze*

"Claire Cook's smart, delightful new book made me laugh on the first page and on every single page all the way through—even when it also made me cry. True, tender, insightful, and hilarious—I loved it."

—PAMELA REDMOND SATRAN,
AUTHOR OF *Suburbanistas*

"Claire Cook has given us a heroine you'll cheer for and a book you won't be able to put down. I loved it."

—KAREN QUINN,
AUTHOR OF *The Ivy Chronicles*
AND *Wife in the Fast Lane*

Beach

Claire Cook

VOICE

Hyperion • New York

The Library of Congress has catalogued the hardcover edition
of this book as follows:

Cook, Claire
     Life's a beach / Claire Cook. — 1st ed.
          p. cm.
     ISBN-10: 1-4013-0324-2
     ISBN-13: 978-1-4013-0324-2
     1. Sisters—Fiction. 2. Middle-aged women—Fiction.
  I. Title.
     PS3553.O55317L54 2007
     813'.54—dc22

                                        2006049227

Paperback ISBN: 978-1-4013-4078-0

Hyperion books are available for special promotions, premi-
ums, or corporate training. For details contact Michael Rentas,
Proprietary Markets, Hyperion, 77 West 66th Street, 12th floor,
New York, New York 10023, or call 212-456-0133.

FIRST PAPERBACK EDITION

10 9 8 7 6 5 4 3 2 1

To Garet and Kaden

ACKNOWLEDGMENTS

A ZILLION THANKS, and more, to the incomparable Lisa Bankoff and Tina Wexler, whose support, advice, laughter, and excitement always make me want to write my next novel just so I can hang out with them some more. Josie Freedman and Michael McCarthy have been right there for me working their movie magic, too, and I'm also very grateful to the foreign rights department and to everyone else at ICM.

I would have followed my brilliant editor Pamela Dorman anywhere, but how lucky am I that she decided to team up with Ellen Archer to start Voice. I'm so proud to be one of the first authors to lend my own voice to their new imprint. Many thanks to Pam and Ellen, and to my fabulous associate editor Sarah Landis and wonderful publicist Beth Gebhard, for their support and guidance, and a heartfelt and alphabetical thank-you to the rest of the talented Hyperion team—Kathleen Carr, Jane Comins, Michelle Ishay, Maha Khalil, Claire McKean, Karen Minster, Shelly Perron, Sarah Rucker, Jessica Wiener, and Katie Wainwright. Thanks so very much to Chris Barba and the Hachette sales group, too.

Gary David Goldberg came into my life to turn *Must Love Dogs* into the movie of my dreams and then stepped it up a notch and became something even more important—a great writer buddy. A huge thanks to Gary for faxing both notes and encouragement.

Thanks so much to Elisabeth Weed for bringing Elias John Amber Hansen with her to the Cape Cod Writers' Center summer conference. Eli was such an original that suddenly a glassblower emerged in the novel I was just beginning to write. Thanks to the many glass artists who answered my questions along the way, especially Don Parkinson of the Sandwich Glass Museum, and also Marj Bates of glassthings.com, who kindly allowed me to crash her workshop. Thanks to Diane Dillon for airline insight and to Charlotte Phinney for support that cuts across the categories. And thanks to Sharon Duran for a funny carwash story that didn't work on paper but inspired a different kind of carwash scene.

Thanks to everyone on the set of the *Must Love Dogs* movie for letting me hang out. I was so sure I'd get kicked off the set for taking notes, but instead everybody from the producers to the actors to the caterers answered all my questions and even started brainstorming ideas for me. I don't think any of them found their way into this novel, but I very much appreciate the encouragement. Thanks to Mike "Moishe" Moyer for being inspirational in the gaffer department, to Cathryn Michon for grrl genius insight into child actors, and to Billy Dowd for answering all my casting questions over a long laugh-filled lunch.

Many, many thanks to my fabulous extended family. It's such a thrill to be discovering more relatives almost every week. And thanks to my wonderful friends, old and new, for cheering me on and talking me up. In fact, so many old friends have come out of the woodwork that I held a random drawing and gave some of you a group cameo in this novel.

A huge thank-you to the booksellers, librarians, and

members of the media who have supported me and spread the word. And I'm forever grateful to my wonderful readers, who through the conduit of my website, www.clairecook.com, have become a kind of virtual extended family.

And my biggest thanks of all, always, go to my husband, Jake Jacobucci, who has turned into one helluva first reader, to our daughter, Garet, for all things cat, and to our son, Kaden, for encouraging Post-its on an early draft: "Good line, Mom!"

Life's a Beach

I WAS SQUEAKY CLEAN AND MY HAIR HAD BEEN CONDI-
tioned for at least two of the suggested three minutes
when the water went cold. I did a quick rinse, then turned
the faucet off. The plastic shower curtain moved a few
inches, and a clean white towel magically appeared. Noah
had already left when I woke up, but maybe he'd only
made a breakfast run. Or maybe he just couldn't stay
away. I smiled.

"Here you go," my mother said from the other side of
the curtain.

I screamed. I wrapped myself in the towel and stepped
out of my tiny square shower and practically into my
mother. "Jesus, Mom, I thought you were . . . someone
else."

"Noah? He left at six-twenty-five this morning. And tell
him to watch that pebble business or he'll break a window." My mother started dabbing my shoulders with another towel.

"Mom, stop."

My mother kept dabbing. There were no limits in our
family. I could clearly remember sitting in the bathtub
with a book one night when I was ten or eleven. My sister,
Geri, had already gone off to college, and my parents had
company for dinner. Suddenly, the door opened and four

adults looked in at me and my bubbles. "Say good night to Mr. and Mrs. O'Brien," my mother said.

Today, my mother was wearing her GIRLS JUST WANNA HAVE FUN T-shirt, and a couple of tiny beaded braids in her thick gray hair made her look like she'd just come back from the Caribbean. I was kind of wishing she were there now. "Listen," she said, "your father and I have found the townhouse of our dreams. The Village of Silver Springs. Fitness center with personal trainers, billiards, bingo, indoor boccie ball, salsa lessons. You know how your father loves to dance."

"It's not just a townhouse, it's a lifestyle," a strange voice said.

I peeked behind my mother to see two women wearing red hats. They were measuring what I liked to think of as my carriage house with a bright yellow tape measure. My cat watched silently from the rumpled sheets of my still-pulled-out sleeper sofa.

On my best days, I could convince myself that, with me at the far end of my parents' driveway, and my sister and her family about a mile away, we had our own little Kennedy compound. On my worst days, I had to admit that I lived in an apartment over my parents' garage.

The women waved. I hiked my towel up a little higher. "Mom," I whispered, "get them out of here. Now."

My mother reached down and scratched my cat under his chin. She said, "Hi, handsome," and he purred his acknowledgment. She nudged yesterday's bra, which had somehow ended up in the middle of the floor, with her toe. "You're going to have to start keeping things a little bit neater around here, honey."

One of the women, the one wearing a jeweled red visor,

didn't seem to be the least bit bothered by the fact that I was dripping all over the apartment she was trying to help my mother sell right out from under me. In fact, she acted like I wasn't even there. "A FROG is a nice bonus feature," she said. "Everybody loves a FROG."

"Excuse me," I said, not that it was any of her business. "But, actually, it's not a Finished Room Over the Garage. It has a bath and a kitchen, which makes it technically more of a carriage house."

Everybody ignored me. "If you bury a statue of St. Joseph in the ground," the visor woman said, "the house will get scooped up right away. Guaranteed."

"Mom," I said with every bit of outrage I could muster without dropping my towel. I wondered if telling these women this wasn't a legal rental unit would make them lose interest, or if it would only get me in trouble with my mother.

"You have to be careful how you bury it," the other woman said. Her hat had a frothy drape of red netting that covered her eyes, so maybe I really was invisible to her. "My cousin said she faced hers away from the house when she buried it, and the house across the street sold instead."

"Upside down and facing the house is the way to go," the other woman said. "If he's upside down, that way St. Joseph will work extra hard to get out of the ground and onto the mantel of your new townhouse."

My mother was actually nodding, as if these two trespassing red-hatted women were not completely and certifiably insane. "Well," I said loudly, "I don't want to keep you. Sounds like you'd better get over to the mall fast before they run out of statues."

Now they were all nodding, so I started inching my

mother toward the door, hoping the other two would follow. They did, though the first woman had unfortunately mastered the art of walking and talking at the same time. "But," she said, "for St. Joseph to be fully effective, you also have to do all the necessary fix-ups, price the house to reflect the current market, and of course, properly stage the home. Cut flowers, cookies baking in the oven, some pine-scent potpourri. *Then* you add the statue."

We were almost there. My mother leaned over and gave me a kiss on the cheek, and I reached past her to open the door. "Sorry we have to run," she said.

"Not a problem," I said as I hiked my towel up again.

"We'll catch up later, honey."

"You bet we will," I said.

When I slammed the door behind them, I just missed the backside of one red-hatted Realtor.

⟢

THE DOWNSIDE OF LIVING in a carriage house over your parents' garage is that you're easy to find. "Your mother," my father said when I answered his knock on my door about three minutes later, "wants to sell the house."

"Gee, Dad, thanks for the warning."

I was dressed now, but steam was still coming out of my ears. I'd just put down the phone after leaving an angry message for my mother. I'd been going over and over the piece of my mind I was going to give her when she finally came home long enough to call me back. She was probably still off saint shopping with her red hat friends. They were a seriously bad influence on her, in my opinion.

My father didn't look so hot. He was wearing shorts

with a yellowed cotton tank-style undershirt, and one brown sock and one reddish one. He was color-blind, and from the time I was six or so I knew that whenever his socks didn't match, it was a sure sign he was fighting with my mother.

"Don't worry," I said, thinking a little levity might help us both. "You can move in here with me."

Not even a giggle. My father looked at me from under his hooded blue eyes. The hair that was no longer on his head seemed to have traveled to his bushy white eyebrows, I noticed.

He looked over his shoulder. "Open the door," he said. "Fast."

I did, and he pushed past me, carrying a big black trash bag. "Gee, thanks, Dad," I said. "But you shouldn't have."

"Hey, Toots, where can we stash this to keep it safe?" He'd clearly been watching too much television since he retired.

Though technically larger than a FROG, it was a very small apartment, with a dollhouse-size bathroom and an illegally added kitchenette. I stalled for time. "Do you mean *we* in the royal sense, or are you suggesting your daughter join you in a life of crime?"

My cat jumped off the couch and circled my father and his garbage bag. Then he pounced. "Down, Boy," my father and I said in one voice. He dug in his claws anyway and teetered on top of the bag, so my father waltzed the bag back to the couch. My father had always been a good dancer.

He put the bag on the couch, and my cat disembarked when he realized the fun was over. My father reached down and pulled up his red sock until it was even with his brown one. "Listen, Dollface. You've got a nice lily pad here, but it's all gonna go away if we don't play our cards right."

Now he was talking like he was in a bad movie. My mother must really be serious about this. "I'm with you, Dad. We have to stop her before it's too late." Apparently talking like you were in a bad movie was contagious.

My father straightened up and put both hands on his lower back. He swiveled his hips around a little, as if he wanted to be sure they were still working. "Don't worry, Toots, I already have a plan cooked up."

Ever since I could remember, my father had always been there for me. I felt my eyes tear up. "Great, Dad. What is it?"

He didn't answer. He was too busy stuffing his garbage bag into my tiny shower.

∞

"DID YOU KNOW Mom wants to sell the house?" I asked my eight-years-and-three-months-older sister Geri when she answered her phone that afternoon. "And she won't even call me back to discuss it."

"You shouldn't still be living there anyway."

"I'm not living here. I'm just staying here for a little while until I figure out what I want to do next."

"Technically, two years is not a little while."

I tried not to do the math in my head. "I have *not* been here for two years."

"Have too."

"Have not."

"Yes, you have. It's time to get a life again, Ginger."

Get a life, Ginger, I mimicked silently. I didn't say it out loud because I thought there might still be a slight chance I could talk her into being on my side, so I didn't want to piss her off unnecessarily. I twisted some silver wire around a piece of bottle green sea glass while I held the phone against my ear with one shoulder. "So you *did* know," I finally said. "Gee, thanks for telling me."

My sister sighed. "Every four seconds a baby boomer turns fifty," she whined into the phone.

I held the receiver away from me and looked at it, thinking it might somehow cough up the missing conversational segue. Geri was still waiting for a reply so I said, "Think of all the company you'll have."

"And every three seconds, more or less," she continued as if I hadn't said a word, "I consider the fact that I'm about to be one of them."

"Excuse me, but what exactly does this have to do with Mom selling the house?" I asked.

"It's always about you, isn't it?"

I added another loop of wire, keeping my eyes closed so it wouldn't come out looking too anal. "Come on, Gerr, you have almost a month left."

"I wish. It's not even half a month." My sister sighed again.

I fished a hypoallergenic pierced earring wire from a Ziploc bag and worked it into a little loop I'd made at what I'd randomly decided would be the top of the earring. I executed another perfect twist with my wire, then walked to the bathroom mirror to hold the earring-in-progress up to my nontelephone ear. Not bad, if I did say so myself. Now all I had to do was make another one that looked reasonably like it.

Geri was still wound up. "They say fifty is the new thirty. I like that. I don't believe it for a minute, but I like it a lot."

"They say tangerine is the new neutral, too, if that helps any."

I swirled my finger around in a jar of sea glass, then placed three likely candidates on the floor in front of me. I covered the receiver and called, "Here, Boyfriend."

Apparently I didn't cover it very well, because Geri said, "Don't call him Boyfriend. It's undignified."

"I can call him anything I want. It's not your business."

While Geri ignored my comment, something she'd been doing fairly consistently since I was born, Boyfriend, my cat of indeterminate age and lineage, stretched provocatively. He eyed me, as if deciding whether he remembered me or not, then vaulted off the couch and leaned his full weight possessively against my lower left leg.

I reached down and scratched him behind one ear. He began to purr, and the vibration made the back of my throat tickle, the way it always did. I nodded toward the sea glass. He eyed all three pieces, then reached a paw out like a hockey stick and shot one across the room.

Boyfriend's taste was impeccable. "Good boy, Boy," I said as I stroked him slowly from the top of his head along the full length of his tiger-striped back. I reached down to pick up the winning piece of sea glass. Boyfriend gave me a dismissive look and headed for his water bowl.

Geri was talking again. "And," she continued, "they also say that a happy family life and the courage to take on new challenges are the best indicators of a successful transition to the second half century of your life. Rachel, open a window if you're going to use nail polish in here, and Re-becca, turn that TV down. Now. Half century. God."

"Deep breaths," I said encouragingly. "If it's still possi-ble at your age."

She gulped in some air. "Can you do me a favor?"

"Depends."

"The kids are all begging to go to that open casting call thing. Even Riley. I still can't believe they're actually shooting a movie in Marshbury."

I had a clear vision of dollar signs. "It would probably be a great experience for them," I said.

"Are you going?"

"Hmm, I hadn't really thought about it." Boyfriend looked up from his water bowl, and I gave him a wink.

Geri sighed again. "Do you think you could take them for me? I really have to get back to the office for a few hours."

I'd never understood why the whole world was in such a rush to have children just so they could ask somebody else to take care of them. What was the big deal about pro-creation? I mean, possums do it. I let Geri wait another second or two, then went in for the kill. "I'd need to hear the magic words first."

"Okay, I'll pay you. Time and a half. You're going to need it. Wait a minute. Riley wants to talk to you."

I got to work on the second earring and waited for my eight-year-old nephew's voice. Eventually I heard it. "Aunt Ginger, how do you move a seventeen-hundred-pound shark?"

"Okay," I said, "I'll bite." He laughed like it was the fun-niest thing he'd ever heard. Riley was my best audience. I gave him a minute to settle down, then asked, "How *do* you move a seventeen-hundred-pound shark?"

Riley waited a beat before he delivered his punch line. His timing was probably genetic. "Ve-ry carefully," he said, in his cute, squeaky voice, which sounded like it had just a touch of helium in it. I heard the thunk of the phone on the counter.

"Nice one, Ry," I yelled, then I braced myself to listen to my sister again.

2

THE EMBARRASSING TRUTH WAS THAT I WAS DYING TO be an extra in *Shark Sense*. I just couldn't resist that kind of thing. It would distract me from waking up every day thinking I'd somehow ended up in the wrong life. I simply knew I was destined for something else, but I really would have thought I'd be further along by now when it came to figuring out exactly what.

I'd maxed out this year's therapy allowance on my lousy health plan in my quest for direction, and honestly, it didn't help all that much. Even my therapist didn't quite get it, or me, for that matter.

However you painted the picture, I was still forty-one and single and, though I'd managed a life full of adventure, I hadn't quite found myself yet. After a few too many years in sales, some more and others less lucrative, my new plan was to transition to the more fulfilling life of an artist. At the moment I made sea glass earrings and sold them for a living, which, by my calculations, meant I was well on my way.

I threw a tank top on over my best jeans and, to complete the look, added a pair of my earrings. The weathered blue glass matched my eyes exactly, plus I liked to wear my own stuff, since you never knew when you'd make a sale. I had to admit that I was still more comfortable thinking in terms of dollars and cents rather than creative opus or artistic oeuvre. It might have been a personality thing. I'm a direct descendant of P. T. Barnum on my mother's side, and by the way, he did not say there's a sucker born every minute. He said there's a *customer* born every minute. I read that somewhere. Since he died in 1891, it's not like he ever said anything directly to me. Even my sister, Geri, isn't quite old enough to have met him.

Speaking of reading, I'd also read an article recently that said you could give yourself a mini face lift by extending your eyeliner vertically at the outer corners. Not that I really needed one yet, but what the hell, I tried it out anyway. I added some mascara and lipstick, then turned my head upside down and gave my hair a good brushing. When I flipped my head back up, it looked full and thick and shiny. I grabbed the hairspray quick, before it got any other ideas. I was one of those lucky tawny-haired people whose occasional gray strands came in looking like highlights. Either that or I was in total denial.

"Sorry, Boyfriend," I said as I wiggled my way out the door without creating any space for him to follow. "I'll make it up to you tonight." As every pet owner knows, leaving the house alone always involves massive quantities of guilt.

Geri and the kids were waiting for me when I pulled into the driveway of her starter castle, her house on steroids, her cookie-cutter McMansion. Okay, I could admit it: I was a tiny bit jealous that she had a house and I didn't, not that I'd ever, in a million years, want to live in this pretentious monstrosity. A hip little bungalow would be more my style, though at this point I'd probably be perfectly happy to settle for a ranchburger.

Geri was instantly recognizable by her crisp white blouse and black power suit. And by the fact that she was communing with her BlackBerry, which seemed to interest her more than life itself. I put my trusty old VW Jetta into park and gave the door a little kick right where it tended to stick. I jumped out fast, before Geri scaled the entrance to her SUV. When you're dealing with family, you *always* get the money up front.

I held out my hand, and Geri handed me a check. I would have preferred cash, but at least I knew it wouldn't bounce, and I'd learned to pick my battles. Rebecca and Riley swept past me to fight for the front seat of my car. Rachel, who knew she had the age card to play, sauntered over to me, giving her jeans a tug in the general direction of her belly button. "What did you do to your eyes?" she asked.

I batted them extravagantly. "You like?"

Rachel squinted up at me. "You look kind of like a geisha. Is that what you were going for?"

I rubbed the sides of my eyes, and Rachel headed off to my car to conquer the front seat. Geri laughed and handed me a tissue. I gave her a little glare and blew my nose in it. She shook her head. "So," I said, "how many more hours till you're fifty?"

"So," she said, "how many more hours till you're homeless?"

✺

IT'S NOT EVERY DAY a movie gets shot in Marshbury, Massachusetts. In fact, it's not any day, at least up until now. So what if it was a horror movie they'd only moved to Marshbury because a great white shark had conveniently managed to get itself stuck in some shallow water off the coast, and could save them a ton of money.

Various officials had been pledging to drive the shark away for over a week when the movie people called. Even the governor had formally called for its eviction, but the fourteen-foot shark seemed to have other ideas. So, the movie people made an offer, and the board of selectmen asked them to double it, and when they did, you've never seen permits issued so fast.

The bad news was it was harder than ever to find a parking place at Scuttle Beach. We cruised the lot a few times, then gave up and headed down the street to park in Noah's driveway. Noah was my human boyfriend. Allegedly anyway.

A line of people stretched almost to Noah's house. We hopped onto the end of it, and over the next hour or so, we followed it across the causeway, along Sea Street, and halfway across the parking lot, where it seemed to be winding its way back from the rickety old bathhouse.

It looked like the whole town had answered the casting call. Of course, the full-page ad in the *Marshbury Mirror* had been hard to miss:

SEEKING ACTORS FOR HORROR FILM IN MARSHBURY, MASSACHUSETTS

Description: Open casting call for Worldwide Studio production of *Shark Sense*. Theatrical Type: horror or possible horror-comedy hybrid. Talent Type: men, women, and children of all ages. Comments: Union and nonunion. Casting will be at the Scuttle Beach parking lot on May 22 from 3–6 PM.

The movie people, who were walking up and down the line handing out clipboards, were hard to miss. It wasn't just the clipboards. They were dressed all wrong for the town—one tall man wore high-top sneakers with a suit. You just don't do that in Marshbury. Some people up ahead of us, three women in red and purple jogging suits who were probably in their seventies, all grabbed greedily at the clipboard he offered. He cleared his throat dramatically and said, "Take your sheet off and pass the clipboard back when you're through." He walked off at a brisk pace.

Rachel was flirting with a boy standing next to us at this point. She was fifteen, so I decided she was entitled. "Becca," I said to her sister, who was unoccupied and also only twelve. "Go tell Riley to get back here quick so he doesn't miss out." Riley had taken off to kick a soccer ball around the parking lot with some friends.

"You snooze, you lose," she said. "And why does Riley have to do everything we do, anyway?" Rebecca kept her eyes glued to her sister, who I hoped was a better role model in the flirt department than her mother had been for me.

The suit-and-sneaker man was back. "SAG?" he was saying repeatedly as he walked past the line, as if he were selling drugs.

I looked down at my chest. "Not yet, thank God," I said.

"Gross! I can't believe you said that in front of me, Aunt Ginger," Becca said. "Mom would kill you."

"Just living up to my reputation," I said. "It takes focus *and* discipline."

Riley bumped his way back into line. "Can we go home now?" he asked.

"Hey, no front cuts, Riley," Becca said.

Rachel dragged her attention back to us and rolled her eyes. "What he means," she said, "is that he's looking for union members. Screen Actors Guild. Does anybody but me read?"

The boy Rachel had been flirting with stepped forward. "Do you have your card?" the man asked him. He nodded and they walked off importantly together.

Rachel watched him disappear. "Easy come, easy go," I said.

"YES, I DO, I do believe in miracles," I said about twenty minutes later when I finally grabbed us a clipboard. I handed a sheet to each of the kids, and they huddled around me reading while I fished in my bag for more pens. "Union rate," I read out loud. "One hundred eighteen dollars for eight hours; nonunion, seventy-five dollars for twelve hours."

"Wow," Becca said. "I think I make more than that with my paper route."

I added up how much I made on my earrings on a bad day. It was close. "Okay," I said. "Just check *all* under availability and write really messy where it asks who your agent is."

"What do you think I should put under *special expertise*? Synchronized swimming?" Rachel asked.

"Oh, you so sucked at that, Rachel," Becca said.

"Put it anyway," I said. "And don't forget that summer we all took sailing lessons."

Rachel scrunched up her forehead. "You didn't take sailing lessons with us."

I was always doing that, forgetting for just a split second that the better part of a generation separated us. "Don't do that—you'll get wrinkles," I said to change the subject. I was pretty sure that forgetting you weren't still fifteen happened to everyone, but I certainly wasn't going to call attention to it.

"What's my inseam?" Rebecca asked. "And what should I put under *hat?*"

"I put baseball," Riley said.

"Am I the only one in this family with a brain?" Rachel asked. "They're looking for your wardrobe sizes, which is why it says 'wardrobe sizes' just above it."

We were almost to the bathhouse. "Just do the best you can," I said. "And listen, here's the deal. If I get in, don't worry, I'll try to pull the rest of you in, too."

There were two women and one man sitting behind a long table in front of the bathhouse. I made Riley go first, so I could listen to the questions and fine-tune my strategy.

Riley must have decided on an offensive approach. "How do you move a seventeen-hundred-pound shark?" he asked as he waved his sheet of paper at them.

One of the women took the paper and looked down at it. "I don't know," she said. "How *do* you move a seventeen-hundred-pound shark?"

Riley crossed his arms and waited just long enough. "Ve-ry carefully."

They laughed. "Got anything else for us?" the same woman asked. She looked down. "Oh that's so cute. He wrote 'baseball' under *hat*. Are you a baseball fan, honey?"

The man stuck out his hand. "My name is Manny, what's yours?"

Riley shook his hand and said, "Pedro."

The man smiled. He was probably in his early thirties, and when he turned his head, I could see he had a pony-tail. "Tell me a little about yourself, Pedro."

"Well, just a few years ago, I was sitting under a mango tree and didn't have fifty cents to ride the bus."

"Ohmigod, he's doing Pedro," Rachel said. The sisters rolled their eyes. Riley had been doing his Pedro imitation for three years now, since the Red Sox won the World Se-ries when he was five.

The people behind the table were all leaning forward and smiling. "And now what, Pedro?" the ponytailed man named Manny asked.

"But now, Boston, I consider her my house. She is my house. And if I don't come back here, it's because she didn't try hard enough to keep me."

"Remind me never to negotiate with you, kid."

And that was it. Riley was in. Or at least Pedro was. And the rest of us were out.

3

RACHEL CROSSED HER ARMS AND HUGGED HERSELF while we walked and Riley ran ahead of us, punching his arms in the air like a triumphant little Rocky. "I so don't get it. What's Riley got that we don't have?"

Becca twirled some hair around her finger and turned to look at her sister. "It's so not fair. I don't think he should get to be in it if we can't. We're a *family*."

We caught up with Riley just as he reached Noah's house. Noah was a glassblower. He made everything from champagne flutes, Christmas ornaments, and witches' balls to elegant vases and the most amazing sculptures. Witches' balls are glass balls that you hang in your window. They have weblike strands of glass inside them to catch evil spirits that might otherwise fly around your house. The name probably helps keep the spirits out, too.

Once a week, Noah opened the studio behind his house for a demonstration. Everybody who could fit would sit down at one of the three old wooden benches. The rest of the people would stand in the back with Noah's dog.

Noah's furnace would be glowing orange, and you could feel the heat even from the benches. He'd put on special sunglasses because, he'd say, the old glassblowers had all gotten cataracts. Then he'd pick up a long metal blowpipe and dip it into the bucket of molten glass in the furnace.

He'd dip that into a pan of brightly colored crushed

glass. Then he'd heat it, and dip it, then heat it and dip it again. He'd sit down at a bench and roll the pipe back and forth along a rail while he shaped the glass blob with a charred applewood block.

Finally, he'd stand up and lift the long metal blowpipe to his mouth. The first time I saw it, I thought he'd blow the glass up like a balloon. But all he did was blow the tiniest puff of air into the pipe and then quickly cover the opening with his thumb. He rolled the pipe around, and the glass expanded so slowly you almost couldn't see it.

Noah's stuff was so gorgeous it often sold before it even made it out of his yard to one of the local gift shops. Today, he'd set up a table on the driveway between the street and my car, and it looked like he'd been doing a brisk business.

"Guess what?" Riley yelled. Noah was finishing waiting on two women. His dog, Sage, who today looked like a cross between a chocolate Lab, an Irish setter, and possibly a dachshund, kept her short-legged self lodged between Noah and her competition. Better Sage than me. One of the women was blond and the other brunette, and if you counted the redheaded dog, they surrounded Noah with the full female spectrum of hair color. The two-legged women hugged their purchases to their chests.

They both said thank you and started walking away. The brunette turned around for one last look at him. "We'll tell all our friends about you," she practically sang.

I couldn't resist an understated eye roll, but nobody noticed, except possibly Sage. It was hard to tell. It was also hard to tell just why Noah always seemed to have this effect on women. He was tall, and basically handsome in kind of a geeky, rumpled way. He had dark hair, pale skin, and great eye contact, but there was also something unfinished about him. Maybe women were drawn to him the way they were drawn to a good home improvement project. A tweak here, a tweak there, and look what you'd have.

Riley was telling Noah his big news. "Nice," Noah said. "Way to go, man." They reached their fists out to each other and touched knuckles in the gesture that seemed to have replaced the high five, and not a moment too soon.

Riley started jumping up and down with excitement as he continued his story. "And they only wanted me. Aunt Ginger even tried to give the lady her earrings, but they still only wanted me."

I reached my hands up to my ears. "Only because she was looking at them," I said. "It wasn't like it was a bribe or anything."

"Yeah, big deal, Riley," Rachel said. "So you're shark bait."

Becca's eyes lit up for the first time since we'd been rejected. "Shark bait, shark bay-yayt."

"Hey," Noah said to me after the girls ran off with Riley chasing them. Apparently Sage didn't see me as any real competition for Noah's affections, because she took off after the kids, which meant we were alone.

"Hey," I said back. I picked up a vase that pulled me in with its swirls of poppy red, indigo blue, and black. People were always saying Noah's work reminded them of a Georgia O'Keeffe painting, but I think what they meant was that pretty much everything he created looked vaguely like a vagina. Possibly this was another reason for his fan club.

Noah stuffed some bills into the empty tennis ball can

where he kept his money. He stepped around the table and lifted my hair off my neck with one hand. He put his other hand on my shoulder and bent forward to give me a kiss just below my right ear. He smelled like propane gas and sweat, which was sexier than it should have been.

Noah's hair was thick and messy, and he didn't exactly have a beard, but I didn't think I'd ever seen him clean-shaven either. When I'd first met him and he told me he was a glassblower, I'd said something witty like *Oh, that's so cool*. And he'd grinned like he was about Riley's age and said, "No, actually it's really hot."

"So," he said now.

"So," I said back. He draped one of his arms across my shoulders a bit awkwardly, and I leaned into him, just a little.

"How's life at the FROG?" he asked.

I shook my head. "Oh, no. Not you, too. I hate that word."

"Okay, how's life at the toad?"

"Much better," I said. "Though I prefer to think of it as a penthouse. You know, with cars as the ground-floor tenants?"

Noah nodded. "Did you know all toads are frogs but not all frogs are toads?"

"Fascinating," I said. "Did you know only the male croaks?"

"Charming," he said. "Listen, I have to get back to the studio. I'm really close on something, and I just want to get a few more hours in." One hand stayed on the small of my back.

I took a step away. "Perfect," I said. "I'm really close on something, too."

"HI, HONEY, WE'RE HOME," I yelled as the kids and I walked into their house. My sister, Geri, and her husband, Seth, were sitting on opposite sides of the sofa, and yes, they were going at it with their BlackBerrys. Since they also each had a glass of red wine within striking distance, I hoped it was the final check of the day. But, who knew, maybe they brought them to bed and woke up repeatedly throughout the night to pound the tiny keyboards with their thumbs. I shivered just a little at the thought.

"Guess what," Riley yelled. "I get to be in the movie."

While his parents congratulated him and his sisters started in again with the shark bait stuff, I tiptoed out to the kitchen to see what my chances were for some dinner before I had to consider cooking my own. I was in luck— meatballs simmered in their sauce on top of the stove. As quietly as I could, I pulled a hunk off the loaf of Italian bread and dipped it in. While I chewed, I gave the sleeve of white paper a twist so the remaining loaf wouldn't start to get stale and even checked the level of the pasta water. I was considerate like that.

"Would you like to stay for dinner?" my sister asked behind me.

"No thanks, I've just eaten," I mumbled.

Geri waited for me to turn around. Eventually I did, but not before I wiped the crumbs off my face. "You really should work on your boundaries," she said.

I opened a drawer, took out a fork, and stabbed a meatball. "You really should work on raising your own children."

It was pretty standard conversation for Geri and me,

since we could never get along for more than a minute or two. Our whole lives, we'd been polar opposites. This might have been more complicated in a family of, say, six or eight siblings, where everybody would have to work harder to stake out niches that didn't overlap, but with just Geri and me it was easy: she was the good girl and I was the rebel. She married her college sweetheart, and I broke up with mine to travel the world. She had kids and found a steady job. I had a series of boyfriends, an assortment of jobs, more trips.

She grabbed a fork and joined me. "Does that mean your nephew will have to miss out on his first chance at stardom?" she asked.

"Okay," I said. "I'll do it. Time and a half stays. And I think an occasional bonus would be a nice gesture." I stabbed another meatball to seal the deal. "Have you heard from Mom?"

"Company!" my mother yelled from the foyer.

⟨⟨⟨

"YOU'RE JUST whistling Dixie here, Toots," my father said. "I'm not going anywhere."

"Don't call me Toots," my mother said.

"Have a heart, Mother," my father said.

"I'm not your mother," my mother said. "And I know you. As soon as we get there, you'll say, *What took us so long?* You're the one who never stops grumbling about how something always needs fixing in an old house, that and the endless yard work. Once we get moved into our new town-house, you won't have a thing to do but enjoy yourself."

My father twirled some pasta around on his fork, then

looked up at my mother again. "But, Dollface, we were just getting comfortable. I wouldn't last a week in one of those brand-spanking-new places. Everything's too perfect." He put the pasta in his mouth and chewed while he looked up at the sparkling chandelier hanging from the cavernous ceiling of Geri's dining room. "There's no soul in new houses," he said when he finished chewing.

"Thanks, Dad," Geri said. Seth checked his watch.

I cleared my throat. "You know, Mom," I said. "I was thinking maybe you should wait. Dad's not ready, and, well . . ." I tried to look pitiful, which wasn't really that hard, ". . . I don't have anyplace to go yet."

My mother leaned forward over her plate. "Honey, we've been enabling you long enough. It's not good for you." My mother was wearing long chunky beads over her T-shirt, and they had just landed on top of her pasta. I certainly wasn't going to be the one to tell her. "I guarantee it, moving out again will be the best thing that ever happened to you. You'll have sixty days once we sell before we pass papers. And the house may not go right away. It's a tough market out there. We're post-bubble now."

"It wasn't actually a bubble," Seth said. "It was essentially a balloon."

"Why don't you and Noah just get married?" Becca asked.

"Shhh," Rachel hissed. "Loser," she said in a whispery voice no one at the table could possibly have missed. "How about because he has to ask first?"

I decided not to try to figure out which one of us Rachel was calling a loser. "It's not that easy to find a pet-friendly rental, Mom. If you don't care about me, what about Boyfriend?"

"Boyfriend and you can move in here with us," Becca said. "My hamster won't mind."

"Yeah," Riley said. "You can have my top bunk. I never use it."

Geri put her fork down. "This is the last time I'm going to say it," she said. "Find another name for that cat."

"What about Neko?" Becca said. "That's cat in Japanese."

"Champ has a nice ring to it," my father said.

There truly was no such thing as a free meal. "Listen," I said. "For the last time, his name was Boyfriend when I got him from the shelter. How would you like it if someone adopted you and changed *your* name?"

Geri shook her head while checking to see that she had her children's undivided attention. "It's completely inappropriate for a grown woman to call her cat 'Boyfriend.'"

"Fine," I said. "Call him whatever you want. It's perfectly okay with me, Grace." The kids giggled appreciatively while I pushed back my chair and picked up my plate. "Let me know as soon as you find out when Riley starts, okay?"

"It's so not fair that Riley gets to miss school if we can't," Rachel said. "Don't you think so, Dad? I mean, it's not like he's exactly a genius or anything."

"Totally," Becca said.

"Ha-ha," Riley said.

"Girls," Geri said.

"By the way," my mother said. "Come by this weekend. Your father and I could use a little help. The house goes on the market a week from Friday."

4

THE SOUND OF A SHOVEL HITTING PACKED CLAY SOIL woke me up the next morning. I knew St. Joseph was involved without even looking, but I crawled out of bed and stuck my head out the window anyway.

"Morning, Mom," I yelled. "Did you bring me any coffee?"

My mother kept digging. "Sure, I'd love some help. Grab a shovel."

I could see where my sister had inherited the more irritating parts of her personality. I pulled on some jeans and an old T-shirt, and headed down the stairs.

"Shoes," my mother said without even looking at my feet.

My mother had always said she had eyes in the back of her head, and here was still more evidence. I stomped back upstairs and slipped my bare feet into some sneakers without untying them, then clomped back down again. My mother handed me the second shovel she'd conveniently brought along. A greenish yellow plastic statue of a guy in a robe watched us from the edge of the driveway. He looked a little bit nervous, I thought.

I caught my mother's eye and pointed. "St. Joseph, I presume?"

She nodded. My mother was wearing yoga pants and a

Kama Sutra T-shirt that said, in smaller letters, SO MANY POSITIONS, SO LITTLE TIME. I blushed. No wonder my father wasn't himself these days.

I jumped on the shovel with my sneaker-clad feet and managed to penetrate the rocklike ground maybe a quarter of an inch. "Are you sure we should be burying him, Mom? I mean, I'm not an expert or anything, but it sounds sacrilegious to me."

"Just keep digging," my mother said.

I did. So did my mother. Eventually we had a hole big enough to bury a little plastic statue. My mother put her shovel down and brushed her hands together briskly. "Okay," she said, "let's give it a go."

I had to ask. "Are you selling the house because of me, Mom?"

My mother was holding St. Joseph now, kind of cradling him in the palm of one hand, as if she were going to rock him to sleep. She shook her head. "I know it's a revolutionary concept, but your father and I would like to have a life of our own before we die."

"Have you checked in with Dad about this?"

She put her hands on my shoulders, and I felt St. Joseph's hard plastic edges digging into me. "Honey, get back out there. Get on with your life."

I didn't mean to say it, but it came out anyway. "I'm scared, Mom."

"Ginger, everyone is scared. You just do it anyway. Never forget, you can be anything you want to be."

"Mom, don't. I hate when you say that. I'm forty-one years old. I think it's a little late."

My mother dropped St. Joseph headfirst into the hole

and picked up her shovel again. "Do you want to know what your problem is?"

"Probably not, but I have a feeling you're going to tell me anyway." St. Joseph was partially buried now, and I thought I could hear him gasping for breath. Or maybe that was me.

"Your problem, my darling daughter, is that you're afraid you're going to miss something. But what you don't realize is that, by not making a decision, you're missing it all."

"Who's missing?" my father asked behind me. When I turned around, I saw that he was carrying yet another garbage bag.

My mother shoveled the rest of the dirt on top of St. Joseph in one fell swoop. "Mind your *p*s and *q*s," she said to him. "What's in the bag?"

"None of your beeswax," he said. "What's in the hole?"

"Coffee, anyone?" my mother asked.

∞

AS MY FATHER booked it up the stairs outside my apartment, I noticed that one of his socks was dark green and the other was maroon today. "You're not going to put that bag in my shower, are you, Dad?" I asked, even though it was perfectly obvious that he was.

He stopped and turned around. He was wearing shorts and sandals with his socks, and his pale flaky legs looked like they could use a good moisturizer. "Psst," he said. "Get in here quick. We don't have much time. Your mother will be back with the java any minute."

I looked down at St. Joseph's freshly filled-in hole and

wondered briefly which one of us was having the worst day so far. "Give me strength," I whispered to him, just in case that was in his saintly job description. Then I followed my father up the stairs.

Even wearing sandals with socks, my father was pretty nimble. The bag had already disappeared. "Okay, Dollface, spill the beans. What did the old broad bury out there?"

I knew better than to get in the middle of this sort of thing. "Um, I'm not really sure. Maybe some daffodil bulbs?" I sneaked a peek at the clock on the stove. I'd promised myself I was going to get in eight hours on my earrings today. Or at least six. "And I don't think you should call Mom an old broad, Dad. Especially in front of her."

My father ran his fingers through his hair, and the sparse strands in the center stayed sticking straight up. This made him look kind of like an elderly Kewpie doll. "Okay," he said, "whatever the old battle-ax buried out there, we're digging it up tonight. As soon as it gets dark, I'll flash a light in your window, and then you meet me out there. Pronto."

"Dad . . ."

"Don't worry. I'll do all the dirty work. All's you'll be is the lookout."

☙

WHEN MY PHONE RANG, it took me a minute to find it because it was buried under my earring supplies. Geri started right in as soon as I said hello. "Are you sure I should let Riley do this? I mean, it's not as though he has any interest in acting, and he's going to have to miss school. And it's not as if he's still in kindergarten. There are *expectations* for second graders."

I cut a piece of earring wire from the spool and did the math for a week's worth of work in my head. I didn't know about Riley, but I could sure use the money. "Well," I said, "you're the mother, but it certainly sounds like a résumé builder to me."

It was almost too easy. "Good point," my sister said. "Okay, yeah. Can you pick him up at eight A.M. tomorrow?"

"Can do." Geri loved it when I sounded efficient. "And I'll figure on time and a half for about twelve hours a day for at least the better part of a week, right?" Boyfriend batted me another piece of sea glass, and I scooped it up.

"No," Geri said. "The casting person said they can only have the kids for eight hours. Seth did a search last night and says it's all about the Coogan Act. Apparently, Jackie Coogan had no rights to the money he made as a child star, so because of the public uproar, the California legislature passed the Child Actors Bill, also known as the Coogan Act, to protect child actors."

I didn't quite get how this related to Marshbury, Massachusetts, but I didn't want to encourage her by asking any questions. Geri's ability to retain detail had always made my eyes glaze over. While she droned on, I pictured a pajama-ed Seth in bed hammering away on his laptop as he surfed the Internet. There were worse things than being single.

"Yeah, well, whatever," I said, shaking my head to dislodge the image. "So, I'll see you tomorrow. Bye."

"Do you think," Geri continued, as if she hadn't heard me, "that a spa weekend would work for my fiftieth? I've always wanted to go to Canyon Ranch. . . ."

There was only one way to end this conversation in a timely fashion. "Hello?" I said, as if I couldn't hear her. "Hello?" I repeated before I pushed the off button on the phone and tossed it across the room and onto my sleeper sofa.

I stood up and stretched. I shook the cramps out of my hands, then picked up Boyfriend and walked over to the window. My mother was digging again, this time in the perennial garden. "It's worth a shot," I whispered to my cat.

"Hey, Mom," I said when I got down there. "Wow, it's so beautiful out here. I don't know how you could ever stand to leave all this."

"Don't start," my mother said. She dug up a big clump of something or other, then started separating the roots with a pitchfork. "Here," she said. "Hold that end and pull."

I did as I was told. Eventually we had a bunch of smaller sections, and we placed one back into the garden and put the rest into old plastic pots. "This phlox is over a hundred years old. When Grandpa worked as a grounds-keeper, he'd bring home a little piece of each plant when he divided the perennials at one of those fancy Cohasset estates."

"Grandpa was a thief?" I couldn't remember hearing this story before.

"He said it was good for the plants to divide them. And if the owner's plant died, that way he'd have a backup." We were adding some garden soil to the pots, and pressing the soil down around the roots with our fingers. My mother wiped her forehead with the back of her hand and smiled. "So, yes, I suppose technically you'd have to call him a thief."

My mother dug up another clump. "There is nothing

like a blue cornflower on a sunny day," she said. I looked at the plant, but all I could see were roots and green leaves. "What I love most about these perennials is that each one has a story."

I picked up the pitchfork and handed it to her.

My mother jabbed it into the plant. "Janice Rourke gave me this one. I wonder whatever happened to her. We had a big falling-out, and I can't even remember why."

"Uh-oh," I said. "You're not going to start traveling around the world looking up your former flower friends to find out what went wrong with the relationship, are you? I think I've seen that movie." I separated a few pots from the stack and started putting a cornflower section into each one.

My mother stabbed the ground with the pitchfork and laughed. "No, but maybe I'll look up my high school boyfriends, at least the ones who are still alive, and give them each a plant. I can tell them they gave it to me way back when and I've treasured it all these years and wanted them to have a piece of it back."

I had the hang of this whole garden thing now, and I was adding soil to the cornflower pots without even being asked. "Yeah, that might work. It's not like they'd remember whether it was true or not at their age anyway."

"You'd be surprised what you'll remember, honey."

"Did you have a lot of boyfriends back then, Mom?" I'd never really thought to ask before. It had always seemed like my parents must have come into the world joined at the hip.

"My fair share."

I wondered what *my* fair share was. Maybe I'd already had it, and I'd kept right on going past the person I was supposed to end up with. Maybe I was with him now. "What made you pick Dad? How did you know?"

Even to my ears, these sounded like questions that should be asked when you were, say, Rachel's age. Maybe I'd even asked them back then. Maybe I'd thought I didn't need to. It was amazing how you could think you knew everything as a teenager, and a couple of decades later, you realized you'd never had a clue.

My mother was just kind of standing there, watching a worm work its way back into the dirt. "The truth?"

"Sure," I said.

"He was cute, and he was crazy about me. And he could dance." She shook her head. "I was so young, it didn't seem all that complicated. You pick a nice boy, and you figure out how to make it work together."

She brushed some dirt from her hands and started a little grouping of pots off to the side. "I will say that the dancing part has held up quite nicely. Never underestimate the joy of being married to the one man at the party who knows how to dance."

Maybe I could call up every guy I'd ever dated and invite them all to a dance-off.

My mother straightened up, a pot in each hand. "Okay, these are for you and Geri. We'll put two of each perennial in Geri's garden. You can dig yours up as soon as you have a house of your own."

I tried to imagine ever having a house of my own. Maybe it could be the bonus prize at the dance-off.

"Unless you want to plant yours over at Noah's?"

"No, no," I said. "Geri's house is probably safer."

5

RILEY AND I WERE FOLLOWING BRIGHT YELLOW PLASTIC signs, which were tacked to utility poles and planted in free-standing buckets of cement at the edge of the road. SHARK SENSE BASE CAMP they proclaimed in tall block letters as they pointed the way with black arrows. As if we needed directions to the beach we'd been going to all our lives.

I was telling Riley the St. Joseph story. "So," I continued, "I waited just the right amount of time. You know, *one Mississippi, two Mississippi*. Then I shoved them all out and slammed the door, and they went flying down the stairs."

It was a slight exaggeration, but Riley laughed his squeaky laugh just the way I knew he would. "That was a good one, Aunt Ginger."

"Thanks. Mom, I mean Gram, was pretty mad, but so was I."

"Mothers always act mad. I bet you even do that with Boyfriend."

I turned on my blinker. "Boyfriend is a cat, Riley. I'm not his mother."

"Then why do you walk him in a stroller?"

"It's not a stroller. It's a, well, sort of a cage on wheels."

"I rest my case," Riley said. He tilted his head back and finished off the milk. "So who's this St. Joseph again?" he asked when he came up for air.

As if I hadn't skipped more Sunday school, or CCD, as it came to be called midstream, than I'd attended. I thought hard. "I think he was Jesus's father."

"Wasn't that God?"

"No, his earthly father. I'm pretty sure he's the patron saint of home and family. And Realtors."

That seemed to satisfy Riley, or maybe he was just distracted by the fact that we were pulling into the beach parking lot. A guard found Riley's name on the list, and then directed us to a roped-off parking area. After we got out of my Jetta, another guard pointed the way to something he called the "holding area." This should have been my first clue that it was going to be a long day.

We milled around with a couple dozen people who looked as lost as we did. I didn't recognize anyone, which raised the distinct possibility they'd brought in ringers from out of town. Either that or I needed to get out more. Finally, a fast-talking woman holding a clipboard and wearing a baseball hat came over and said something about AD.

I leaned down and whispered to Riley. "Did she say she's ADD?"

Riley looked just like Rachel when he rolled his eyes at me. "AD means Assistant Director, and if they say 'background,' that means they want the extras. But I'm not really an extra, I'm Boy Number Four."

I patted him on the head. "Don't worry, honey, you'll be Boy Number One before you know it."

Riley looked up at me. "Is that a joke, Aunt Ginger?"

Riley seemed to be losing both his comic sensibility and his faith in his guardian. "Sorry," I said. "It's early. But, how do you know all this?"

"They sent us stuff. We got two whole pages of intrucksions and a permission slip."

How nice of his mother to share them with me. Especially the *intrucksions* that, by the way, reminded me that despite being extremely advanced, I'd still said *cimmanon* at Riley's age. Fortunately, it seemed like the AD person was repeating the pertinent information. If we absolutely had to leave the holding area at any time, we should let her know. Refreshments and the bathhouse restrooms were available. If we stayed long enough, we'd be given lunch. That last part sounded vaguely threatening to me, as if we'd only get lunch if we behaved ourselves, but maybe I was just being paranoid.

"Each scene," she continued, reading from her clipboard, "as you may or may not realize, is filmed from a number of different angles, which are later edited together. Each angle requires the same careful camera placement and lighting as all the others. The illusion which must be maintained in the final product is that it is all happening at one time, in one place."

She took a moment to look down at Riley and the other kids, who probably had absolutely no idea what she was talking about. "It is important for you to remember what you do and when and where you do it in relation to everyone else. You'll have to repeat it within the same scene, and it must look identical each time. We call this 'matching action.' Now, any questions?"

A cute little boy about a head shorter than Riley put his hand up.

The AD woman nodded at him.

"Are you the teacher?" he asked.

I DIDN'T HAVE A SCRIPT, of course. Geri was probably reading the guardian's copy this very minute, assuming there was such a thing. But the way it looked from here, Rachel and Becca weren't too far off with the shark bait thing. Riley, aka Boy Number Four, stood in a small circle of kids on the sand close to the edge of the water. I hoped none of them would get a sudden urge to go swimming, since the very shark that had brought the movie to town was out there.

Actually the shark was in a small bay about a hundred feet or so away from the beach. It was separated by a shoal of eelgrass, but I imagined that with the right camera work you could still make it look pretty scary. And, honestly, it *was* pretty scary to think of that dorsal fin pacing back and forth above the surface of the water just over in the lagoon. I looked over at the group of journalists, scientists, and tourists clustered on the rocks behind a cordoned-off area that was being protected by police and assorted officials.

I was sitting just out of camera range at a child-size picnic table under a freestanding awning, the kind you might put in your backyard if you wanted to have a cookout and didn't have a shade tree. I glanced over my shoulder to see what looked like half of Massachusetts standing back behind the ropes. The movie crowd was double the size of the shark crowd, and twice as many cops stood by to make sure nobody made a break for the action. I couldn't resist giving a smug little wave to the people who couldn't get in. It was like being back in high school, but this time I was part of the in crowd.

The *Marshbury Mirror* was a weekly, so we all relied on *The Daily Catch* for breaking news. I picked up a copy of today's paper, which someone had kindly left within my reach.

SHARK NEEDS REST, MORE ELBOW ROOM

After attaching a satellite-tracking device to the great white shark with a 6-foot spear, researchers coaxed the 1,700-pound female to within 100 feet of an outlet to the open ocean. A spokesman for the Executive Office of Marine and Wild Life Affairs said the move put a lot of stress on the shark, so a rest was recommended. He said this would conveniently coincide with Worldwide Studio's location shooting of *Shark Sense*, scheduled to begin this week.

Locals appearing as extras in the movie include Marshbury Harbormaster Craig Bates, Marshbury School Committee President Mary Mulberry, and the twin daughters of Marshbury Beautification Commission Chairperson Allison Flagg.

I wondered what it would take to get a job in Wild Life Affairs.

I looked up from the paper. "Can you give me another inch on that dolly track so I can get a wider reveal?" I heard some important-looking guy sitting in front of a video monitor ask. I thought about sauntering over to see if I could talk my way into a small part in the movie, but when I stood up, another AD-looking guy gave me a warning stare. I smiled sweetly at him. He kept watching me and didn't smile back.

I sat back down and took a sip of my coffee. There was a

flagpole dug into the sand in the center of the kids' circle, and brightly colored ribbons fluttered from the top of the pole. A couple of adults stood next to the pole with their hands on their hips, talking in low voices to one another.

"I'm Allison Flagg, the twins' mother," said the woman sitting next to me at the picnic table.

"Hi," I said. "Ginger Walsh. So, what's holding things up?"

She reached over and deadheaded a beach rose. "It looks to me like the educational consultant and the multicultural dance people can't agree on the proper way for the kids to do the maypole dance."

"Wow," I said, "you can tell all that from here?"

She adjusted her terrycloth visor and looked out from under it at me. "My twins have worked before. Identical twins are quite valuable in the movie business."

"I'll have to remember that next time," I said, for lack of a better comment. "Maybe I could even try for identical triplets."

"Which one is yours?" she asked.

I pointed. "The cute little guy with blue shorts and freckles. Actually, he's my nephew, Riley."

"Oh," she said. "No children of your own yet?"

"Nope," I said. "Totally child-free."

Allison Flagg rested her hand lightly on mine and lowered her voice. "I know a great fertility specialist. And I have some extra eggs frozen if you need to borrow any."

6

I SPLASHED WATER ON MY FACE IN THE BATHHOUSE, trying to cool off. Why was it that perfect strangers thought they had the right to butt into my private life? It just made me so angry that they somehow thought they knew me better than I knew myself. And the worst part was: *What if they did?*

The find-a-guy-to-make-babies-with thing had never been a part of my dreams. Even when we were kids and Geri handed down her Ken doll to me, I ignored him and wanted G.I. Joe, honorably discharged from service and suitably dressed for an exotic adventure. And when it came to real live boys, Geri and her very first boyfriend seemed like an old married couple. I was pretty sure I remembered being lulled asleep upstairs by the sound of them discussing health insurance on the living room sofa below.

I, on the other hand, had to admit to an early fetish for AFS students. Hans from Denmark, Pato from Guatemala, Joshua from New Zealand. By the time I graduated from high school, my photo albums had a real United Nations feel, and I had big plans for my first passport.

A friend and I bought backpacks and headed for Europe as soon as we graduated from college. We planned to visit at least a dozen countries, staying at youth hostels and traveling by train, but we never made it out of England. We met two guys on the beach, Archie and Owen, or something like that. They took us to a fancy spa, complete with gambling, dancing, and therapeutic waters. They told us they were the spa managers and hired us to work for them selling discount packages back in the States. It was a fifty-fifty split, which would have been a great deal, except that it turned out they didn't actually work for the spa. Looking back, it was the first of a long line of men and sales jobs that always promised more than they delivered.

I yanked a sheet of paper towel from its dispenser and managed to pat my face dry without dislodging my eye makeup. I walked out of the bathhouse. As I rounded the corner of the building, I almost plowed right into a curly-haired guy in jeans and a black T-shirt. I stepped to my right. He stepped to my right, too. We both stepped to my left.

"Dance?" he asked.

"Too early for me. But thanks." He had hazel eyes and his hair was kind of a sandy color.

"So," he said. "Having fun yet? It gets pretty boring, doesn't it?"

He had a point, but just in case it was a trick question, I said, "Oh, no, not at all. I'm completely fascinated."

He held out his hand and said, "Tim Kelly."

"Hi. Ginger Walsh." He was probably my age, give or take. "So, what do you do?"

"I'm the gaffer."

"Is that like a gopher?"

His eyes clouded over. "No," he said like he'd said it many times before. "It's like an electrician."

"Wow," I said. "I've always wanted to meet an electrician."

He laughed. "You're here with one of the kids, right?"

"Yeah, my nephew."

"You want me to get better lighting for him?"

Tim Kelly was seriously cute. I smiled. "I'll talk to his makeup artist and get back to you."

"Good," he said. "I'll look forward to it."

I made a wide circle so I could casually bypass Allison Flagg and sit at another mini picnic table. It was just a few feet closer to the action, but it made a big difference. I could see and hear everything much more clearly now, and even managed to give Riley a thumbs-up when he looked over. The technical advisors had apparently worked through their philosophical differences about the maypole dance, and each of the dozen or so kids was holding the end of a long ribbon. The girls' ribbons were pink and the boys' were green.

The girls and boys faced one another, and most of them managed to put their right feet back successfully. Then they bent their right knees, straightened them back out again, and slowly rose up on their toes. That seemed like a lot to expect from a group of kids who looked to me to be between the ages of six and eight, and when they had to do the same thing with their left feet, things got pretty shaky.

There were a bunch of rehearsals, and sometimes the kids were better and sometimes they were worse. They were playing what sounded like waltz music, which I thought might have been their first mistake. Something a bit more up-tempo might have helped all of us. I could feel my lower back stiffening from sitting so long. Finally, the AD guy who'd given me the dirty look yelled "Quiet."

Then somebody said "Rolling," and after that a woman walked over and held a clapper in front of the kids. She touched the top part to the bottom part and said "Marker."

Who knew? I'd always thought they said "Take one" or "Take four hundred and seventy-three," but everything was actually written right on the clapper. And it wasn't until he said "Action" that I realized the ponytailed guy from the casting call was the director. At least I thought the director was the one who got to say it. I felt like I'd landed in a foreign country and didn't speak the language.

Allison Flagg was going to be hard to shake. She sat down at my picnic table and held out an empty bank deposit slip with a phone number written on the back of it. "He's the best there is," she whispered. "They call him the fertility god."

"Catchy," I whispered, without taking it. "Who's that?" I asked to distract her, pointing to the ponytailed guy.

She reached over and tucked the bank slip between two fingers of my clenched fist. "That's the director. Manny Muscadel."

One of the dance people pushed a button on the CD player and the educational consultant said, "Okay, kids. Now."

The director was sitting with a small group of people in a semicircle in front of a video moniter. "Cut," he said when one of the girls tripped and the rest of the kids piled up like dominoes. He took off his headphones and buried his head in his hands.

Many, many attempts later, the sun was directly overhead, and I didn't know about the kids, but I'd never been so bored in my entire life. A dance guy clapped his hands and said, "All right now, let's focus."

Riley started shaking his hand until little waves ran up the length of his ribbon. I tried to catch his eye. Geri would kill me if he got fired.

The director pushed himself out of his director's chair. "That's good. Have them all do that. And then just make them circle around the pole a little."

"Technically—" the dance guy began.

"Just let them jump around and pretend they're having fun. We can cut in the top of the pole with the ribbons weaving in and out afterward."

So the kids got to shake their ribbons and skip around the pole, girls going one way and boys the other. Riley jumped up and clicked his heels together a few times, and then a couple of other kids started doing it, too.

"Cut," the director said. "Print." He looked over his shoulder at the other people in the chairs. "You know, there's a point when one more take and it's child abuse."

NOT THAT THERE was much competition, but lunch was by far the high point of the day. We piled into fifteen-seater vans and were transported all the way to the other side of the parking lot. There was a huge white tent, and several long tables loaded with chafing dishes were set out in front of that. We grabbed plastic trays and real plates and cloth napkins and silverware. I just couldn't pick one thing, so I filled my plate with tiny piles of shrimp and pesto salad, steak tip salad, chinese chicken salad, and salad salad.

Riley made his way over to the adjacent fast-food trailer, where they handed his hamburger and french fries out to

him through the trailer window. We carried our trays inside the tent and found a place at one of the long,
cafeteria-style tables. There were white tablecloths on the
tables, and it felt a little bit like being at a wedding with
people we didn't know very well. I'd been to a lot of weddings like that.

After a six-hour morning that dragged on for what felt
like six days, our lunchtime flew by. I was trying to decide
if I really should go back for dessert. I knew I couldn't eat
it, but I thought I could probably get away with wrapping
it up and putting it in my pocketbook so I could eat it for
dinner. I bet people who worked on movies never even
had to go to the grocery store. I was surprised I didn't see
lots of really fat people, and when I looked around the
tent I noticed everyone was in relatively good shape. I
didn't see many actors around either. Maybe there was a
no-cal trailer somewhere. I'd have to find out, because by
midweek I'd be ready for it.

"How long does lunch last anyway?" I asked the people
sitting around us.

"Thirty minutes after the last person is served," somebody said.

"Thanks." I lowered my voice to talk just to Riley. "At
least you'll get to do something else this afternoon. That
maypole thing is getting old."

"You can say that again," Riley said.

"That maypole thing is getting old."

Riley laughed. "I knew you were going to do that, Aunt
Ginger."

We dropped off our trays on our way out of the tent.
"Maybe just one tiny bit of chocolate," I suggested.

Riley saw them first. A whole row of gumball machines.

One was filled with peanut M&M's, one with cashews, another with a kind of snack mix. And, get this, you didn't need any money to make them work. "Score," Riley said. "I'm glad I have pockets."

Riley and the other kids went back to their circle, and Allison Flagg stalked me to our cozy little picnic table. I ignored her and focused on my M&M's. As soon as I ran out, it was déjà vu all over again. One of my old boyfriends was always quoting Yogi Berra, and I still had occasional flashbacks. He'd say the one about the future not being what it used to be or something about when you come to a fork in the road, take it. It wasn't really why we broke up, but by the fourth or fifth time he rolled over after making love and said, "I usually take a two-hour nap from one to four," I was pretty much over Yogi. Not to mention the boyfriend.

They'd only done that stupid maypole dance about a million times, and now they had to do it about a million more times to get the close-ups. Why would anyone even want to be a movie actor? I was ready for a two-hour nap from one to four myself, but apparently lunch had had the opposite effect on some of the kids.

One of the little boys started jumping up and down. "Sugar high, sugar high," he kept saying.

The director pushed himself out of his chair, and once he was out of the way I could see that it said MANUEL MUSCADEL. He walked over to the technical advisors for what looked like a consult. The educational consultant pulled the sugar-high kid out of the circle, and one of the ADs took his place.

"What happened to the other kid?" Riley asked him.

"Don't worry, he'll be back in a minute," the AD said.

"Just do everything I do, okay?" He was well over six feet tall and looked like he'd wandered off the set of *Big* and into the wrong movie.

I leaned over to Allison. "I don't think that's going to work."

"It's a close-up. You won't see him at all. He's just in there to try to control the kids who are *amateurs*."

It worked pretty well. Until they brought a boom mike in and held it over the kids. "Just talk for a while," the director said. "Say the normal kinds of things you would say."

One of the little girls jumped up to touch the microphone.

"Don't touch that," the dance guy said.

"Are *you* the teacher?" the same little boy asked.

"*I'm* the teacher," the educational consultant said. "Don't touch that."

"Testing," another kid said to the microphone. "Testing one two three."

One of the twins stood up. "Tomorrow," she belted out. "Tomorrow. Tomorrow's a day today . . ."

"Somehow that doesn't sound quite right," I said to her mother.

Riley jumped up. "And now it's time for a commercial break."

"She was still singing," Allison Flagg said to me.

The sugar-high kid was back. "Sugar high, sugar high," he chanted as he hopped around.

Riley stood on his tiptoes to get closer to the boom mike. "In the rare case an erection lasts more than four hours," he said, "seek immediate medical attention."

7

"HE SAID WHAT?" GERI ASKED AFTER RILEY WAS OUT OF earshot and I could tell her. "You're kidding, right?"

"Nope." I opened Geri's refrigerator and closed it again. I couldn't possibly be hungry. "He's a natural mimic, that's all. I think he gets it from my side of the family."

Geri shook her head. "You're the aunt. You don't have a side of the family. But it's not like they don't show the commercial all day long."

"Yeah, I think I even saw it on Nickelodeon once. Anyway, he got a big laugh, and I heard somebody say he thought the kid was ready to direct."

"Do you think he knows what it means?"

"Directing?"

Geri gave me a look. "Uh, no."

"Oh, that. How would I know? He's your kid. I just drive him."

"Well, it's certainly a teaching moment. And one I'm going to hand right over to Seth as soon as he gets home."

I refused to allow myself to picture Seth discussing four-hour erections with Riley for even one millisecond. Geri sat down at her kitchen counter and opened a plastic file bulging with newspaper clippings and computer printouts. I knew I'd better wrap it up quick or Geri would be obsessing about her fiftieth again. "Well, anyway, Riley was fine, especially compared to the sugar-high kid. After listening to that one, I was thinking maybe I'd get my tubes tied, just for extra insurance."

As soon as it came out of my mouth, I regretted it. Geri's eyes lit up. "You know, if you got rid of Noah now, you could still have kids," she said.

I wondered if my sister and Allison Flagg were in cahoots. "What is it with the kid stuff today? Is there something in the water? Plus, *if* I wanted to have kids, which I don't, why couldn't I have them with Noah?"

"Come on. Noah's far too self-absorbed to have children. He can't even remember he has you."

"Thanks," I said.

She nodded. "Of course, it's your fault as much as his. People treat us the way we let them."

"Why do you hate Noah so much?"

Geri flipped through her file for a minute, then looked up again. "It's not so much that I don't like him personally. I just can't stand his type. You know, artsy-fartsy, full of himself, too-cool-for-school. He thinks he's such an original, but he's really just as much of a cliché as the rest of us."

"Wow," I said. "You have way too much time on your hands. Maybe you should have a few more kids yourself, just to keep from overanalyzing people who are none of your business. You're not even close, by the way. Noah's nothing like that. And, just to set the record straight, from where I sit, Seth isn't exactly a prize."

Geri didn't even have the good sense to be insulted. She just leaned toward me the way brides do when they're throwing a bouquet. "It's not too late if you change your mind, you know. How about that fifty-six-year-old woman who just got pregnant?"

"Give me a break, I'm only forty-one. And, anyway, didn't it turn out she was faking it?"

"That doesn't mean it's not possible."

When it came to these conversations with my sister, you pretty much had to give her something. "Okay," I said, "I'll have kids."

Geri's eyes lit up. "Really?"

"Sure, if you take care of them for me. I mean, fair's fair."

Geri put her hands on her hips. "As if you could afford my rates."

"Okay, listen. For the very last time, not that it's any of your business, let me say that I absolutely do not want children. Basically, I just want to still *be* one."

Geri got up and turned the burner on under the teakettle. "It's quite possible that you're beyond help," she said. She turned around to face me and leaned back against the kitchen counter. "Why exactly would you like to return to your childhood?"

I'd thought this through before. "So that when Mom sat down beside me like she did a couple of times a week practically from the moment I was born and said, 'Ginger, never forget, you can be anything you want to be,' I could turn to her and say, 'Mom, knock it off. It's not true. It's too much choice. It's too much pressure. And if you don't stop it right now, you're going to mess me up for life.' "

"She said the same thing to me and look how I turned out."

"Oh, puh-lease."

"Well, look at Mom. She's exactly who she wants to be. And I think she and Dad are happier than they've ever been."

"Are you crazy? Dad's flipping out because he doesn't want to move. He's hiding stuff in my apartment."

Geri shook her head. "That's just how they do things. Mom gets the big ideas and Dad freaks out, but Mom pulls him along anyway, and when he gets there he acts like it was his idea in the first place."

"That's so twisted."

"No wonder you're single."

It was time for a quick subject change followed by an even quicker getaway. I clapped my hands together. "I know. Let's talk about your birthday."

"Really?" Geri made us each a cup of tea without asking me and placed mine on the counter in front of me. She picked up her overstuffed folder and held it to her chest as she sat down at the kitchen island.

I held out my hand, and she handed over the folder so I could flip through it. "Where do you find all this stuff?" I asked.

"I don't know. Magazines. Newspapers. And I go online at work and print things out."

I gave her a shocked look. "You? On company time? Aren't you too perfect for that?"

"Everybody does it. I mean, we're a nonprofit." Geri took a sip of her tea. "Well, do you see anything?"

I closed the folder. "Boring," I said. "Why don't you get a Brazilian bikini wax to celebrate? I saw an ad for a place called Hot Cheeks that just opened in the mall. You could invite all your friends and put aftershave and painkillers in the party bags."

"Have you ever had one?"

"Not that I can remember. But I bet it would hurt enough to make you forget about fifty."

"Good point. Okay, I'll add it to the list."

I stood up to leave. I wasn't planning to say it, but it just slipped out. "So you really don't think there's any hope for Noah and me?"

Geri reached out, and I handed her the folder. "Well, maybe," she said, "but I think one of you would have to hire a dating coach first."

WHEN I FINALLY GOT HOME, my father and my cat were seated on the floor of my apartment. Boyfriend gave me a disdainful look that clearly said, *Don't look at me, I didn't let him in.*

"Hiya, Toots," my father said without looking up.

I bent down to scratch Boyfriend behind his ears. "Hi, Dad," I said. "Thanks for stopping by."

"Anytime," my father said. "Champ and I have been having a fine time for ourselves."

"Whatcha got there, Dad?" I asked as casually as I could manage.

My father finally looked up at me. He dropped his voice to a whisper. "Keep it under your hat, but I think we have at least one original here."

"Dad, is that more stuff?"

"Toots, you would not believe what people give away at the Take It or Leave It."

"Dad, did you bring those back from the dump?"

My father shrugged. "Don't look at me. Your mother's

the one who keeps loading up the car and sending me over there."

Marshbury still had a landfill, and "going to the dump" was a big part of the town's social life. Politicians campaigned there, Girl Scouts sold cookies there, and hordes of seagulls dined there on a daily basis. It was pretty disgusting if you stopped to think about it.

Take It or Leave It was just what it sounded like, a section of the dump where you could drop off the junk you no longer needed, and help yourself to other people's junk. Which, of course, you didn't really need either. It was the most popular part of the Marshbury landfill, and there were people who seemed to hang around all day, and would even come over to help you unload your car when you pulled up. It was possible that my father was turning into one of these people.

I took a few steps over to my bathroom and pushed the door open. There were so many garbage bags jammed into my little square shower that it looked like some new style of Dumpster. I wished it were an oversize trash compactor instead, since at least then I'd stand a better chance of taking a shower in the foreseeable future.

I turned back to my father. "Dad," I began.

"Listen, Dollface, this is no time to be a party pooper."

I sat down on the floor between my father and my cat. At least my father was wearing two white socks today, though one had two bands of hunter green near the top, and the other sock was circled twice in brown. In front of him were several old toys and what appeared to be a hose from a vacuum cleaner. "Dad," I began again.

He leaned forward and picked up one of the toys. It looked like an earless plastic cat collapsed on a wooden guitar. "I'm ninety-nine percent sure that what we've got here is an authentic Tailspin Tabby." He pointed to a string. "Here, pull this."

I did, and the earless cat stood up. "Amazing," I said. Boyfriend ignored the imitation feline and started licking his paw.

"I know," my father said. "It's one of the original Fisher-Price toys. Early 1930s, I'd say. It drives me bananas to think this could have fallen into the wrong hands. It's a piece of history, for crissakes."

"Well, it is a little bit broken." I picked up the hose. "What's this for, Dad?"

"A vacuum cleaner. The rest of it's still in the car. Just the ticket if yours goes on the fritz."

It was highly unlikely my vacuum would ever be over-worked enough to do any fritzing. I nodded at the jack-in-the-box and the rusty red scooter leaning up against my couch. "Dad, what's Mom going to say when she sees all this stuff?"

"Your mother," my father said, "is nothing but an old fart. She wants to move me into a place with a julienne balcony. What the heck am I going to do with a julienne balcony?"

"I think it's called a Juliet balcony, Dad."

"And those devil friends of hers in those red hats of theirs. One of them tries to kiss me every time she comes over to see your mother. On the lips."

A car backed out of the garage underneath us. My father reached for the scooter and used it to push himself back into a standing position. Then he climbed on and took a wobbly ride over to the window. "Looks like the coast is clear. Grab a flashlight, we're digging it up."

For what it was worth, I tried playing dumb. "Digging what up, Dad?"

My father parked his scooter over by my door. "Come on," he said. "Let's move."

It was easy to tell where to dig, since a circle of grass sat on top of the hole like a hat. My father shoved it off to the side with the tip of his shovel while I held the flashlight and looked over my shoulder a few times like a good look-out should.

It was a lot easier digging a hole in the same place the second time around, I observed. "Just wondering," I said, "but what are you going to do with whatever it is when you find it?"

"We'll cross that bridge when we get to it, Toots."

I looked over my shoulder again. I considered whether I should let my father in on the whole St. Joseph story or not. I mean, what if he brought the statue to Take It or Leave It, and the dump sold it instead?

"Hey, Toots," my father said, "can you wipe that grin off your face and give me a hand? I'm afraid somebody might have gotten here first."

I took the shovel from my father and handed him the flashlight. First I sifted through the dirt pile, careful not to injure any hiding saints. Then I dug into the hole and scraped away at the hard-packed edges.

St. Joseph had disappeared.

8

I WAS CURLED UP ON THE COUCH WITH BOYFRIEND ON my lap, not really watching something on TV, when I heard the first pebble on the window. Noah hated the phone. I had to admit I wasn't too crazy about the pebble thing either.

"Hey," Noah said when I opened the door. He was holding a pizza box in one hand and a gallon of milk in the other, and his hair was wet.

"Oh," I said. "Did we have dinner plans?"

"Oh," he said. "Sorry. I probably should have stopped by first to ask. I guess I figured if you weren't here, then I'd just catch up with you tomorrow or something."

"And if I were here, you'd already have the pizza."

He managed to shrug and nod at the same time. Boyfriend came over to eye the gallon of milk. Noah reached into his pocket and took out a little tin frog with a key sticking out of its side. He wound it up and reached across the threshold to place it on the floor. Boyfriend stalked it from a distance as the frog chugged its way into the room.

I stepped back and let Noah in, too. I mean, what else could I do? It's not really that rude to just show up, if you bring a gallon of milk and a toy for somebody's cat, is it? "Cute," I said. "But aren't frogs supposed to hop?"

Noah took the two steps required to reach my kitchenette and placed the pizza box and milk on the counter. "I guess it depends on the frog," he said. "Maybe we could go out for an ice cream later? You know, dessert? Or we could just leave the pizza here for the cat and the frog, and go get dinner somewhere."

"That's okay," I said. "But, I'm just curious. Do you remember the last time you were here, when we discussed the concept of advance planning?"

Noah turned around slowly. "Well," he said, "I really meant to do that, but then somehow most of the week slipped by, and it just seemed to make more sense to come over." He smiled. "Pizza?"

I took the slice he handed me. "Well," I said, "at least this time you remembered I don't like mushrooms."

The first time I met Noah was about two years ago. I had quit my job at an all-inclusive resort in Panama and moved to North Carolina to sell furniture. It turned out that wasn't my thing either, so I quit that job and moved home.

I was coming out of a Childfree by Choice meeting. Actually, I never made it all the way inside. I just lurked around in the back of musty old St. Mary's Hall, listening for a while, staying safely behind the second set of double doors. Then I picked up a two-sided flyer and tiptoed back outside. I liked the idea that there might be some other people in the world my age whose lives didn't revolve around either their kids or last-ditch efforts to get pregnant, but I wasn't exactly the clubby type. Plus I'd just moved back to Marshbury and I was afraid of being recognized by someone I went to high school with.

It was a Friday night in the summer, so Marshbury's Main Street was closed to all but pedestrian traffic. A couple of sawhorses at either end did the trick. Marshbury merchants set up long tables on the sidewalks in front of their shops, and a farmers' market featuring local produce took up the center of the street. Craftspeople and a couple of mortgage brokers occupied the remaining space.

I sat down on a bench at the edge of the sidewalk and started reading the flyer. Wow, these people were serious—they even had T-shirts you could order. CHILD-FREE BY CHOICE. PARENT YOURSELF. FAMILY OF ONE. NO KIDDING. I COULD HAVE KIDS, BUT I JUST DON'T LIKE THEM. Not only that, but there were *activities for married or single adults who have never had children.* I scanned the list. The Chocolate Trolley Tour sounded good, but it also seemed like something I'd bring one of the kids to so I didn't have to go alone. Riley loved chocolate.

I looked up. A guy was staring straight at me from one of the booths. "AA?" he asked.

"Excuse me?" I said.

He nodded toward the hall. "Did you just come out of an AA meeting?"

I sat up a little straighter. "Nah, they make me too thirsty."

He brushed some hair away from his face and smiled. "Not very PC," he said.

"I have that tendency," I said. I folded up the flyer and stuffed it into my pocket.

He watched me do it. "So," he said. "What kind of meeting was it?"

"I can't remember," I said.

"Hmm," he said. "Well, I guess I could go in there and find out. For both of us."

I shrugged. "I guess you could. But then someone might steal your stuff."

"Good point," he said.

"Childfree by Choice," I said. "I was just lurking."

He tilted his head to one side. "Childfree by Choice in a Catholic church? Isn't that philosophically inconsistent?"

"Church hall," I said. "Maybe there's an equal opportunity rental clause."

"Actually," he said, "I was just wondering if the meeting was about to get out. Whether I should wait around for a few minutes or pack it in now."

Somehow I ended up helping him break his booth down. He introduced me to Sage, his cute, redheaded mutt, who followed his every move with such clear adoration that it seemed to me it would be a lot to live up to. I'd never really thought about it before, but Boyfriend's indifference was a whole lot less pressure.

"Do you live in Marshbury?" I asked.

"Yeah, I've lived here a couple years."

"And before that?"

"I apprenticed in Seattle, which is supposed to be kind of the new Mecca for glassblowers."

"What's the old Mecca?"

"Venice. You should see the stuff they have over there. Anyway, Seattle didn't work out for personal reasons, so Sage and I went looking for a place where I could make enough money to support us. I knew this was it as soon as I saw it. Great beaches, good vibe. No other glassblowers."

I didn't know anything about glassblowing, but as I wrapped newspaper around a bunch of bowls I seriously wished I could afford, even I could see Noah was talented. I held up the waviest of the bunch. "This is amazing," I said.

Noah shrugged. "You can turn most of your mistakes

into a wavy bowl. You just hang it upside down and start spinning. It's basic angular momentum—when an object is spinning, everything flattens and goes to the outer edges."

He'd pretty much lost me, so I picked up a cute little folded-over glass plate that held Noah's business cards. "Great idea," I said, thinking maybe I could get him to make me one as soon as I figured out what my next business cards would say.

Noah shook his head. "You would not believe how many of those silly things I've sold. I was always forgetting to put out my cards, so one day I just thought I'd recycle a mistake. . . ."

"Wavy bowl," I said. "Next time just turn it into a wavy bowl."

"Thanks," he said. "I'll remember that. So, what do you do for a living?"

I told him how I'd just quit another stupid sales job because I found out that pretty much everyone who worked for this particular Boston rental car company had, like me, been told they were management track. And that I'd only moved Boyfriend and me into my parents' garage apartment as a temporary thing until I could afford something more appropriate with my soon-to-be manager's salary, but now it looked like I'd be there until I came up with something else to do. Or until hell froze over, whichever came first.

Already I could see that Noah was one of those rare people who listened with full attention. His eyes didn't dance around over my shoulders, on the lookout for something more interesting. When I finished, he picked up a paperweight, deep blue with an explosion of raised yellow swirls that reminded me of Van Gogh's *Starry Night*. "What if you started making something?" he asked. He made it sound so easy.

"Like what?" I asked.

"I don't know. Whatever interests you." He handed me the paperweight, and I considered it like a crystal ball.

"Too intimidating," I said, though I was tempted by a quick vision of Noah's sweaty arms wrapped around my sweaty body as he taught me everything he knew. "But how did you choose glassblowing?"

Noah shook his head. "My father wanted me to be an accountant, but one summer I took a glassblowing workshop. Then I went back to school in the fall and figured out I could earn as much making bongs as I could putting on a suit."

I searched his table for drug paraphernalia.

He laughed. "Don't worry. I've become almost gentrified since college. But I still love glassblowing. It's the greatest thing I could imagine doing. It's my life."

Judging by the new Honda Element we loaded everything into, it looked like it must be pretty lucrative, too. At least by my standards. Or maybe he had a trust fund. "Can you make a living at it?" I asked.

"Yeah," he said. "If you work seven days a week and don't sleep a lot. I mean, I'd do it for free, but it's a lot more gratifying to make money at it. Plus, my dog likes to eat."

"You'd really do it for free?"

"Sure. That's the way it has to be. If you're not really into something, you don't put the time in, so you don't get good at it. Passion is the key to everyone's gifts."

I tried to remember that, so I could write it down later. Noah and Sage and I started walking along the street toward the water. Noah showed me a secluded little shelf of rocks between the big town pier and some private docks. As we climbed down there, I wondered if I should be more worried about the possibility of him being an artistic serial killer.

But we just sat crimelessly on the rocks and looked out at the ocean, which was that really rich shade of blue it reaches before it gets dark out. Some early evening sailing was still going on just past the mouth of the harbor, and closer to me I could feel electricity dancing between us.

Noah gestured with his head and said, "Look." On the far side of the harbor, an amazing orangey pink sun hovered just over the lighthouse. We watched it sink slowly behind the tip of the lighthouse and peek out around the sides. Then, all of a sudden, it burst through the glass part of the lighthouse and lit the whole thing up, as if someone had flipped a switch. We watched without moving until it dropped behind the lighthouse and the light went out.

I turned to look at Noah, and he was smiling as if he'd made it happen just for me.

"Thanks," I said, just in case.

He laughed. "You're welcome. But I'm not sure I can take full credit. My magic days are over."

"You were a magician?" I asked, mostly just to keep him talking.

"I was pretty geeky all right, but I think I drew the line at magic tricks. I spent most of my formative years playing Dungeons & Dragons. Do you know what a larper is?"

I was back in serial killer fantasyland again, and I took a moment to visualize my escape route just in case I needed one. "Uh, no," I said. "What?"

"A larper is someone who dresses up as his, or her, character. Think swords made from foam wrapped around PVC pipe with duct tape."

"Whew, I bet you got a lot of dates with that stuff."

"No kidding. Not a lot of prom action going on for me."

"What were you? I mean who was your character?"

Noah rubbed his hands over his face. "Tassrigoth the Elf."

"Wow, that's a lot to recover from. I only played princess for about a month in kindergarten, and then my mother started telling me things like if a princess has a college education she won't need to be rescued and even princesses should have a prenup. It kind of took the fun right out of it."

Nobody said anything for a few seconds, which always makes me nervous, so I reached for something to fill the silence. "You're not married or anything, are you?" slipped out before I thought it through.

He shook his head. "Nope," he said. "And apparently I never was."

I waited for the rest of the story, but it didn't come. "Apparently?"

"My in-laws pulled some strings and had it annulled. So, essentially, my marriage never existed. I've always been single. That's a no. Not married. Or anything." He rubbed his hands back and forth on his jeans, just above his knees, and looked out at the water.

Eventually he asked, "So, what about you? Are you married or anything?"

"Nope. Almost a couple times, I think, but now I'm not even sure I'm remembering it right."

He nodded, and Sage rested her head on his knee. This was getting really depressing, so I thought I should try to lighten things up. I hunched over and sighed an exaggerated sigh. "So, anyway," I said in an old lady voice, "I guess I'm just destined to end up as the crazy maiden aunt living with my cat in an apartment over the garage."

Noah sighed, too. "Yeah, I know. Sometimes I just pretend I'm a monk."

One of us had to move things along here, and clearly it wasn't going to be Noah. I leaned back and turned toward him, eyes wide, going for kind of a flirty disbelief. "You're celibate?"

He laughed and I laughed. But I'd been around the block enough to know that early in a relationship with anyone, friend or lover, the other person reveals himself. It might take you a month or a few years before you believe it, but he's already told you who he is and what you can expect from him.

I didn't expect a lot from Noah. I wasn't even sure if I wanted much from him. If you were to graph our relationship over the two years we'd known each other, it wouldn't have a lot of peaks and valleys. We saw each other fairly regularly, took long walks, went to the occasional movie or art show. We had great sex. I wasn't sure if we knew much more about each other now than when we first met. Maybe we both just happened to be in the same place, and we were marking time together until one of us drifted away to something else. Or maybe I just couldn't admit to either of us that I wanted more, because then I'd have to notice if I didn't get it.

9

"SO, DID YOU SAY IT?" GERI ASKED FIRST THING SATUR-day morning.

I held the phone in place with my chin so I could use both hands to move my father's garbage bags out of my shower. "Yes, I said it. I said, *Did we have dinner plans?* Just the way you told me to."

"Then what happened? You didn't let him in, I hope. And if you did, I certainly hope you didn't *do* anything."

My older sister had a disturbing interest in my sex life. I shoved the garbage bag out into the main room and pulled the door closed. I looked in the mirror and, yes, I was glowing. "Of course not," I lied. I reached into the shower stall and turned on the water.

My sister blew some air through her lips and made a sound that horses make. "Don't you know anything?" she asked. "From a strategic point of view, the worst thing you can do is sleep with him. At least make him work a little."

It didn't seem worth pointing out that sex was the one thing Noah and I had figured out. It was only when we got out of bed that things seemed a bit vague.

"You know, if you don't believe you deserve better treat-ment, you'll never get it. Look at me. I got everything I wanted."

"Yeah, and now you have Mom's hips."

"Don't try to change the subject. Is he still there?"

"No, why?"

"Why? *Why?* So what, he just shows up, gets laid, and then leaves before he even cooks breakfast for you?"

I wasn't sure whether to hang up on my sister, or turn the shower off so I wouldn't run out of hot water before I even got in. "Oh, please, not that it's any of your business, but he had to go home to take his dog out. He's very conscientious like that."

"Sure. Too bad you're not his dog. I hope you at least talked him into helping out at Mom and Dad's today."

"Why? They're not his parents. Listen, I have to go. I'll see you over there."

❧

"HEY, DAD," I said, about twenty minutes later when I wandered over to my parents' house. "Is there any coffee left?"

"It was nice of that young fellow of yours to help us out before he left," my father said. "He swept the whole porch."

"What? You made Noah sweep the porch?"

My mother let the screen door slam behind her. "He didn't seem to mind at all," she said. "I told him he should show up during daylight hours sometime, so you could bring him over here for dinner."

"I can't have this conversation without caffeine," I said.

My mother caught up to me in the kitchen. I poured myself a cup of stale coffee and she climbed up on a stepladder. "We'll whip the house into shape this weekend, and then get to work on your place early in the week."

"Dad's already helping me with my place," I said.

"We've got it under control." I took a sip of my coffee, then poured the rest of it down the sink. "Where's the coffee?" I asked.

"Same place it's always been."

I opened the cupboard next to the refrigerator and grabbed the old tin coffee canister. It wasn't hard to find, since there were only about three items left on the shelf. "Hey," I said. "Where did everything go?"

"We're trying to make the cupboards look bigger." My mother climbed down and placed some old bottles on the counter, then climbed back up again.

I filled a new coffee filter with extra coffee and added water to the coffeemaker, then went over to help my mother. She handed me some more bottles.

I managed to get them onto the counter without breaking them. They were tiny. The dark brown and green ones looked like they might be antiques, and a clear one looked like the bottom of a baby food jar. Some of them had corks in the top, and others were topped with a circle of fabric tied with a piece of ribbon. "Hilton Head," I read out loud from a faded yellow label. "Sanibel. Virginia Beach. Paine's Creek. Pegotty. What are these?"

"Sand," my mother said. "From every beach your father and I have ever walked."

"Oh, that's so sweet," I said. It was strange to think of my parents having collections I hadn't bothered to notice. I started picking up bottles and reading them. I lined them up across the length of the old flecked counter my parents had never gotten around to upgrading.

My mother climbed down from the stepladder and leaned back against the counter. She picked up one of the bottles. "We sure walked a lot of beaches in our day."

I picked up another one. "Detroit?"

My mother giggled like she was Becca's age. "That was from your father. He brought it back from a business trip. I'm sure there are lovely beaches in Detroit, but he scooped the sand from the ashtray in the hotel lobby." She shook her head. "I think that's my favorite one of all."

"Do you have a box I can pack these in?" I asked.

My mother handed me a half-full garbage bag. "Just dump them in here."

I couldn't believe it. "Mom," I said.

"Honey, we can't take it all with us. There's nothing worse than a couple of old people with a whole big house full of clutter crammed into a little townhouse."

"You're not old," I said. "But, okay, I'll just split these bottles with Geri when she gets here."

∽

WHEN I FINALLY GOT HOME from my parents' house, it was dark and Boyfriend was meowing at the door like he hadn't seen me in a month. I squatted down and scooped him up in my arms. "Sorry," I whispered in his ear.

He started grooming my cheek with his sandpapery tongue. "Yeah, I know, I'm a mess," I said. I was carrying a bag containing my half of the sand-filled bottles, along with a few empty ones my mother and I had found on the same shelf. I placed the bag on the kitchen counter and reached around with one hand until I found an empty bottle. You never knew when you might pass a beach.

Boyfriend and I headed down the stairs, and I yanked up one of the heavy garage doors. I dragged out Boyfriend's pet carrier on wheels, and stood back to take a look at it under the outdoor lights.

I'd ordered it online about a year ago and didn't remember the description having the word *stroller* in it anywhere. "Riley's way off base. I don't think this looks anything like a stroller, do you?" Boyfriend didn't seem to disagree, so I unzipped the top and plopped him inside. He knew the drill and, avoiding the canvas-covered back half of the carrier, immediately circled around and got comfortable up front, where only an open weave of green netting stood between my cat and the world.

I put the bottle inside in case he got bored and needed something to play with, and pushed him down to the end of the driveway at a brisk pace. We bumped our way up to the sidewalk. "Maybe a little bit like a shopping cart," I suggested, "or even a chariot." I realized I was talking out loud to my cat in public. I was far too young to be a crazy cat lady, so I reined it in.

Possibly winged chariot was even closer, since Boyfriend and I practically seemed to fly along the sidewalks of Marshbury. It was dark already and the stars were twinkling away up in the sky. After a day of packing and cleaning, it felt good to move, and I was a little less stiff with every couple of steps. If I didn't have Boyfriend, I'd probably be asleep already. I took a deep breath of the late spring air. "Thanks for getting me out tonight," I whispered.

Even though Noah had been gone since this morning, I couldn't quite shake him. All day long I kept starting to turn to tell him something, and then I'd remember he wasn't there. So instead I'd tweak it around in my head a few times until I'd get it just the way I would have said it if he'd still happened to be around.

I always missed Noah right after he left. I knew I'd be okay after a night or two alone. I had some DVDs I'd rented and hadn't even watched yet, plus I had orders from two local shops and was way behind on my earrings. I just had to let it all fade. He'd be back in a few days or a few weeks, and the longer he was gone, the less it would feel like it mattered.

Of course, the flip side was that why couldn't a grown woman, even one pushing a cat along the sidewalk in the dark, shake off her inertia and stop by to visit her pseudo boyfriend if she felt like it? I mean, after all, hadn't Noah just shown up at *my* door last night? Maybe I'd show him the empty bottle and tell him about my parents' sand collection. It would be such a romantic story that we'd just naturally start planning a beachy adventure of our own.

Boyfriend and I came to an intersection. I thought for a minute, then took a left. Half a block later we were crunching our way along Noah's crushed mussel shell driveway. Noah's little beach house, one of the few on the block that hadn't been ripped down and replaced with something bigger and trendier, was dark, but the studio he'd built in his backyard was all lit up.

I pushed the pet carrier on wheels up to the window so I could peek inside first. I didn't really think Noah would be in there with another woman, but you didn't get to be my age without a few jolting experiences in your life, and it never hurt to be sure.

Noah was alone. His glassblowing furnace was open and blazing. He must have just turned on his CD player,

because a scratchy recording of Gregorian chants blasted
out at full volume and made me jump. He was wearing
jeans with huge, frayed white rips in them and an old
T-shirt.

He leaned back against the wall, and then kind of slid
down until he was sitting cross-legged on the floor. I was
half waiting for him to start chanting along with the Gre-
gorians. Or even to start wrapping duct tape around PVC
pipe so he could have a swordfight with some elves or
something.

He sat there for a little while, then stood up again and
tied a washed-out red bandana around his head, tangling
some of his hair in when he knotted it in the back. He
reached for his sunglasses and put them on, and I waited
to see something along the lines of one of his open studio
demonstrations. Instead, he started to dance. It took me
completely by surprise, and I stepped away from the window and pulled Boyfriend with me.

I peeked in again, from the side. It wasn't quite a dance
after all. More like tai chi or some kind of yoga in motion.
Whatever he was doing, it was filled with long, graceful,
continuous movements, and I could have sworn there was
a little bit of imaginary swordplay in there, too.

He picked up a long blowpipe with a big knob of sea
green glass on the end and clamped it across his work-
bench. Then he grabbed another smaller rod and dipped it
into the furnace, and when he pulled it out he rolled the
button-shaped gather of hot glass around in an old tin
filled with crushed cobalt glass. He kept the first pipe
spinning with his knee at the same time he twirled
molten glass from the second pipe around the original
blob of glass. Then he picked up some metal tongs and

reached into the glass and twisted and pulled at it until it froze into a series of waves.

He stopped and put everything down, stepped back, and looked at the knob from all sides, gave it a spin, then he did some more almost dancing around the room.

He came back and unclamped the blowpipe and plunged the knob into the furnace. He placed it back in the clamp again and kept it spinning with one hand. With the other, he reached into another tin and pulled out a handful of something that might have been pieces of gold and silver foil and sprinkled them like confetti over the knob.

He put the blowpipe back into the furnace again, and sweat soaked through his T-shirt. He pulled it back out and dropped the glass end down until it almost touched the ground. The monks were still chanting, and Noah looked like he was lip-synching into the other end of the pipe. Maybe he was. Then he started to swing the pipe in a huge circle, crossing his wrists, as if he were twirling a fiery baton.

Finally, he lifted the pipe and placed his creation into the empty center of a sphere made from several lengths of copper tubing circled around and around and dangling from a clamp. He blew some air into the blowpipe and quickly covered the opening with his thumb. The blob of glass expanded slowly and magically until it filled up the copper orb and became some new kind of ringed planet.

Watching Noah like this was somehow more intimate than having sex with him. I felt like a stalker. In fact, I probably looked like a stalker. I glanced down at Boyfriend, and I had to admit that, even in the dark, the thing I was pushing him in was suddenly looking, well, *strollery*.

We bumped our way back over the mussel shell driveway and out to the sidewalk. I was trying to figure out what I was feeling. Number one, Noah was lost in his own little world. Number two, by the looks of things, he certainly hadn't spent the day missing me. Number three, I really, really wanted to feel the intensity he was feeling, out in his studio all by himself, about something. But what? And, number whatever it was, why didn't Noah feel that way about me?

It was just around the corner, and I thought about walking over to the beach to fill the little bottle with sand, but how pitiful would that be? I could just see the label now: GINGER ALONE WITH CAT, SCUTTLE BEACH. So, instead, I pushed Boyfriend through the starlit streets back to the garage, and then I carried him up the stairs.

I pulled out the sleep sofa. Boyfriend jumped up to his side of the bed, and I went into the bathroom to wash up. The shower curtain was open and I saw that my father had left me another garbage bag. Great. The perfect ending to a very long day.

I crawled into bed and fell almost immediately into a heavy sleep. When my alarm woke me up, it caught me in the middle of a dream about running into Noah. I was working behind the counter of a cell phone kiosk that happened to be sitting on the side of the road. It was so real I could even read the sign: SHE SELLS SEA CELLS DOWN BY THE SEASHORE. Noah was pushing triplets past me in a great big baby stroller, and walking along beside him was Allison Flagg.

10

RILEY AND I WERE LATE GETTING TO THE *SHARK SENSE* Base Camp, but it didn't matter, since it was taking them forever to get the first shot of the day set up. One of the ADs brought all the kids down to the edge of the water, only to send them back to the holding area a few minutes later. Then she finally told us we could all take a bathroom break and go raid the craft services table. I grabbed a bottle of water and a handful of strawberries, but Riley was more interested in the joke book he'd brought along.

We sat on a big rock at the edge of the beach while he read, and I could tell by his squeaky laugh when he hit a good one. I finished the strawberries, wiped my hands on an inconspicuous section of my jeans, since I'd forgotten to take a napkin, and started rooting around in the sand for treasures.

When I'd first started making my earrings, I found out you could buy a whole color-coordinated bag of Authentic Sealike Glass, encased in plastic netting, for $2.69 or 2/$5.00 at Oceanside Craft Mart. I'd push my wobbly red cart up and down the aisles and throw in a spool of twenty-gauge wire and some hypoallergenic pierced ear-ring wires. Then I'd fish through the piles until I found a bag of pale green sealike glass and maybe one of pink, which was even prettier than a color you'd really find on the beach. I'd add a bag of assorted color sealike glass, just so I'd have some variety. The stuff looked amazingly good, and I figured that anything it lacked in authenticity was more than made up for by the convenience.

But now I wasn't so sure. Maybe there was something special about a piece of glass that had actually been tumbled smooth by waves pounding it into the sand until it became a treasure. When Geri and I were kids, we'd spend long afternoons at this beach, hunting for sea glass, and even digging shiny glass shards out of the rocks. I remembered how we'd fight over the cobalt pieces, and once Geri told me they were only hunks of old Noxzema jars, just so I'd give mine to her. I didn't care where they came from. I just knew they were beautiful.

When the tide was out at Scuttle Beach, as it was now, it was way out. This surge in tidal flow meant that there was always a lot to find on the rocky shore. I kicked a sunbleached lobster claw out of the way and picked up a tarnished, circular ring of metal. I looked around some more and found a small pumpkin-colored rock with little bits of white shell imbedded in it.

I'd locked my shoulder bag in my car, so I put them in my pocket and started walking the beach. I almost missed a perfect square of chocolate brown sea glass until the sun hit it and it sparkled right at me. Maybe this was how Noah felt when he saw shapes in liquid glass. Maybe I was finally finding my inner artist.

〰️

"CUT," MANNY YELLED. He buried his head in his hands. "Why didn't I just quit while I was a production assistant?" he mumbled softly.

I was close enough to hear him. It's not like I was eavesdropping, but I'd been sitting on the sand and slowly sliding my way down toward the line of director's chairs. I'd found a couple of really cool shells and an old watch with a fogged-out face, and so far not a single AD had sent me back to my place. Maybe I was low enough to be under their radar.

"Let's take ten, everybody," Manny said. He looked down at me. "You don't happen to have a bat and ball, do you?"

"Sorry," I said. "But I can go get one. We're close to home."

"Make that twenty," he yelled.

Tim Kelly was suddenly beside me. "Want some company?" he asked.

The gaffer was wearing jeans and a blue T-shirt today, and his sandy hair was already curly. I'd happened to notice it started off fairly straight in the morning but got curlier as the day went on. "No, thanks," I said. "I'm all set."

He shook his head. "Too bad. Is there a boyfriend I should know about?"

"Sort of," I said. "How about you?"

"Nope. I'm pretty much heterosexual."

"Funny," I said. "But I meant girlfriend."

He crossed his arms over his chest, and I tried not to check out his shoulders. "Define girlfriend," he said.

I had a better shot at defining trouble. Even though I wasn't actually wearing a watch, I glanced down at my wrist anyway. "Well, will you look at the time," I said before I walked away.

After I grabbed an old bat and ball from my parents' garage, I headed up the steps to say a quick hello to

Boyfriend. Sitting just outside my door was one of Noah's vases. It was deep turquoise with long strands of sea green cording, and it was filled with purple lilacs.

"See," I said to my cat when he met me at the door. "He really is trying."

SINCE IT WAS RILEY'S BAT, he got to hit first. Manny was pitching, and I was catching. A bunch of the kids were out in the field, which was actually one end of the roped-off beach.

Manny threw the ball so wide I had to run after it. "I don't swing at garbage," Riley yelled to him.

"God, I love this kid," Manny said. I managed to throw the ball back to him without seriously embarrassing myself, and he tried again.

I scooped up the ball, and Riley put the bat behind his head and twisted his torso from side to side. "We need a pitcher, not a belly-itcher," he yelled.

"Let's see you hit my knuckle curve," Manny yelled.

Riley swung and hit the ball out into the water. He ran around the beach stone bases, pumping both hands up in the air, while Manny's personal assistant waded in to get the ball.

Eventually, a worried-looking guy wearing a suit waved us all back to the set. "Bummer," Manny said as he handed me the bat and still soggy ball. "Oh, well, it was fun while it lasted."

Riley ran in from the outfield, and the three of us started walking back together. I could never resist this kind of opportunity. "You know," I said. "I was just thinking, since I have to be here anyway. Just in case you need any more extras or anything. . . ."

Manny stopped. "Oh, no. Not you, too."

"You can have my part, Aunt Ginger," Riley said.

I put my hand on his shoulder. "That's okay," I said.

"My own mother even offered to use her frequent flyer miles to bring herself out here. 'Just a small part, Manuel,' she said. 'Nothing anybody else would miss.' "

"Sorry," I said. I held up the bat and ball. "I think I'll put these back in the car. Just so we'll know where they are."

Allison Flagg followed me out to the parking lot. "You know," she said, "I'm only saying this because the other mothers are starting to talk about you. They think you're kissing up to the director to get some lines for your nephew."

I threw the bat and ball into the trunk, then slammed it shut. "Guess they're on to me," I said before I walked away from Allison Flagg.

Maybe I didn't have much of a life right now, but at least I had more than a stage mom did. And if I could just get focused, possibly I could have even more than that. I wondered if your ability to change had a shelf life, like your looks and your fertility, and even the amount of time you could live in an apartment over your parents' garage before they sold it on you. I hoped not, but just in case, even I could tell it was time to use it or lose it.

"THANKS FOR TAKING me out a book on your card, Aunt Ginger," Riley said beside me. "I needed some new jokes."

"You're welcome." I put on my blinker and pulled into

his driveway. The backseat of my car was piled with anything and everything I could find at the Marshbury Public Library about jewelry and jewelry making and beach art and found art. I wasn't sure exactly where I was going, but for once in my life I was determined to stick with it until I figured it out. "Just don't forget to return it."

Riley pushed open the car door and jumped out. "I won't," he yelled over his shoulder. "See you tomorrow."

"Hey, loser," Rachel said as she came running out the door, "it's your turn to set the table."

For a minute, I thought she was talking to me. So much for personal growth. Then Riley stood on his tiptoes and punched her in the shoulder, and Becca ran out after her sister. "Yeah," Becca said, "just because you're shark bait doesn't mean you get out of doing chores."

"Mo-om," Riley yelled as he ran past her.

Rachel came over and stood by my door until I rolled my window down. "Mom wants you to come in for a minute," she said as she hiked up her jeans.

Becca peered into my backseat. "Cool," she said. "Are you gonna make more stuff?"

"That's the plan," I said.

"I have some extra beads I'm not using," Rachel said.

"I think I have some polymer clay in my room that hasn't dried up yet," Becca said.

I pushed my car door open. "Bring it on," I said.

Geri was sitting at the kitchen island, and no surprise, she was immersed in her burgeoning birthday folder.

I walked over and opened her refrigerator. "Can I get you anything?" I asked politely. When she didn't answer, I checked out some kind of as-yet-uncooked chicken thing to see if it was worth waiting around for, and grabbed a bottle of water. "What are you doing home, anyway? You haven't put in eighteen hours yet today, have you?"

Geri ignored me. "What about this? I invite everyone to a party and tell them to wear black and white, and then I show up in red."

"So, what, you can stick out like a sore thumb?"

"Never mind," Geri said.

"Guess who left me flowers today?" I said.

"Hel-lo?" my sister said. "We're not talking about you. I'm having a midlife crisis here." She sighed. "Anyway, it's the very least he could do. What do you mean, he *left* you flowers?"

"When I got home, they were waiting outside my door," I said. "It was very sweet."

"So, when are you going to see him again?"

"You know," I said, "I really think we should stay focused on your birthday."

I drummed my fingers on the table while Geri hunted some more.

"Will you stop that?"

"Sorry," I said. Rachel and Becca were taking forever getting me their stuff. "What does Seth think you should do?" I asked as if I cared.

"He says we should go away for a weekend and you can babysit for us."

That sounded boring even for Seth. "Don't you have any friends turning fifty this year? Maybe you could all do something together."

Geri actually looked up. "Yeah, I'm still in touch with some friends from college. We got out our calendars a couple times, and it looks like we might have a window in late August. . . ."

Geri went back to her endless search, and I took a sip of water and started thinking about friends. I'd had lots of friends over the course of my life, but I seemed to be without many actual *active* friendships now. Most of them had been the casualty of marriage and kids, and others had turned out to be all about work and had evaporated pretty quickly once I left that particular job. And still others turned out to be based on the shared interest of going places to meet men, and that whole thing just got old for me. I must have drifted away from the rest of them when I headed back to live in the compound. You don't want just anybody to know you live over your parents' garage.

"Hey," I said, thinking maybe I should work on my conversational skills in the unlikely case I ever made any new friends. "Wanna hear something strange?"

Geri didn't say anything, which I took as a yes.

"Mom buried a statue of St. Joseph to help the house sell, and when Dad went to dig it up, it wasn't there."

"That's nice," Geri said.

"You don't happen to have any extra statues kicking around, do you? I'm just thinking I should put another one in the hole so they don't start blaming each other. That way if Dad looks, he'll think he just missed it the first time, and if Mom checks, she'll think it's still there." Even at my age, I hated the sound of my parents fighting.

Geri sighed and looked up. "The drawer to the left of the silverware."

I found it on the first try and pulled it all the way out. "Wow," I said as I rooted around in a tangled mass of CCD books, church bulletins, dried palm frond crosses, and an ancient mantilla that must have belonged to Geri when she was a kid, since I'd had one just like it. "What's this, your God Help Us drawer?"

Geri closed her folder and pushed her chair back. She reached around in the drawer and handed me a small plastic statue.

"I don't think this is the same one," I said. "The other guy didn't have anybody sitting on his shoulder." I'd always been able to distinguish the boy saints from the girl saints by their beards, but beyond that, one cheap plastic statue looked pretty much like the next one to me. Possibly it was a matter of so many saints, so much skipped Sunday school. Yes, we've all heard of St. Joseph, but could we pick him out of a lineup?

"Do you want it or not?"

"Yeah, okay. I mean, I guess it's pretty dark in that hole anyway." Before she could close the drawer again, I grabbed a pair of rosary beads. The beads looked like real tigereye, and they were linked with intricate silver fili-gree. I held them out of my sister's reach. "Can I have these, too?"

Geri tapped her toe on the kitchen floor. "For what?"

"I don't know, I was thinking I might start praying again."

"Yeah, right." My sister held out her hand. "Give those back to me right now. You cannot turn them into earrings."

I held the rosary beads behind my back.

"You'll rot in Hell," my older sister said.

"No you won't, Aunt Ginger," Rachel said as she came into the room with Becca right behind her. They both had their hands full. "Everybody's making rosary jewelry. Paris Hilton has a whole line."

"She's already going to rot in Hell," Geri said. "Your aunt still has a slight shot at Purgatory."

When I got home, I decided to give St. Whoever He Was a quick burial before it got dark. I was happy to discover that when it came to digging holes, the third time in the same place was a total piece of cake.

11

I PUT THE SHOVEL BACK IN THE GARAGE, BRUSHED OFF my hands, and headed upstairs with my library books and hand-me-down art supplies. I took a few steps into the apartment and stopped. For a split second I thought I'd been robbed, but then I realized that Boyfriend had been shredding again.

Boyfriend loved to shred. His favorite thing was to wiggle the toilet paper, or even the paper towel roll, off the holder. He'd wrestle it down the hallway, thumping it with his hind feet as if he were subduing a dangerous criminal. Then he'd pull a long sheet off the roll, wad it up, and carry it around the house with him. Sometimes he'd leave it on my pillow as a present.

"Oh, Boy," I said out loud as I surveyed the damage. He'd pretty much covered the apartment in little nests of toilet paper. I wondered if my HMO had a therapist who'd be willing to give my cat and me a group rate.

I decided I'd deal with the mess in the morning. I changed Boyfriend's water and poured some more dry food into his bowl. And then I saw it. The cardboard box I kept my earring supplies in was lying on its side under my tiny kitchen table. Boyfriend had managed to unravel the better part of a spool of wire and empty my bag of sea glass into the center. All that was left in the box were a

pair of needle-nose pliers and two packages of hypoallergenic pierced earring wires.

I'd planned on bringing my earring supplies with me to
kill some time on the set tomorrow, and maybe even
make a few sales while I was at it. But it would take me
forever to straighten everything out tonight, and I was just
too tired to deal with it. "It's okay, Boyfriend," I said. It
wasn't really my cat's fault. I was the one who'd taught
him to play with sea glass in the first place.

I took a step back. I tilted my head to one side. The sea
glass shards weren't just dumped on the wire, they were
nestled in it, with tendrils of wire crisscrossing in the
most surprising ways. It looked like a sculpture of sorts.
You could solder it to some sheet metal for a wall hanging,
or I could even see it as kind of a chandelier if you added
some strands of little white lights. It was balanced and yet
unexpected, with that certain je ne sais quoi that made it
recognizably, if inexplicably, art. Carefully, I lifted the
whole thing up onto my kitchen table.

Wouldn't you know it, even my goddamned cat was
more talented than I was. I put the beads and the polymer
clay down on the table. Maybe one of us could put them to
good use.

"KNOCK-KNOCK!" a strange voice yelled just before my
door opened.

I was sitting on my pulled-out sofa bed. I'd been trying
to decide whether to make dinner, drag myself the three
steps it took to get to my bathroom to wash up, or just go
to sleep in my clothes.

My mother walked in, flanked by the dreaded red hatters. I considered making a quick dive under the covers, but they'd already spotted me.

The woman closest to me was wearing a red fisherman's hat. It was covered with buttons. One of them said, A WOMAN WITHOUT A MAN IS LIKE A FISH WITHOUT A BICYCLE. I wondered if all the other buttons had an aquatic theme to match her hat, too. Before I could read any more of them, she said, "Oh, dear. You'll never find a husband with these housekeeping skills."

I thought her mouth and her button were seriously out of sync, but I wasn't sure it was worth pointing out.

The other woman was wearing a red straw hat that, in my opinion, was a bit Easter bonnet-y for late May. The brim was topped with red and purple flowers, and a miniature bird's nest with three tiny red eggs was tucked in tidily. "Maybe a younger one," she said. "They're not as keen on cleanliness."

I glared at my mother. She ignored me and walked over to my bathroom and started dragging out garbage bags. "Your father will be over in the morning to take these to the dump. I told him you'd made a good start bagging things up, but you needed some help getting rid of them."

I couldn't think of a thing to say that wouldn't get my father in trouble.

The fisherman's hat lady was sniffing now. "Clutter can kill a sale," she said, "but we have to think about all five senses. Pet owners can't smell their own pets, so pets are a particular liability. You might want to consider boarding the cat until after the open house. That way we can take the kitty toys and the litter box right out of here."

Boyfriend jumped up beside me and burrowed under

the sheets. Maybe we could find a kennel that would take both of us.

"Size really does matter," the Easter bonnet lady said. The three of them giggled, and I rolled my eyes. "The rule of thumb," she continued, "is to get rid of half of everything, and the place will look twice as big. Especially in the closet. And the underwear drawers. Only the sexy items should stay. People think they're buying a house, but they're really buying a fantasy."

My own personal fantasy was that they'd all disappear before any of them found my underwear drawer.

"Selling a house," the fisherman's hat lady was saying, "is a lot like making love. Setting the mood is half the battle." She walked over to a window and pulled up the old venetian blind. "People will pay a premium for good light. We'll want to keep these blinds up and the windows open from now on, dear."

"Pink lightbulbs will help, too," the other woman said. "You should be using them anyway, hon. Now that you're no longer a spring chickadee, they're much more flattering." She grabbed the handle of my father's scooter and pulled it away from the wall. "I didn't realize we had children here. We'll have to make them scarce, too."

"No children," my mother said. "I have no idea where that old thing came from, but I'm sure Ginger can send it off to Take It or Leave It with her father."

"Be careful what books and magazines you have lying around," the Easter lady said. "Nothing risqué and nothing partisan. Voting for the wrong candidate can cost you a sale."

"Does that mean I have to get rid of the autographed picture of the president I sent away for?" I asked.

"Well," the fisherman lady said, "normally I like to turn down the bed and put a chocolate on the pillow to give the air of a fancy hotel, but I think we're better off leaving the sleeper sofa folded up to optimize the floor space. We'll play some nice Paul Anka music, though."

She took a few steps around and sniffed some more. "And we still need to discuss flowers. Fragrant flowers will make a big difference in here. And maybe a drop of vanilla on each of the lightbulbs."

"Don't forget the plug-in fireplace you mentioned," my mother said.

"We'll drop that off later in the week," the Easter lady said.

"Can't wait," I said.

My mother had worked her way over to my kitchen table and was staring down at my cat's creation. "My goodness, Ginger. This is lovely. I had no idea you were so talented."

The other two women joined my mother. "Marvelous," one of them said. "But get it up on a wall or get it out of here."

"PSST," MY FATHER SAID from my doorway about two minutes later.

I conked my head against the back of my sleeper sofa. "Come on in, Dad."

My father dropped two new garbage bags in the middle of my floor and bent down to give Boyfriend a pat. "How's it going, Champ?"

Boyfriend licked my father's hand briefly, then went back to grooming himself.

"Don't worry," my father said when he straightened up again. "I didn't miss a word. You can hear everything that goes on up here from down in the garage."

"Great, Dad. I'll keep that in mind."

"You would not believe what I found today at the Take It or Leave It, Toots." My father untwisted the tie on one of the bags and dumped its contents on my floor. Before I closed my eyes I saw a toy jukebox, a sheriff's badge, and a KISS THE COOK sign.

When I opened them again, my father was setting up a Chinese checkers game on the foot of my pulled-out bed, and my cat was batting a yellow marble around on the floor.

"We're missing a few marbles here," my father said.

"Speak for yourself," I said.

"Hey, that's a good one, Dollface. You get that from me, you know." He slid the game closer to my end of the bed. "Okay, you can be red and I'll be blue, and we'll fill in the missing ones with the greens and just remember who they belong to. That way Champ can have the yellow ones all to himself."

"Dad?"

"Okay, age before beauty. I'll start." My father moved a blue marble diagonally forward until it rested in the next tin dimple.

I picked up a red marble. "Dad? Mom's not kidding, you know. She's really going to sell the house. Maybe you should get rid of some of this stuff, and then we can rent you a storage unit for the rest of it."

"This isn't chess, you know, Toots. Come on, make your move."

I put the marble down, and my father moved another blue one right away. "If I have to move," he said, "I think I'd rather live on a houseboat. Maybe I can take your mother on a cruise and get her used to the idea."

"I'm not sure we have time for that, Dad."

"Okay, then we'll pretend to be sick. First I'll go, then you'll come down with the same thing." He scratched his head and picked up another marble. "We'll have to synchronize our symptoms, though. That mother of yours is one smart cookie. How about a headache first and then it travels south from there?"

I moved another marble and tried to picture where I'd be in a few months. Not, I hoped, on a couch in my parents' townhouse. Riley's top bunk might be slightly less depressing. The only thing I knew for sure was that I was a lot of sea glass earrings away from my own apartment. I could try to talk myself into considering another sales job, but the money was so unreliable, especially in the beginning. And I knew I'd go crazy in an office job. I just couldn't spend my life cooped up behind four walls, living someone else's dream. I had to figure out something more fulfilling.

My father pushed himself off the edge of the sofa bed and started pacing. "Or maybe you and that young man of yours could get engaged, Toots. You could say you've always dreamed of a garden wedding. The old broad would never be able to resist that one."

I buried my head in my hands.

"You don't have to go through with it if you don't want to, Dollface. A long engagement is all we need. He's a nice young man, though. A good sweeper, too."

My father squatted down and rolled a yellow marble. Boyfriend stalked it, then went in for the kill. "Way to go, Champ," my father said.

He paced another few steps and leaned over my kitchen table. "Wooh, baby," he said. "Will you look at that. What do you know, Champ. Looks like our Toots is quite the artist. A regular Picasso."

12

WHEN RILEY AND I GOT TO THE SET THE NEXT DAY, everybody was passing around the latest issue of *The Daily Catch*. "What happened?" I asked one of the AD people.

She shook her head and handed me her paper.

SHARK FLIES COOP

After a 23-day visit to the shores of Marshbury, a 14-foot, 1,700-pound female great white shark slipped out under the cover of darkness last night. Though a satellite tracking device, attached earlier, will allow scientists to observe the great white's movements, it is unlikely that even Worldwide Studio will be able to talk the shark into returning to finish the filming of *Shark Sense*. When asked whether this constitutes a breach of contract on the part of the shark, Director Manny Muscadel had no comment.

Riley was reading over my elbow. "Uh-oh," he said when he finished.

"Yeah," I said, "who knew sharks could fly?"

He laughed, but not with his usual abandon. "What are they going to do?"

I didn't have a clue so I just shrugged. Riley headed down the beach to join the other kids. I read the article one more time, just in case I'd missed something. When I looked up, Manny was standing in front of me.

I put the paper behind my back. "Too late," he said. "I've already seen it."

I wasn't sure whether to smile or not. I bowed my head. "I'm so sorry for your loss," I mumbled.

He rubbed his thumb and forefinger back and forth across his jaw. There was a jagged piece of toilet paper stuck below his right cheekbone. Maybe it was the fact that his sneakers were untied, but even with clear-cut evidence that he shaved, he looked about twelve. "Well," he said finally. "Now I know why Spielberg built the shark for *Jaws*."

"Is it still around? Maybe he'd let you borrow it."

He didn't seem to hear me. "I just figured we'd save so much money this way."

"Or maybe you could bring in a sea lion or something?"

He shook his head. "The studio's pulling the plug."

For a minute I actually thought he meant they were pulling the plug on the whole ocean. Or at least the whole movie. Just to be safe, I went with a sympathetic shake of my head.

" 'Come back,' they said. 'There are plenty of sharks in LA.' " He buried his face in his hands.

I wasn't sure what to do. I put a hand on his shoulder, then lifted it up. "But you'll still get to make the movie, right?"

He looked up from his hands. "Yeah, I guess, if I can make what I got here fit with what I can do on the left coast. And stay within budget." He reached up to straighten the brim of his baseball hat, and I could see that his hands were shaking. "Listen," he said. "I was hoping you could help us out."

"Sure," I said. "Anything. Whatever you need." I wondered if I should offer to help him tie his shoes before he tripped, or if he'd be insulted.

"It's the kid. Who reps him?"

I looked at him blankly.

"Never mind. I'll have the casting people look it up. But the kid, the kid is great. We'd like to take him with us to LA."

When I glanced up, Tim Kelly was leaning over the back of a director's chair watching me. He wiggled his eyebrows and grinned. I looked away, but not before he saw me looking.

WE'D CALLED HOME during the lunch break, so everybody was waiting for us when we got to Geri's house.

My mother put an arm around Riley and started walking him into the living room. "So," she said. "Sit right down and tell us everything. Don't leave out a single detail."

I leaned back against the kitchen counter. "I think one of the movie guys likes me," I whispered to Geri. "The gaffer."

"Hel-lo?" my sister said. "Today is not about you. My son is going to Hollywood." She leaned forward. "What *is* a gaffer anyway? Is that like a gopher?"

"No," I said. "It's like an electrician. Everybody knows that."

"Well, pardon me, but I didn't. So, are you going to

dump Noah and start dating the gopher? I have to say, it's about time."

I started heading for the living room. "Gaffer," I said. "And don't be ridiculous."

"We got to start the screaming part today," Riley was saying as I sat down next to him on the couch. "Do you want to hear mine?"

"Let's save it for outside, okay, honey?" Geri sat down on his other side. She had a legal pad with her, and it actually looked like she might be about to make a list that didn't involve her birthday.

Seth looked up from his laptop. "Okay, the casting director referred me to an agent, and the agent says they'll pay first-class travel, put up Riley and whoever goes with him, and pay a per diem."

"Seth," Geri said. "Aren't you getting a little ahead of yourself? We're not even sure yet we're going to let him go."

Rachel crossed her arms over her chest. "You can't let him go. We still have school left."

Becca twirled some hair around her finger. "If Riley goes, we should all get to go. We're a *family*."

"Oh, honey," Geri said. She tapped her pen against her lip a few times, then added a few words to her list. Geri put her pen down and looked up. "I think you girls should stay with your father, and I'll go with Riley. If he's going to go, he should have his mother with him."

"I was thinking I should be the one to go," Seth said. "A boy needs his father."

"His grandfather and I could go," my mother said.

"Yes, indeedy," my father said, nodding over at my mother. "We're retired."

Rachel pushed back her chair and stood up. "I hate you all," she said.

"Me, too," Becca said. She stood up.

"Excuse me?" I said.

Everybody turned to look at me.

"Excuse me?" I repeated, just to be sure I had their full attention. I cleared my throat. "You should all be ashamed of yourselves," I said. "If anyone deserves to go with Riley, we all know who that is. We're a team. I put the time in. I know the ropes." I was running out of tired expressions, so I looked from Geri to Seth, then back again. "Besides, neither of you could stand to be away from work for more than five minutes. And, if you did go, you'd still have to hire me to help out with the girls, and I'll tell you right now the answer is no."

I took a deep breath. Wow, standing up for myself felt great. Maybe I should do it more often. "So there," I finished.

"Good girl," my mother said.

My father winked at me. "Way to go, Dollface."

"You're right," my sister actually said.

Since I appeared to be on a roll, I figured I might as well see what else I could accomplish. "Of course, I'll need somebody to take care of Boyfriend."

Geri let out a puff of air.

"Ix-nay on the Oyfriend-bay," Riley said.

"My hamster and I could take care of Kareshi," Becca said.

"Didn't you say he was Neko in Japanese?" I asked. "I kind of liked that."

"*Neko* is cat," Becca whispered. "*Kareshi* is Oyfriend-bay."

"Just for future reference," Geri said. "I happen to be fluent in pig latin."

"I can take care of Champ," my father said. "I'm right next door."

"Thanks, Dad," I said.

"Sure, I could," my father said. "And I could even stay over there with him so he won't be lonely."

"Excuse me?" my mother said. "You're sleeping in your bed where you belong."

I peeked over at my father, then looked back at my mother. "I was also kind of hoping that putting the house on the market could wait until I got back."

My father put his arm around my mother's shoulders and said, "We can always sell the house when she gets back. What's a couple of weeks amongst friends, right, Toots?"

"Don't call me 'Toots,'" my mother said. "All right, let me think about that. Maybe we can wait a week or two on the house, but don't forget we've still got piles of junk to take to the dump, which is your department."

My father wiggled his bushy white eyebrows. "Yes, sirree, Bob," he said.

"Okay," Geri said, "there's one big thing left. Riley, do you want to go?"

Riley looked up from the joke book he was reading. "Yeah, sure. As long as they have those gumball machines there."

After we worked out a few of the details, my sister walked me outside while she checked her BlackBerry for messages. She was still in her work clothes, a perfectly co-ordinated pinstripe suit and white blouse affair that I'd never be able to put together. "Guess what?" she asked, once her thumbs had stopped dancing.

I opened my car door. "What?"

"You're not going to believe this, but I went online at work today and looked up the statue I gave you."

"Why wouldn't I believe that? It's not like you ever seem to do any actual work there."

My sister ignored me. "Guess who he is?"

I sat down in my car and put the key in the ignition. Geri held my door open. "I give up," I said.

Geri opened her eyes wide, and made a little *ooh-ooh, ooh-ooh* sound. "St. Christopher."

"So?"

"He's the patron saint of travelers. Get it? You buried him, and now you're going on a trip?"

My sister needed to get out more. Or maybe stay home more. "You don't really believe that, do you?" I asked.

"Who knows? But to be on the safe side, I think you should dig him up and take him with Riley and you. Just to keep an eye on things."

⟁

WORD SPREADS FAST in Marshbury. I stopped by Harborside Drugs on the way home to pick up a few odds and ends just in case I couldn't find a drugstore when we got to Hollywood. I put an assortment of tampons, teeth-whitening toothpaste, breath-freshening gum, Altoids, Dramamine, travel-size deodorant, Twizzlers, plus a copy of *Shape* magazine to make up for the Twizzlers, on the counter.

The woman behind the register was about my age and looked vaguely familiar. She folded down the corner of the page she was on in her *People* magazine and placed it on a shelf behind her. "So, Hollywood, huh?" she said. "Need a secretary?"

I laughed politely and looked at her more closely. "Did we go to high school together?" I asked.

She pointed my package of Twizzlers at me like a gun. "How quickly they forget."

I tried to get a look at her name tag but her hair was covering it. "Polly?"

"Penny Cabozzi." She scanned the Twizzlers without looking. "Everybody's moving back, you know. Deb and Linda Shea, Mary Carroll, Donna Duffey, David Ogden, Nan Fitzpatrick, George Newman. Oh, and Austine Frawley."

"Great," I said. I wondered if they all lived over their parents' garages, too. Maybe we'd go down in history as the FROG generation.

Penny Cabozzi leaned toward me over the counter. "Listen," she said loudly. "I think you should know that bitch Allison Flagg is going around town telling everyone that the only reason they're taking your nephew to Hollywood is because you slept with someone from the movie."

"You're kidding," I said. "She's not also saying that I want to have kids, is she?"

She scanned my tampons and lowered her voice. "No, but I know a great doctor if you're having problems. They call him the fertility god."

I looked over my shoulder, hoping I could say, *Wow, will you look at that line* but, of course, there wasn't anybody behind me. "Actually, I'm child-free. By choice."

She scanned the Dramamine and picked up the deodorant. "Sure you are. Anyway, don't worry, I've been sticking up for you. I've been saying that if Ginger Walsh slept with anyone, you can bet she'd have the part and not her nephew."

"That's so sweet," I said as I grabbed my bag. "Thank you."

"You're welcome. Let me know when you need a manager."

13

WHEN I GOT HOME, BOYFRIEND LEANED INTO MY LEG and meowed. I was feeling guilty about leaving him already, so I grabbed one of the books, a big fat one on the history of jewelry, and pulled him onto my lap for a nice long cuddle. He started rubbing his chin back and forth along the edge of the book.

"Hmm," I said. "Did you know the Imperial Romans had a major toy dog thing? It says here they were perfumed, coiffed, dressed in jewelry, and carried around on plush cushions. Julius Caesar even asked if Roman women had begun giving birth to lapdogs instead of children."

I thought it might be an interesting alternative to human babies, and possibly less of a commitment, but my cat only yawned and stretched. I reached around until I found one of the Chinese checkers marbles, which were pretty much everywhere, I noticed. I rolled it across the floor like a tiny bowling ball, and Boyfriend vaulted off my lap after it.

I turned a few more pages. Apparently we owed the invention of the diamond engagement ring to the Archduke Maximillian of Austria, who presented a rough diamond set in elaborate gold to his fiancée at the end of the fifteenth century. "Jerk," I said out loud.

The oldest recorded exchange of wedding rings happened in Egypt about 4,800 years ago and was considered a supernatural link with eternal love. I shivered. I mean, were there any other creations in history that had made more women who didn't happen to be wearing one or the other or both feel bad? I mean, you might as well brand us on the forehead.

It wasn't that I didn't want to be married or engaged, or even engaged and then actually married. I didn't need a man to complete me or any of that old stuff, but I really liked the idea of having a partner in crime. I even liked rings. I'd come close a couple times. Once, right out of college, I'd gotten as far as wearing the world's tiniest graduate-school-budget diamond for several months. He studied and worked. I worked and went to the library with him when he studied. I flipped through the travel magazines I couldn't afford to buy and dreamed of trips we couldn't afford to take. I waited until I was just about to die of boredom, and then I gave him back the ring and got the hell out of Dodge.

I closed the book and put it down. Maybe I should forget about the whole of jewelry history and just rely on my own imagination. I walked around the room, collecting the supplies my cat wasn't using, and sat down cross-legged on the floor with them. I closed my eyes and tried to clear my mind of all but pure creative thoughts. I made a quick attempt to chant like a Gregorian monk, but when Boyfriend gave me a worried look, I decided to go with profound silence.

I opened a square, cellophane-wrapped packet of polymer clay the color of green tea. Maybe I could roll little balls and thread them onto the bamboo skewers I'd bought when I was feeling ambitious and thought I might attempt shish kebabs someday. If all went well, I'd slide them off the skewers after I baked them, and I'd have beads that I could paint and combine somehow with my sea glass. Or I'd even take it up a notch and mix them with recycled rosary beads, and maybe make something memorable to give Geri for her birthday. I mean, what were sisters for? If things went less well, of course, I'd have blazing bamboo skewers in my oven.

What I really needed was something that was unique and original, a new beachy jewelry twist that was mine alone. Something teenagers would wear. Rachel and Becca were always spending money on trendy jewelry. What about alternating little flip-flop charms with sea glass and beads? Or why not decorate real flip-flops with sea glass, the way I'd seen them embellished with puka and cowrie shells? I could make up some samples and show them around Hollywood while I was there.

For some reason, the familiar sound of a pebble against my window really hit me the wrong way tonight. I mean, did I interrupt Noah when he was working? I decided to ignore it. I ignored the next one, too. And the next. Then my phone rang. It was all getting to be too much to ignore, so I picked up the receiver and directed the obligatory *hello* into it.

"Do you think you might consider opening the door and letting Noah in?" my mother's voice asked. "Your father and I have enough to do without buying all new windows."

"I think you must have the wrong number," I said courteously before I hung up. No wonder I couldn't seem to stick with anything for long. It was clearly environmental.

My bad mood was giving me a headache, and the sound of another pebble hitting glass was definitely not helping. "Can you get that?" I asked my cat.

Boyfriend was busy puffing himself up to twice his normal size. His fur stood on end, as if somebody had rubbed a balloon back and forth over it, and his eyes glittered like emeralds. "I'll take that as a no," I said.

"Hey," Noah said when I opened the door. Sage looked past me at Boyfriend and gave a short, tentative bark. Boyfriend hissed and dove under the sofa bed.

"I think they're starting to get used to each other," Noah said. When I didn't say anything, he took a step past me and added, "The Sage-ster and I have stopped by a few times this week. Long days in the movie biz, huh? How's it going? Riley having a good time?"

I made a noncommittal sound, and Sage stopped wagging her tail and went over and sat by the door. For a minute, Noah looked like he might follow her, but then he sat down on the couch and picked up the book I had been reading. "How about those jewels," he said as he opened it. "Real fascinating stuff." He glanced up at me, then back down again. "Coral, for instance. According to ancient lore, the way it was created was that Perseus placed the severed head of Medusa in a bag on a heap of seaweed."

"Men," I said. Sage made a few digging motions with her paws right where the floor met my door. Then she circled around and flopped down.

"Excuse me?" Noah said.

At this moment, I could totally relate to Medusa. I could feel snakes sprouting in my hair and tusks growing between my teeth, but I couldn't seem to help myself. "Never mind" was the best I could do.

Noah put the book down. "Anyway, the head's power passed into the seaweed, which turned rigid and shriveled up like stone, and became coral." He rubbed his chin and watched me. "Why so glum, chum? Is something wrong?"

I walked around to the back of the couch, and got down on my hands and knees and looked underneath to make sure Boyfriend was okay. His eyes sparkled at me in the dark. "*Chum?*" I mouthed to him.

"Wow," Noah said. "Did *you* do this?"

I pushed myself up to a vertical position. Noah was standing over my kitchen table. I noticed Boyfriend had added the metal ring and the seashell-studded rock I'd brought home from the set to the messy sculpture he'd made with my earring supplies. I looked more closely and saw that he'd also wrapped some of Rachel's beads in wire, and they jutted out in perfect counterpoint to several pieces of jade green sea glass. There were a couple of wadded pieces of paper in there, too, but other than that, the effect was pretty remarkable.

Noah leaned forward to get a better look. "This is amazing," he said. "So free, yet balanced. It's organic, but also completely new and fresh. I had no idea you were this talented, Ginger."

My headache had taken on a rhythm of its own. I tried closing one eye to ease the pounding. Then I closed both of them. "Not as talented as Boyfriend," I managed to mumble.

"Thanks," Noah said. "But I mean it. And you should allow yourself to accept the compliment. Just say 'thank you.'"

I opened both eyes. "What kind of jerky thing was that to say? I didn't mean you. I meant my cat did it."

Noah raised one eyebrow. "What kind of jerky name is *Boyfriend* for a cat?"

"What did you say?"

"You heard me. I hate that name."

"Oh, right, and *Sage* is just so perfect. You'd probably name *your* cat something stuck-up, like *Buddha*. Or *Enlightenment*."

"For your information, Sage is named after an herb. And, also for your information, I wouldn't even get a cat."

"What?"

Noah slid his hands into the pockets of his jeans, and then pulled them out and crossed his arms over his chest. "Cats," he said slowly and clearly, "are for people who don't really want to go out of their way. They're as close as you can get to not having a pet."

"Oh, please, what about goldfish?" Some little-used part of my brain, way in the back somewhere, signaled me to quit while I was ahead. I ignored it. "And, anyway, Mr. I-Can't-Have-a-Relationship-Because-I'm-an-Ahhtist, you know what dogs are? Dogs are as close as you can get to having a person in your life without really having one."

"I thought you liked the way things were. How come you never told me?"

"I did. Repeatedly. At least I think I did. How come you never told me you didn't like cats?"

Noah ran both hands back through his hair. "You always do that."

"What?"

"Whenever I try to talk about us, you always change the subject."

"Oh, right, and you're so emotionally available."

"What's that supposed to mean?"

"Nothing. Anyway, I really want to know. What do you have against cats?"

Noah put his hands back in his pockets and took them out again. He walked over to Boyfriend's sculpture and looked at it some more. "Okay, dogs give you more, that's all. They come when you call them. They play Frisbee. They'll sit in your car with the windows open and wait for you forever, and no matter how long it takes you to get going, they're still excited beyond belief to go anywhere with you."

Sage tilted her head at Noah and wagged her tail. "Cats are completely self-sufficient," I said. "They're happy to see you, but they don't really need you because they have a life of their own."

Boyfriend batted a yellow marble out from under the couch. "Dogs have your back," Noah said. "Their feelings for you are completely unconditional."

"Cats are discriminating. You get what you earn with a cat."

We stared at each other. One of us seriously needed to smooth things over here, but it certainly wasn't going to be me.

"So," Noah said. "I guess tonight's not really going too well."

I took a deep breath. "Maybe next time you should call first."

"It never bothered you before."

"Well, it does now."

Noah and his dog were almost down the stairs before I remembered to yell, "And by the way, thanks for the flowers."

"Don't mention it," he yelled back.

14

I PACED THE FULL LENGTH OF MY APARTMENT. FOR seven steps in one direction, and seven steps back again, I replayed my fight with Noah over and over in my head. It was a really stupid fight. Not that I'd had many really smart fights in my life, but still. Bottom line, though, he was old enough to know you don't throw pebbles at a girl's window. You call.

Now the worst thing was that he didn't know Riley and I were going to Hollywood. Or maybe the best thing was he didn't know we were going. It was hard to tell. Possibly it didn't matter. I mean, it's not like I wouldn't be back in a week or two. Though maybe a little time to miss me wouldn't be a bad idea. But what if he didn't even notice I was gone?

Okay, the other way to look at it was that what if he'd already written me off, and then I'd get back and find out he'd had all that time to move on, and I wouldn't know I was supposed to start moving on, so I hadn't even started. That would really suck.

But, wait. This wasn't about the guy. It was the perfect time to go. For me. While Riley worked, I could devote myself entirely to my art. My apartment would be in the hands of fate, or at least my mother, and completely out of my control. I wouldn't be hanging around comparing myself to my talented boyfriend, or possible ex-boyfriend. Or even to my talented cat. I'd bring my books and supplies. I'd scour the shops and galleries for ideas. Maybe I couldn't figure out how to have a relationship to save my life, but all that suffering might end up being great for my art.

I felt better already. I reached over and picked up my cat. I carried him down to his pet carrier on wheels and took him for an extra long walk. The summer crowds would be arriving in Marshbury this weekend, just like they did every Memorial Day weekend. July and August would be worse in terms of numbers, but still, you'd feel the difference right away, and everybody's lives would change at least a little until after Labor Day. You knew the best time to shop and which back roads to take to avoid the worst of the traffic during the summer months, and you adjusted. When I first moved home again, the summer rhythm had come right back to me, as if I'd never been away.

It was too dark to walk the beach, but the stars and the streetlights gave us enough light to walk around the beach parking lot. I picked up a couple tiny pieces of driftwood from the sandy edges, and put them into the compartment with Boyfriend. He immediately batted one of them into the netting. "Score," I said.

It was surprisingly quiet. Maybe all the tourists were stuck in traffic. We took our time walking back, enjoying the empty streets while we still could. I stood outside the open garage door and looked up at the sky. It was probably really silly, especially since it was Geri's idea, but I had this sudden urge to dig up St. Christopher. Maybe he could be my good luck charm for the artistic travels on my horizon.

Boyfriend meowed loudly. "Just give me one minute," I

whispered. I turned on the garage lights, inside and out. I could make out the green circle of grass from here, so I grabbed a shovel and got to work.

Ten minutes and a trip up to my apartment to get a flashlight later, and I was sure. St. Christopher had completely disappeared. I unzipped Boyfriend from his carrier and ran up the stairs with him as fast as I could. I locked the door behind us and dialed my parents' number.

"Mom?" I whispered when she answered the phone.

"Why are you whispering?" she whispered.

"Mom, can you come over here?"

"Ginger, tell me what happened."

"Well, Dad and I tried to dig up St. Joseph. Actually, I was only the lookout. But St. Joseph wasn't there and I didn't want you and Dad to get into a fight, so I asked Geri for another St. Joseph, but all she had was a St. Christopher, so I buried him instead. But he turned out to be the patron saint of travelers, and Geri thought that might be why Riley and I were going to Hollywood, so I tried to dig him up to bring him with us for good luck." I looked down and saw actual goosebumps on my forearms. Maybe this was how people became born-again. "And now he's gone, too."

"I'll be right there," my mother said before she hung up.

❦

MY MOTHER WAS wearing slippers and her old terrycloth bathrobe. She must have just finished washing up, because a stretchy aqua headband held her thick gray hair off her shiny face, and I could smell Pond's cold cream as soon as I opened the door.

I threw my arms around her. "Mom," I said.

I stepped back and rubbed my hip bones. "Ouch. What was that?"

A greenish yellow plastic statue was peeking out of each of my mother's two square bathrobe pockets. "Mom?"

My mother pulled out the statues and placed them on my kitchen counter. "This place could use a good cleaning," she said. "And why is that scooter still here?"

"Don't try to change the subject," I said.

She sat down at my kitchen table, and I did, too. Maybe it was because I was used to seeing her in yoga pants instead of a bathrobe, but my mother looked almost old tonight. "Seller's remorse, I suppose," she said finally, "but as soon as we buried St. Joseph, I just wasn't sure I wanted to rush things along. So many memories."

"But what about St. Christopher?"

She shrugged. "How did I know that's who he was until I got him home? My night vision's not what it used to be."

"Don't say that, Mom. You have eyes in the back of your head."

My mother smiled.

"Does this mean we get to keep the house?"

"Honestly, Ginger. Sometimes you sound like the world's oldest living adolescent."

My eyes teared up. "I know. I know. I just can't seem to get my bearings." I put my elbows on the table and leaned my head into my hands, and Boyfriend rubbed up against my legs. "It's embarrassing, Mom. I'm forty-one years old, and I haven't been this completely and utterly lost since I was sixteen." I looked up. "But I really do want you and Dad to be happy. You should do whatever you want to do about the house. I'll be fine."

My mother put her hand on my arm. "Of course you'll be fine, honey. I think the best thing for all of us is to sell the house. We'll do it fast, like pulling off a Band-Aid."

I nodded. The kitchen table felt warm and safe under the light of the little yellow lamp hanging over us. I tried to imagine sitting around a table at my mother's age, and wondered who the other people would be. I couldn't get a picture.

My mother picked up a piece of sea glass from the table and put it back in Boyfriend's sculpture. Boyfriend jumped up on my mother's lap, and she started petting him. "Hi, handsome," she whispered.

"You know, Dad says one of your red hat friends is always kissing him."

My mother smiled. "Oh, they're awful. They'll be lined up at his door in five minutes if I go first."

"Do you really think Dad will be okay in the townhouse, Mom?"

"He'll be fine, honey. It just takes him a while. I tell you, that father of yours would hang a tea bag out to dry on a clothesline just so he wouldn't have to say good-bye to it."

Boyfriend jumped off my mother's lap and circled around and jumped up on mine. "Hey, Champ," I said.

"Deep down inside, I know it's the right thing to do. There'll be dances and parties and a first-rate gym, and we won't have to mow the lawn. And your father and I have always wanted to live in a house that's brand spanking new."

I nodded.

"The only thing I'm worried about are the cliques and the claques and everyone knowing everyone else's business."

"Don't tell me people still do that at your age? I was hoping things would get easier by then."

My mother blew out a puff of breath with the same horsy sound Geri always made. "It's an active adult community, fifty-five-plus, not a nursing home. There are some real youngsters there. Some of them aren't much older than you and your sister."

"Gee, thanks, Mom." Boyfriend jumped off my lap and headed off to chase down a marble. "Mom?"

She covered her mouth and yawned again. "Excuse me. What, honey?"

"Did you ever wish you hadn't had kids? I mean, not now maybe, but when you were younger? You know, was there ever anything you really wished you could have done but couldn't, because of us?"

She clasped her hands together and stretched them up over her head. "Well, when you were little I used to tell you I wanted to be the first woman president, but the truth was I would have loved to dance on Broadway. I had such dreams of being a Rockette."

I leaned forward over the table. "You gave that up for us, Mom?"

"No, I gave that up because my legs were too short." She pulled her stretchy headband back down over her ears, then rested one hand on mine. "You make a decision and you don't look back, honey. Have a family. Don't have a family. But, meanwhile, you've got a great big world out there to enjoy."

"It just seems like everyone else is already out there living their lives, you know, buzzing right by me, two by two."

"You've got a boyfriend named Noah, honey. You can probably get a good seat on the ark."

My fight with Noah bubbled up again, and I sat with it for a minute. "I'm not sure this is even about Noah, Mom."

My mother stood up and retied the belt on her robe. She put St. Joseph back in her pocket and handed me St. Christopher. I stood up, too, and she placed her hands on my shoulders and kissed me on the forehead. "Ever since you were tiny, you always had to find the hardest way to do everything. Remember, Virginia, you choose your life or it chooses you."

I was pretty sure I recognized this as just another variation of her You Can Be Anything You Want to Be speech, but I let it go. My mother was the only one who ever called me Virginia. Geri was named Gerianne after a favorite great aunt, and eight years later I was named Virginia after the state where I was conceived during one of the romantic getaways my mother was always dragging my father along on. It seemed a statement on the trajectory of my mother's growth. Had I been born a few years later, I might well have been named Pilates.

"Got it," I said, though I wasn't quite sure I did. "Hey, Mom, do you think there's a patron saint of disappearing statues?"

"God only knows," my mother said. "Come on, your father was sound asleep when I left. Let's go give St. Joseph a quick burial."

15

"PSST," MY FATHER SAID BEHIND ME.

"Hi, Dad," I said without turning around. I had every bit of clothing I owned spread out on my pulled-out sofa, and I was trying to figure out what could be packed right away and what should probably be washed first.

"Just tell me, what was the old bat doing over here last night?"

"Just tell me you didn't bring another garbage bag with you, okay, Dad?"

"Better than that, Dollface, better than that."

I wasn't sure if I turned and then heard the meows, or if I turned because I heard the meows. My father pushed Boyfriend's pet carrier on wheels all the way into the room. Even I had to admit it definitely looked like a stroller right now. My father was grinning from ear to ear.

I leaned over. Two tiny kittens, one mostly black and one mostly white, were curled up on a pink blanket under the green mesh. The white one opened its mouth, and the sound it made was actually more like a mew than a full-blown meow. "Awhh," I said. "Where did you get them?"

"The Take It or Leave It," he said. "No way that mother of yours would put two defenseless kittens out on the street. Champ and I will take care of them while you're gone, and when you get back, you can help us out."

"You brought cats home from the dump, Dad? What if Boyfriend catches something from them?"

My father pressed on the handle and started bouncing the stroller up and down. "Don't be ridiculous, Toots. I got them from a very respectable lady who had them in a fancy wicker basket. They've had their first shots and all the rest of that rigmarole. Good thing, it's highway robbery what those vets charge these days."

Boyfriend was eyeing the carriage and circling it with the long careful steps of a leopard hunting its prey. "Dad, I think one cat might be enough."

My father leaned over to pick up Boyfriend, who sprang across the room like he'd been shot at. "Oh, they'll be thick as thieves before you know it," my father said. "Come on, now, spill the beans about last night and then we'll go buy some kitten chow."

"It was just girl talk, Dad. No cloak-and-dagger stuff at all."

"You're not pulling my leg now, are you, Toots?"

"Cross my heart," I said.

I was trying to stay away from them, but I couldn't help myself. I unzipped the zipper that ran down the center of the netting, and reached in and took out the black kitten, and then the white one, and I cuddled them both to my chest. They were so tiny. We'd had kittens growing up, but Boyfriend had been a full-grown shelter cat when I adopted him, so it had been a long time since I'd smelled that kitten smell.

Eventually I zipped them back in their stroller. "I am so out of this, Dad. When Mom finds out, just tell her you got them after I left, okay?"

IT WAS LATE AFTERNOON by the time I made it over to Geri's house. When I walked into her kitchen, she put her BlackBerry down in a ceramic bowl on her granite kitchen island, where it nestled in right next to Seth's. I nodded at them. "Life is but a bowl of BlackBerrys," I said.

She ignored me and picked up her phone and pressed some buttons.

I opened the refrigerator and had to settle for an apple. My sister needed to shop more often. I held it up. "Is this washed?" I asked.

"Shh," Geri said. She pushed a button on the phone. "Ohmigod, will you listen to this."

She handed me the phone, so I did. "I don't know if you're involved in casting for the movie," a woman's voice said. "But this is Laura Meeker and my son is on Riley's soccer team and I understand there are roles for school-age children. My son is a redhead and would look great with Brad Pitt. Even though Brad Pitt isn't a redhead, but you could dye it. My son, not Brad, of course. Is Brad Pitt really in the movie? That's what I heard. Anyway, I know it's a little forward of me to ask, but I thought it was worth a try. I can send you a head shot if you'd like. Again, this is Laura Meeker and my son usually plays defense and his name is Josh and he and Riley are very compatible. We're at 781-555-5335."

"Wow," I said as I handed the phone back to Geri and took a bite of my possibly unwashed apple. "Are you going to call her back?"

Geri shook her head. "No way. She didn't even invite Riley to Josh's last birthday party. And it's not like she didn't invite half the soccer team." Geri put the phone back and opened the refrigerator and got herself a piece of string cheese. "I hate this stuff," she said as she chewed. "Anyway, I think that's call number seven or eight. My favorite was from one of Mom's friends who offered me money to dump you and hire her."

"And you didn't take it?"

"It wasn't that much money." Geri was back sitting at the counter and making a list on a legal pad.

"Hey," I said. "You didn't happen to hear that I slept with someone to get Riley his part, did you?"

Rachel came into the room and opened the refrigerator. "Oh, that's so old news," she said. "So, have you and Noah said good-bye yet?"

"Possibly," I said.

Geri opened her eyes wide. "Did he break up with you?"

I opened my eyes wider. "What makes you think he'd be the one to break up with me?"

"Listen," Geri said. "I can FedEx you anything Riley forgets, and Riley's teacher will fax his last bit of homework for the year to the hotel and you can bring it in to the set teacher. Call me every day when you get up. Riley has a cell phone so he can call me, too."

"Riley has a cell phone? I barely have a cell phone."

"Of course he has a cell phone. All kids have cell phones. They're like umbilical cords. When the girls go to sleepovers, Seth and I make them send us periodic photos so we know they haven't tiptoed out of the house while the parents weren't paying attention."

"The way you and I used to in high school?"

Apparently Geri wasn't in the mood to reminisce. She wrote a few more words on her list, then put her pen down and looked up. "Okay, what happened with Noah?"

I took a bite of my apple and chewed it slowly. "We had a fight."

"And . . ."

"And I'm not even sure if he knows I'm leaving. Although, come to think of it, Allison Flagg probably told him when she told him I was sleeping around. And that I wanted to have kids." This was the downside of living in a small town like Marshbury, where everybody knew everybody else. If you weren't paranoid when you moved in, it didn't take long.

Geri peeled off a long string of cheese and popped it into her mouth. "So, call him."

"Why should I have to be the one who calls?"

"Because you're the one leaving for Hollywood in the morning?"

GERI HAD PICKED ME UP at my apartment and brought me to her house, so she could go over things with me one more time. It was the Monday of Memorial Day weekend, and Seth was going to drop us off at the Harbor Express, because he was heading into work for a few hours. The Harbor Express was a water ferry and the most civilized way to get from Marshbury to Logan Airport these days, because the Big Dig had turned Boston into a big tunnel repair nightmare.

Of course, talking to Seth on the way to the ferry wasn't

going to be a picnic either. My sister seemed to be perfectly content in her marriage, but he bored me to tears. I
didn't even like the way he parted his hair. One straight
line, just like the rest of him.

Geri was planning to do something special with the
girls today, who were still not happy about Riley going to
Hollywood without them. And we all agreed that the last
thing Riley needed was a high-drama family send-off at
the airport. "So, well, thanks a lot, Seth," I said as Seth finally pulled into the Harbor Express parking lot.

He flipped the trunk switch and jumped out to get our
suitcases. "Not a problem," he said. "Take good care of Riley for us."

"Will do," I said. We both leaned forward and gave each
other a fake little hug.

Seth and Riley gave each other a real hug. "Be careful
out there," Seth said. "Don't take any wooden five-dollar
bills, okay?"

Riley's eyes were scrunched closed. "Love you, Dad."

"Love you, too, kiddo."

We sat in the front seat of the ferry so we could check out
the Boston Harbor Islands we passed. Riley knew the names
of all of them. He pointed. "That's Bumkin, way over
there," he said. "And that's Peddock's. And there's Sheep."

I pointed. "And there's Hippopotamus."

Riley's laugh wasn't up to his usual standards. "You
okay?" I asked.

"Yeah, sure," Riley said, but he didn't look so sure. He
was wearing long pants and a button-down shirt, which
somehow made him look smaller. His freckles really stood
out today against his paler-than-usual skin, and his hair

had separated into stiff sections from an overly generous application of gel.

I was actually feeling just the tiniest bit nervous myself. I opened the big envelope Geri had given me, and pulled out two ticket folders clipped together along with a receipt from the travel agent. I gasped. "Riley, do you have any idea how much these tickets cost? Three thousand eight hundred and sixty-eight dollars. And seventy-one cents. Each."

"Is that a lot, Aunt Ginger?"

"Put it this way, I didn't even know tickets *could* cost that much."

Good thing we were early, because I had to think this through. It wasn't that I was cheap, but I was holding almost eight thousand dollars in my hot little hands. I could bank some of it, so I'd have the security deposit and the first month's rent on a new apartment. I could even trade in my Jetta and put some of the money toward a less used car. Of course, I wasn't the kind of person who would ever take advantage of my nephew.

"Riley, I'm thinking maybe you and I should buy a car together. I'll drive it until you're old enough. You're eight, right?" It sounded weak even to me. "I'll drive you and your friends anywhere you want to go," I added to sweeten the deal.

Riley wrinkled his nose and scrunched his eyes. "Does this mean we're not going to Hollywood?"

No, even I could see this wasn't really fair. Riley could bank his half for college and I'd forget about the car. Although maybe I could still get the door fixed on my Jetta. "Don't worry, we're going, honey. I'm just going to try to make us each a few bucks on these tickets."

﹏

"YOU WANT TO BE *downgraded?*" the man behind the check-in counter asked.

I smiled my most encouraging smile. "Well, yes, I think so, but I just want to be sure I can get the difference." I opened my eyes wide and tried to look pleading but not desperate. "Cash would be great," I added.

"Excuse me?" he said in kind of a snippy tone. He slid one of the tickets out of its envelope with his thumb and forefinger, as if he didn't want to smudge any incriminating fingerprints.

I had this horrible feeling he was about to call security, so I backpedaled a little. "But, really, a check would be just fine. Thanks so much for anything you can do. Sir."

He gave me a look that said he was all-powerful and I was a mere ant in the picnic of life. "Listen, hon, we change these tickets and the best that can happen is the travel agency gets a refund check. I'm not even sure about that."

He slid the ticket back into its envelope and flicked his wrist to hold it out to me. "Take the first class, hon," he said. "It might be your only chance."

Riley and I found our way to the security checkpoint line, which seemed to stretch back for miles. As we waited, people sighed and looked at their watches and talked about how ridiculous this was and how there had to be a more efficient way to do that. We inched forward for maybe ten minutes or so, and I began to notice occasional people walking by us as if the line didn't apply to them. "Save my place," I said to Riley the next time one of them went by.

I followed a man in a suit until I saw a sign on a waist-high metal pole that said FIRST CLASS and BUSINESS CLASS. The man strolled past the pole as if he owned the place, and I practically ran back to Riley.

I grabbed my carry-on. "Follow me," I said to Riley.

Riley and I wheeled our suitcases right past all those poor suckers. "I don't think you're allowed to take front cuts," Riley said.

"You get what you pay for," I said.

We were through security before we knew it, and we sat in plastic chairs and watched the television sets next to our gate until we heard a voice say, "Boarding flight two-sixty-four. First-class passengers only."

Riley and I waltzed past the pilot and the smiling flight attendants to seats 3A and 3C. I reached up to put our bags in the roomy overhead bins and noticed the seats next to us were 3D and F. Seats 3B and E apparently did not exist, which meant that two entire people had been done away with to make room for our navy blue leather recliners.

"Score," Riley said beside me as he reached around in the pocket on the back of the seat in front of him. "We don't have to pay for the headphones."

"Champagne?" a flight attendant asked.

"I might need some," I answered, nodding over at Riley, who had his headphones on and was making squeaky sound effects as he played a video game built into his armrest. The flight attendant actually laughed, rather than ignoring me the way they usually did in coach.

I looked at my watch. 12:23. "Hmm. Maybe not. I've never had a drink this early. Except in college when I'd been up all night."

He winked and lifted some champagne off his tray, in

an actual glass, no less. "No worries. It's cocktail hour somewhere. Why, it's after five PM in London, after six in Amsterdam."

"What time is it in LA?"

"Nine-twenty-three AM. But who's counting?"

"Thanks," I said as I took the glass.

"And how about you, sir?" I tapped Riley's shoulder, and he pushed a button on the armrest and lifted up one of his earphones. "Can I get you a soda?"

"Coke, please," Riley said. "Do you have endless refills?"

The flight attendant laughed again. "For you, absolutely."

While Riley and I sipped our drinks, those poor coach people started getting herded in like cattle. Through a little break in the never-ending line, I noticed that three of the four people in the front row of the plane had their shoes off and their stocking feet up on the carpeted wall in front of them. I elbowed Riley and pointed at them.

"Are they allowed to do that?" Riley asked.

"I think they're worried about thrombosis. It must be a first-class thing."

"What's trombonesis?" Riley asked.

"It's when a blood clot breaks off from your leg and kills you." I guess I said it a little too loudly because the man across the aisle gave me a look of terror. "Sorry," I said. I lowered my voice and whispered to Riley, "I don't think we have to worry about it. We come from a long line of coach stock."

I held up my glass. "Anyway, cheers. May the road rise up to meet you."

Riley conked his glass into mine. "May the wind always be at your back."

"May the roof above us never fall in," we said together.

"Owe me a Coke," Riley and I said, which was exactly what his mother and I both had to try to say first when we were kids and said something at the same time.

"I don't have to," I said to Riley. "They have endless re-fills."

The champagne was almost to my lips when my cell phone rang. It was probably Geri, calling to tell me to turn it off. Which I supposed wasn't actually a bad thing, since I'd forgotten all about it.

"Hey, Riley," I said. "Don't forget to turn off your cell phone, okay?"

"I already did," he said.

I put my champagne on Riley's tray and shuffled through my shoulder bag to find my cell phone. "Hello," I said eventually.

"Get off the plane right now," Geri's voice said.

"Are you crazy?" Just in case she was not only crazy but serious, I reached for my champagne and chugged it. The bubbles tickled my nose and I sneezed.

"Bless you. Listen, I mean it. Is the plane door still open?"

It was, but I wasn't sure I should admit it. "Why? And we can't just leave. What about our baggage?"

"They'll have to get it off. The new FAA rules state that your luggage can't be on the plane if you're not."

Leave it to my sister to do the research before she called. Our flight attendant was pushing his way past the passengers still flocking onto the plane. I handed him my phone.

"Here," I said. "It's for you."

16

RILEY KEPT WATCHING ME AS WE ROLLED OUR SUIT-
cases up the ramp toward the terminal. "This better be
good," I said into my cell phone. "You have no idea how
comfortable those blue leather recliners were. And, let me
tell you, that baggage guy got pretty ugly before he found
our suitcases." I covered the mouthpiece. "Everything's
fine," I said to Riley. "Just a second, and I'll fill you in."

"What?" I said again after Geri finished telling me. Riley
and I were back in the terminal now, and I slowed down
when we came to a swarm of people milling around outside Legal Sea Foods. I was having a hard time focusing,
since I was pretty much occupied by the fantasy that
maybe I could scalp our ticket stubs before the plane took
off. "LAX?" I imagined myself whispering into the crowd.

"Hello? Earth to Ginger," my sister said into my ear.
"What is your problem? Listen, you've got to get over to
Cape Air ASAP. It's in the same terminal—just head over
to ticketing. Let me talk to Riley, okay?"

"How about if you tell me one more time first?"

"How about if you try listening for a change? All right.
Some production assistant called to say Riley's call time
was eight AM tomorrow and said they'd fax over the location directions. I said we had the directions and a car was
picking you up at LAX and taking you to the hotel. He
said, 'Oops.' Which I eventually found out meant they'd

completely forgotten you and Riley were heading out to LA." Geri took a gulp of air. "You with me so far?"

"I think so."

"Good. Okay, so apparently the shark resurfaced on the Cape over the weekend, and the producers got some permits pulled fast and they've been scrambling around to get everything down there so they can shoot before the shark takes off again."

"They forgot about us?" I couldn't believe it.

"Listen, get over yourself, will you? It could have been worse. You could have flown all the way out there, just to turn around and fly all the way back again."

"But at least then we could have said we'd been to Hollywood." My carry-on was slipping off the top of my suitcase, so I stopped to push it back up again. "And why don't we just drive to the Cape?"

"Don't you think Riley's been through enough already for one day without having to come back to Marshbury and start all over again?"

"Riley? What about me? I'm right here next to him." I looked over to make sure he was still there. He was.

"Do you see the ticket counter yet?"

I thought I could make out a single Cape Air sign at the end of the long row of counters. "Yeah, I think so, but—"

"Just give them your names. It's all set. When you get to the Cape, a car will take you to the hotel, and the hotel will have a rental car waiting for you. I'll fax you everything else you need. Now let me talk to Riley. The poor kid probably has no idea what's going on."

"Okay, here he is," I said. "Oh, if you happen to go into Harborside Drugs for anything, just don't tell Penny

Cabozzi I didn't end up going to Hollywood after all, okay?"

I tried to wrap my brain around the fairly jolting change in plans while Riley talked to his mother and we waited in line at the ticket counter. I'd had such a clear picture of me poking around the shops and galleries in Los Angeles, absorbing art like a sponge. Of course, since the Cape was a lot closer, maybe Geri and Seth could take turns coming down after work, and this way, I could actually have more time to absorb. And having a rental car for a week or two would save some wear and tear on my Jetta, so that was a bonus. Although, then again, the Cape was certainly a lot less exotic than Hollywood, plus I'd only been there about a million times. Allison Flagg was probably laughing already.

But, then *again*, if Noah actually tried to track me down, at least I'd be easier to locate on the Cape. I had a quick image of a frantic Noah trying to find me and not being able to. Of course, this wasn't the real Noah, but a Noah who actually used the telephone, had never thrown a pebble, understood the concept of advance planning, and had his canine-human issues thoroughly worked out.

"Next," a woman behind the counter said. A Nantucket basket filled with paper luggage tags sat on the counter in front of her. I thought it was a nice touch, but not nice enough to make up for missing Hollywood.

"Yup," Riley said into my cell phone as we headed over to her. "I will. Okay. Okay. I won't. Love you, too, Mom. Bye."

I had my license out already, and I handed it over to the woman and gave her Riley's name. She tapped away at the keyboard for a minute, then glanced up. "Looks like you'll just make the one forty-five. You can check your luggage at the gate."

"Thanks," I said. "And I'm sure you already have this, but we're supposed to be in first class."

She laughed. "On a nine-passenger Cessna, you can be any class you want to be, hon."

When I unzipped my shoulder bag to tuck my license back into my wallet, St. Christopher poked his little plastic head out.

"Thanks a lot," I said before I zipped him back in.

ONCE MEMORIAL DAY HIT, it was slim pickings when it came to last-minute hotels on the Cape. Ours was jammed in between the Dew Drop Inn and the Ahoy Matey Motel. The Fisherman's Lodge wasn't exactly the first picture that popped into your head when you thought of Cape Cod. A guy who looked like a lumberjack held open a mammoth rough-hewn wooden door for us. I wondered where he'd have stashed his rifle if we had said yes to his offer of help with our bags.

Riley stopped to check out a pair of fake beavers gliding under a fairly authentic-looking beaver dam in the pond in the middle of the lobby. Behind the dam a craggy waterfall splashed and sparkled under fluorescent lights. "Cool," Riley said. "I bet this is even better than Hollywood."

"Mmm," I said. I was so tired I felt like I'd walked to Hollywood and back on my hands. Plus, my teeth were still rattling from the bumpy little plane ride. Cape Cod was a lot like Marshbury, only with more traffic. It had taken us forever to get to the hotel from the airport. We rolled our way up to the desk, passing a fishing-pole rental kiosk, a hair salon, and an Internet work station along the way.

"Hi," I said. "We're checking in."

A bored-looking woman turned back around from putting a note in one of the dark wooden mailboxes that took up the entire wall behind the counter. She had pink hair and a thick silver ring at the base of her nose, and she was wearing a T-shirt that said GONE FISHING. My guess was the T-shirt hadn't been her idea. I thought about asking her if she'd made the ring herself and then seeing if I could get some tips about the local art scene, but I decided I needed a nap first. Or a swim.

⚬

THE PHONE WAS RINGING when Riley and I pushed open the door to our hotel room. "What is your problem?" Geri screamed into my ear when I answered. "I've been trying to reach you for hours."

I looked at the clock radio next to the phone. *Hours* seemed like a bit of an exaggeration. My hotel towel was soaked right through, and water was running down my legs and dripping onto the carpet. We'd cranked up the air-conditioning before we headed down to the pool, and I was starting to shiver already. If I hung up now, I could change fast before Riley came out of the bathroom. "Can I call you right back?" I asked.

"No, you cannot call me right back," Geri yelled.

I didn't say anything.

"Why?" she asked in a quieter voice.

"Because I'm soaking wet and I need to put some dry

clothes on?" I said. Then I hung up. I kept my towel on and peeled my bathing suit off under it, and pulled on some drawstring pants and a sweatshirt. Just so I didn't traumatize Riley in case he was a faster changer than I expected, I opened the closet door and hid behind it while I was changing. Apparently, junior suite meant that your living quarters and bedroom were basically different ends of the same open room.

The phone rang again just as Riley was coming out of the bathroom wearing shorts and holding his bathing suit and towel in his hands. His hair stood up in little points all over his head. "Where should I put these?" he asked.

I grabbed them on my way into the bathroom. "Oh, answer that, will you? I think it's your mother."

I rinsed our bathing suits and squeezed them out and hung them over the shower curtain rod along with our towels. I watched myself in the mirror for a while, and wished my toothbrush and toothpaste weren't still in my suitcase. I wasn't hiding, at least not in the strictest sense of the word. I was just giving my sister time to get over herself.

There was a child-size knock on the bathroom door. "Coming," I said in a cheery voice. I crossed my eyes at myself in the mirror.

"Mom wants to talk to you," Riley said. He handed me the phone and I made myself take it.

"Do you mean to tell me he hasn't even eaten yet? And have you signed in for your car yet? There's supposed to be a rental car desk in the lobby."

I held the phone away from my ear and started moving my lips as if I were Geri. Riley laughed, then put his hand over his mouth and opened his eyes wide.

"And if Riley's call sheet hasn't arrived yet, can you check at the front desk to see if it's been faxed over yet? You should get a map and directions, too. Otherwise, call me back and I'll track them down for you. And turn your cell phone on, will you, and make sure it's charged. Riley's, too. And keep them on, okay?" She took a deep breath and let out a long sigh. "Jesus, how old are you anyway?"

"Not even close to turning fifty," I said before I hung up again.

Riley was still standing there looking at me. I shrugged. "Sisters," I said.

"Yeah, I know. You should hear mine when they get going."

⟡

I OPENED THE DOOR to our minibar, then closed it again. It was a little-known historical fact that the first minibar was invented sometime during our family vacation era. If it had been a few years earlier, I might well have been *named* Minibar, so I supposed I should count my blessings. The truth was I'd never quite gotten over the trauma of being told it was off-limits. As an adult, the high point of my hotel experience was eating a six-dollar candy bar for dinner. But I had Riley to think about on this trip, so most likely we should have something a little bit healthier first.

When Geri and I were kids, I remembered my mother taking everything out of the minibar and replacing it with small cartons of milk and a box of powdered sugar donuts we'd bought at the store for breakfast. I don't remember why the donuts went into the refrigerator, since they probably had enough preservatives in them to last for centuries. Possibly it was fear of ants, which by the way, is myrmecophobia. I'd had to memorize phobias for some class in college, though I no longer remembered which one. My favorite was triskaidekaphobia, fear of the number thirteen. I just liked the way it sounded.

So anyway, Geri and I would stare at the displaced contents of the minibar with unrequited love, sometimes for days, until we left the hotel. One day Geri and I were both walking around the tiny hotel room, each cradling a candy bar as if it were a doll, when my mother looked up from her magazine.

"Don't worry, we're just looking at them," Geri said. "It was Ginger's idea."

My father glanced up from the sports section. "We'll get you those exact same candy bars tomorrow when we stop for gas," he said. "Scout's honor."

"Maybe you girls could draw pictures of them to make sure you get the right ones," my mother added. My mother was always trying to turn pretty much everything into a teaching moment. "Your crayons are right over there in that shoe box."

Geri was old enough to be insulted, so she stomped off to the bathroom, but I sat down at the built-in desk and attempted to draw the Junior Mints I lusted after. But when I finally got them the next day, it just wasn't the same. I knew now that my parents had probably spent every extra cent they had on that vacation. At the time I thought they just didn't understand the magic of the minibar.

I found the menu and brought it over to Riley's bed. "Take your pick," I said. "Just get a vegetable in case your mother asks. Then we can scavenge in the minibar for dessert."

We unpacked our suitcases while we waited for Riley's chicken fingers and my shrimp Caesar salad. To set a good example, I even put my clothes in the drawers.

"This is for you, Aunt Ginger," Riley said behind me.

I turned around, and he handed me a red plastic and silver metal thing. It looked like a mini cement mixer. "Thanks," I said. "But how did you fit this in your suitcase?"

"Easy. I just took out some shirts and stuff."

I circled it around in my hands. "What is it anyway?" I asked.

"It's a rock tumbler. You can use it for your jewelry. You just add water and sandy stuff, and it makes the rocks smooth. I hardly ever use it anymore."

He'd even saved the *intrucksions*. I started flipping through the newsprint pages. "Do you think I could use this to make sea glass?" I asked.

"Sure. I bet it would work lots faster than rocks. Techlically, I think glass is made up of water and sand."

"Woo-hoo," I said. "Let's go find some bottles to break."

17

RILEY AND I HAD NO TROUBLE AT ALL GETTING OUR
routine worked out the next morning. I ordered breakfast
while he jumped in the shower, then I jumped in while he
listened for the room service knock. If I had a son, he
would probably be a lot like Riley. We even both liked to
read while we ate our breakfast. Riley got to work on his
joke book, and I flipped through a well-worn and slightly
moldy copy of *A Child's Guide to the Biz* my father had
picked up for me at Take It or Leave It.

"Okay," I said. " 'Rate the following attributes in order of
their importance to your career. Stamina, charm, punctu-
ality, looks, connections.' "

"Boring," Riley said.

"Yeah, I agree. Poor Gramps, must have been slim pickings in the book section at the dump." I turned my book
facedown on our little round table and took a bite of my
omelet. "Your turn," I said. "Flip me one."

Riley flipped through the pages of the new joke book
which, along with a cute stuffed shark, had been a going-
away present from my parents. "If you're being chased by
a dozen sharks, what time is it?"

"I don't know, what?"

"Twelve after one."

"Pretty funny," I said. I looked over at the clock radio.
"And thanks for the reminder. We'd better hit the road."

Even if you factored out the part about not being in Hollywood, it was more than a little bit disorienting to be following the same bright yellow plastic signs on Cape Cod that Riley and I had followed in Marshbury last week. Once again, they were tacked to utility poles and planted in freestanding buckets of cement along the edge of the road. SHARK SENSE BASE CAMP their tall block letters proclaimed as they pointed the way with black arrows.

"So," I said when we got there. "Same thing, different beach."

Manny Muscadel didn't look any happier here than he'd looked the last time we saw him in Marshbury. He worked his way through the maze of cameras, lights, microphones, big thick cables, and all sorts of other equipment, right over to Riley and me.

He reached out, and he and Riley touched knuckles. "Oh, good, you're here," he said to Riley. "Do you and your people have everything you need?"

Riley and I both started to giggle at the idea of having people. I pulled it together first. "Thanks, we're all set," I said. "Too bad about those tickets to LA, though. It's really a shame it's too late to get the money back?" I thought the questioning tone of my voice might leave things open in case he had any suggestions.

Manny shrugged. "Not a big deal in the scheme of things." He rubbed his jaw back and forth with his thumb and forefinger. "You have no idea."

Since that was less than helpful, I couldn't resist a fact-finding attempt for future reference. "Hey," I said, "has anybody ever tried to cash in one of those first-class tickets and flown coach instead?"

Manny adjusted his ponytail and actually smiled. "Sure," he said. "I used to do it all the time."

Some lessons in life were just too painful. If I ever saw that snotty reservations agent again, there was no telling what I might do.

Manny turned to Riley. "Did you bring the bat and ball?"

Riley looked at me.

"Sorry," I said, "but we can go find one later."

"Thanks," Manny said. "I'd appreciate that." He circled his fingers around and around on his temples, then reached back and pulled at his ponytail again. His baseball cap was crooked, and he looked like he hadn't slept in a very long time.

"Are you okay?" I finally asked.

He looked over his shoulder, not unlike the way my father did before he brought another garbage bag into my house. "Come on," he said. "Let's find somewhere to sit down."

I picked up a few stray pieces of broken glass at the edge of the parking lot. When we got back to the hotel, I could add them to the pieces tumbling around on top of our bathroom sink. We'd managed to find and break one green beer bottle before we went to bed last night, but I wanted more variety. I hoped the housekeeping people wouldn't unplug the rock tumbler when they came in to clean. It was a tiny bit loud, so I also hoped they wouldn't think it was a bomb or anything.

Manny sat down on a big rock and I sat on the library book I'd brought to read today, *Fantabulous Found Jewelry*. He buried his head in his hands and rocked back and forth for a moment. "So," he said when he looked up. "We've got the shark again, but I gotta be honest, I'm not sure we have much else."

Riley crossed his arms over his chest. "What seems to be the problem?" he asked. Riley was sitting on an even bigger rock, kicking his legs back and forth. I noticed that his socks didn't match. Apparently my high school biology teacher was actually right about color-blindness often being passed from a father who had it through his daughter, who didn't, to her son, who did. I should probably start checking Riley's socks before we left the hotel, though it was actually a good look for him. I wasn't a fashion expert, but I thought the mismatched socks made him look kind of like a male Punky Brewster.

"Well," Manny said. "My original plan was that the movie would go deep to the primordial fear we all have of swimming in the ocean. I wanted to capture that exact moment when the horror is so pure it becomes transcendent. Excruciatingly beautiful, really, in its own way."

Riley nodded. "That's good. I like it."

Manny nodded. "And I thought it should be about evil getting loose on the innocent. About vulnerability and the onslaught of ferocity. And the velocity of that ferocity."

"What about the monstrosity of that ferocity?" Riley asked.

"Yeah, yeah, that's it," Manny said. "You're right on the mark."

"Well," I said. "This might just be *curiosity* . . ."

Manny looked at me blankly.

"Never mind," I said. "I was just wondering, don't you have a script?" I'd actually picked up a thing or two reading *A Kid's Guide to the Biz* over breakfast that morning.

Manny started rubbing his temples again. "Clint says a script is only a blueprint."

"Mmm," I said. I wasn't sure it was a fair comparison, but not having a script hadn't worked so well in my own life.

Manny gripped the sides of his rock. He looked like he was trying to hang on to a life raft. "Who am I kidding? I'm dead in the water here. The studio doesn't care how many directors they have to bring in."

It didn't seem like the best moment to ask whether Riley would still have a job, so I just nodded sympathetically.

Riley leaned over so he could punch Manny in the shoulder. "You can't get a hit if you're not in there swinging," he said in his squeaky little voice.

Manny jumped up and ruffled Riley's hair. "Thanks, buddy," he said.

"Man," Riley said as soon as Manny walked away. "That guy's high maintenance."

IT DIDN'T EVEN SURPRISE ME to see Allison Flagg a few minutes later. She'd probably tracked down the shark herself just so the twins could still be in the movie. After Riley went off with the other kids, I saw her whispering to a group of women.

I took a deep breath and walked right up to them. "So, who did I sleep with today?" I asked Allison Flagg sweetly.

I turned on my heel and smacked right into Tim Kelly. He grabbed my hand and danced me a few steps sideways in the sand.

"Dip?" he asked.

"Sure," I said. "Why not?" He dipped me, and I saw an upside-down blur of Allison Flagg and her new best friends.

When I was right side up again, I peeked over my shoulder. They were really whispering now.

"Well, that was helpful," I said. I let go of Tim Kelly's hand and bent down and picked up a shard of blue glass. "Hey, you don't happen to have an electric drill and a diamond drill bit I could take back to the hotel tonight, do you?"

Tim Kelly laughed. "What for?"

"I want to drill holes in some sea glass. I tried it once before and the glass shattered, but last night I was reading that the trick is to use a diamond bit and to drill underwater."

Tim Kelly raised one eyebrow. "I don't know what kind of books you're reading, but trust me, you should never use an electric drill underwater."

"No, see, you make a donut with a tiny piece of modeling clay and press it over where you want the hole to be, then you fill that with water and drill."

He nodded. "Okay, that sounds safe. But I have to warn you, my tools never go anywhere without me. We're a package."

I looked at him. He looked at me.

I took another deep breath. I recognized this. It was the fork in the road where I always took the wrong turn. "Thanks," I said. "But I don't allow gaffers in my hotel room. I'm becoming an artist." I closed my eyes and made myself think of Noah. "It's a lot like being a monk," I heard myself saying.

"Hot *and* funny," Tim Kelly said before he walked off. "Just my type."

⟨⟨⟩⟩

ALLISON FLAGG CAUGHT UP to me as I was heading up to the top of the beach. "Well," she said. "You certainly don't waste any time. Usually it takes a day or two for the OLAs to get started."

I wanted to ignore her, but I wanted to know what an OLA was more. "Not that I'm really interested," I said, "but what exactly is an OL-whatever-you-said?"

She gave a furtive look around and dropped her voice to a whisper. "On location affair. Everybody looks the other way and pretends it's not happening, but nobody misses a thing. Movie locations are a lot like adult summer camp, and when the summer's over, everybody goes back to the real world."

It was kind of an intriguing concept. "Give me a break," I said. "It was only a dip. The most you can accuse me of is an OLD. Get it, on location dip?"

"Time will tell," Allison Flagg said.

I walked up to the top of the beach and stood beside the bathhouse. I had a clear view of Riley from here. They were wrapping his real arm tight against his body and attaching a bloody stump to him. At least one of us was having a good day.

I found my cell phone in my shoulder bag and called Geri. She answered on the first ring. She probably had her cell phone Velcro-ed to her, although then where would she keep her BlackBerry? "Is something wrong?" she asked.

"You're turning into Mom," I said. "Why does something always have to be wrong?" It was cooler on the Cape than it had been in Marshbury yesterday, but you could still smell full-blown summer in the air. And the light was gorgeous. The light was always the best thing about being near the ocean. I wasn't sure why. Maybe the light was actually brighter, or maybe it just seemed like there was more of it because of the reflection of the water. God, I was forty-one and there was still so much I hadn't figured out yet.

"Why does something have to be wrong?" Geri repeated. I could hear the clicking of Geri's keyboard over the phone. I had to give her credit—she had great typing skills. "How about because you actually called me?"

"Oh, yeah, good point. Well, Riley's fine. They're covering his arm in blood right now."

"Did he have a good breakfast?"

"No, but he can just chew off the other arm if he gets hungry."

"I was just asking. You know, it's not that easy being here while you two are down there having all the fun."

I leaned back against the cold cement wall of the bathhouse and imagined myself stretched out on a towel on the beach below. Maybe even next to Noah. I tried to picture his face, but I couldn't quite get it. Then I tried to picture his dog. Clear as a bell.

I sighed. "Allison Flagg is here."

"Is she still talking about you?" Geri asked. The clicking had stopped, and now I could hear her crunching away on something that sounded healthy. It was quite possible she'd lost the ability to do one thing at a time.

"That would be my guess," I said. From here, I could

just barely make out Allison Flagg, who had rejoined her posse. Maybe she'd have to head back to Marshbury soon. I mean, surely the Beautification Commission had important work to be done.

"Welcome to my world. You should hear those soccer parents. Oops, I have to go."

"Nice talking to you, too," I said to the dial tone.

The phone rang again just as I was starting to put it away. My heart did a little flip, maybe that tiny optimist part of me thinking it might be Noah. The rest of me wasn't surprised when I heard my father's voice.

"Hiya, Toots."

"Hi, Dad."

"Just wanted to let you know Champ here and I are holding down the fort and everything is fine and dandy."

"That's great, Dad."

"Here, somebody wants to say hello. Come on, Champ, you don't want those young whippersnappers to show you up, do you?"

"Hi, Boyfriend," I said in one of those sappy voices people use to talk to their pets on the phone.

"It's me again," my father's voice said. "Listen, Champ and I were just wondering. You haven't seen that Ann-Margret yet, have you?"

"Uh, no."

"Well, let us know if you catch sight of her, okay, Toots? And if you're talking to you-know-who, don't let on we were asking, okay?"

I finally made the Ann-Margret connection. "Hey, Dad, we're not in Hollywood. We're on Cape Cod."

"Did I know that?"

"I'm not sure, Dad. I just barely found out."

"Well, you'd think the old goat could have told me. Listen, I better go check on the babies."

"Awhh, how're they doing?"

"Better than the bee's knees. See ya later, Dollface."

"Bye, Dad," I said to my second dial tone of the morning.

18

I SPENT THE NEXT CHUNK OF THE MORNING ALTER-
nating between watching Riley and hunting for stray
pieces of glass. Then I tracked down the gumball machines for Riley, who would be thrilled to hear they hadn't
accidentally been left behind in Marshbury.

During a break between shots, Riley and I headed up to
use the restrooms at the bathhouse. His bloody stump
took a bit of getting used to, but I was fine, as long as I
didn't look directly at it. "Nice job," I said.

"Thanks," he said. "It's pretty fun today." He held up
his stump. "Do you think they'll let me take this home
with me?"

"We can ask."

"Cool."

The twins came up beside us. Just as I looked over and
started to smile at them, one of them shoved Riley hard.
He took a few hops, trying to stay on his feet, but the pros-
thesis must have thrown off his balance, because he top-
pled over into me, and we both went down.

As I was chomping a mouthful of sand, I distinctly
heard a duet. "Liar, liar, pants on fire."

I pushed myself up onto my knees, then jerked my way
into a standing position. It hurt a lot more to fall now than
it had just a couple of years ago, I noticed. The sand

wasn't as much of a cushion as you'd think it would be, and I felt like I had tiny shards of glass imbedded in my knees and palms. Maybe I could dig them out and turn them into sea glass.

Riley was already up. The twins were probably out of earshot, but he yelled after them anyway. "See ya, wouldn't want to be ya."

"You okay?" I asked.

He held up his stump and waved it back and forth. "Look what they did to me," he said. Then he smiled.

We walked up the hill and stopped where the signs pointed one way for men and the other for women. "Meet you back here," I said. "Hey, other than getting shoved around, are things going okay with the other kids?"

Riley gave me a thumbs-up with the hand he could control. "Yeah, we all work together. It's a beautiful thing."

I wasn't buying it. "Are you sure?"

Riley lowered his voice to a squeaky whisper. "They said you did sex with someone so I could be in the movie. So I told them then their guardian did it with two people."

"What?"

Riley grinned. "Get it, Aunt Ginger? There's two of them?"

I reached for something a good parent might say. "Riley, you know I didn't really do anything to get you your part in the movie, don't you? You got it all by yourself. One hundred percent."

Riley nodded. "Yeah, I know that. But it was a good line, wasn't it?"

I TRIED CALLING GERI to tell her she might want to check in with Riley to make sure he wasn't being scarred for life by the twins, but she didn't answer. I thought I was handling things pretty well, though. Riley was probably starting to think of me as a third parent by now.

After that I just hung around out of Allison Flagg's line of vision and read my library book. There was a great idea for linking fishing swivels together to make bracelets. The best thing about it was I could probably get some right at the Fisherman's Lodge. If I could manage to drill some holes in my sea glass, I could even thread some small pieces of it onto the swivels, maybe alternating them with beads. I'd make a few samples and visit a couple of the Cape shops while I was down here and see if they'd take any on consignment.

Of course, I should get back to work on my sea glass earrings, too. I'd managed to pack up some of my supplies, at least the ones my cat wasn't using, so I had two small bags of sea glass, plus most of a spool of twenty-gauge wire and half a bag of hypoallergenic pierced earring wires, with me. There was a whole chapter in this book about wire-wrapping techniques, so maybe I could master something new in that department.

So far I was fairly limited. I'd perfected kind of an asymmetrical wire wrap, with an extra little loop. I could also do a wrap that made the piece of sea glass look like a tiny present. And then there was the double-wrap present technique, which added a second strand of wire right next to the first, and let's not forget about the asymmetrical wrap with two extra loops instead of one. I had a lot to learn.

I kept reading. I could hardly wait to try twisting and coiling and even hammering the wire to make spiral cages for the sea glass. There were some figure eight techniques that could work, too, as kind of a backdrop for the sea glass. It might also be interesting to try to make something called a jig by hammering nails into a piece of graph paper glued onto a block of wood to try some more complicated wire patterns.

Wow, there was even a section in the book about making jewelry with electrical supplies. Little tiny metal things called condensers could be used to create earrings if you ran wire down the middle of them. Who knew?

I looked up. The gaffer was staring at me from over by the video monitors. He put down the big cord he was holding and waved. I looked down again and kept reading.

Riley and I both managed to eat our lunch without anyone shoving us. We even sat right down at the table with Allison Flagg and the twins, just so they didn't think they could push us around. Some of the women at the table actually seemed pretty friendly. One of them pointed to my book. "There's a great place for jewelry near the town square. It's called Sand, Sea and Sky. You should check it out."

"Thanks," I said.

"In your spare time," Allison Flagg said. One of the other women giggled.

I didn't even bother to look at her. "All set, Riley?" I said as I pushed my chair back from the table.

We stopped at the gumball machines on our way back. Riley stretched out his arms and gave one of them a hug. "I missed you guys," he said.

That gaffer was everywhere. "Hey, are you still following me?" he asked as he walked over to us. He flipped his sunglasses up to the top of his head.

"Are you almost ready, Riley?" I asked. I'd never really noticed before how handy it was to have kids around. They were a great social buffer.

"Okay," Tim Kelly said. "You can take my drill. But just for one night."

Riley gave me a handful of M&M's and went back for more. "You don't happen to have any old electrical condensers you don't need, do you?" I asked. "Little ones?"

The gaffer shook his head. "Give 'em an inch. . . ." He turned around so we were both facing the same way, and draped an arm across my shoulder. "I knew it. You're much brighter than you pretend to be."

"Brightest bulb in the pack," I said as I slid out from under his arm.

He grinned. "Are you trying to turn me on with all this electrical talk?"

I groaned. "Yuck. And you were almost likable for a minute there. Listen, thanks so much about the drill. I really appreciate it. Well, better get back to work." I took a few quick steps toward Riley.

"Right," he said. "Let me know if you need me for anything."

I was pretty sure I could think of a couple things if I tried, but I was definitely not going there.

⟶

RILEY GOT BUSY AGAIN and I tried to. Every paragraph or two, I'd find myself peeking over the top of my book to look for the gaffer. I imagined stretching out beside him on a beach blanket, rubbing sunscreen on his back. Handing him the bottle so he could rub some on mine. . . .

I was saved by the ring of my cell phone. It was my father. "Just to let you know," he said as soon as I said hello, "we took our daily constitutional and walked way the heck over to the Take It or Leave It so I could show the babies where they were adopted."

"That's nice, Dad. You didn't try to put Boyfriend in the stroller with them, did you?"

"Champ decided to stay home, but I told him I'd keep an eye out for a double stroller. We'll work things out, don't you worry. By the way, you don't have any of that Bactine ointment hanging around anywhere, do you?"

"Ask Mom." I stood up so I could get a better look at things on the film front. Riley was splashing around in the water now, and everybody on the beach was screaming. It looked pretty scary, even from here.

"Listen, Champ and I were just thinking maybe we'd drive the babies down to see you. How's that sound to you, Toots?"

That got my attention. "Dangerous?" I suggested.

"Oh, don't be a stick-in-the-mud. We were thinking the babies could stay with you, and Champ and I would take the ferry over to Nantucket. Some lady at the Take It or Leave It told me you could make a million dollars in one month on the things they throw away at the dump over there. None of those rich people want to bother to haul their old stuff off the island, so they just leave it for the taking."

"Dad, Boyfriend doesn't like to ride in the car. What's Mom up to today? Maybe you should ask her to take a ride with you."

"Keep this under your hat, but I think the old broad is spying on me."

"What?"

"The babies and I are pretty sure we saw her over at the dump today."

"Maybe she was just getting rid of some things."

"Everybody knows that's not her department. Anyhoo, did I tell you what we found at the Take It or Leave It today?"

I was wearing a watch today. I looked at it. "No, what?"

"A ship's wheel coffee table exactly like the one in our rumpus room. We'll have a matched set once I talk you-know-who into it. They just don't make tables like that anymore. Right now we've got Champ's food and water up on top of it. I don't think he likes sharing with the babies, so they've got their own chow area on the floor over by the kitchen cabinets."

I was trying not to picture all that stuff in my apartment. "Great, Dad."

"Well, okay, Toots, that's it for now. We'll talk to you later. Over and out."

My phone rang again before I could even put it away. I pushed the green button. "What, do you guys take a number, like at the deli?"

"Is that any way to talk to your mother, Virginia?"

"Oh, Mom, sorry, I thought you were Geri. I haven't talked to her since this morning. You don't think she's sick, do you?"

"Do you know that father of yours is keeping kittens at your place?"

"You're kidding."

"I knew you knew. Wait till I get my hands on him."

"Mom, let's change the subject, okay? What else is going on up there?"

"Well, I finally gave up waiting for you-know-who to do it, so I got rid of that awful old coffee table in the rumpus room. I talked the paperboy into helping me load it into the car and drove it over to the dump myself."

"That's great, Mom. Listen, I'm right in the middle of one of my jewelry books. Can I call you later?"

☙

I WAITED AROUND outside the special effects trailer while Riley had his bloody stump removed for the day, and then we went over to the electrical trailer to get the drill. Even though it had been a long day, we decided we'd drive into town and walk around before we headed back to the hotel.

We grabbed some bottles of water at the crafts services table for the ride and started across the parking lot toward our rental car. Riley was carrying the drill and a pair of safety goggles, and I was looking through a handful of tiny metal condensers. Some of them had definite possibilities. I looked over my shoulder to make sure Tim Kelly wasn't following us, but the coast was clear. The gaffer had actually been pretty nice about handing everything over.

"Uh-oh," Riley said.

It looked like our rental car had had a long day, too. There was a thick brown streak smeared across the windshield of our white Chevy Malibu, and a small mound of the same stuff sat dead center on the hood. "Ohmigod," I said, "is that what it looks like?"

Riley took a step closer and sniffed. "I think it's only smushed brownie."

I stood beside Riley and leaned forward carefully. "I think you're right." I reached into my bag and pulled out a tissue, but it seemed woefully inadequate. "Got any good ideas?" I asked.

"How about the windshield wipers?"

"You're pretty smart for an eight-year-old." We climbed into the car, and I kept my finger on the windshield fluid button until it seemed safe to turn on the wipers.

Several tries later and we'd created a small window in a sea of chocolate flecks. Now we had a great view of the big pile of brownie on the hood. "I'm not touching that," I said. "It really looks like dog poop."

Riley laughed. "I think we should keep it on there."

"I think we should take a picture and send it to the Marshbury Beautification Commission. They should know what their chairperson's daughters have been up to."

19

RILEY SEEMED FINE TO ME, BUT I KNEW IT WAS MY RE-sponsibility to make sure he was taking the brownie poop in stride. "I don't usually tell this story," I said once we were on the road, "but when I was in sixth grade I got a big part in a play, and somebody put a dead rat in my locker."

"Cool," Riley said. "How'd they kill it?"

There really was a gender difference. In all these years, I'd never once stopped to ponder that question. "I don't know," I said. "Machine gun?"

"Nah, that would splatter it."

We were almost to the harbor, so I rolled down the window and took a whiff of salt air. "Maybe it was dead already. Bubonic plague?"

Riley considered this. "Maybe it was rat poison."

"Well," I said. "Better it than me, I guess." I rolled the window back up to see if I could trap the salt smell inside with us.

We parked the rental car right on Main Street and pre-tended we didn't notice the tourists staring at the hood of our car as they walked by. We got out and poured what was left of our bottled water on the main deposit of brownie. Riley picked up a stick and gave it a little poke.

He started to laugh. "I think it turned into a fossil," he said between squeaks.

"Well, you're going to have to drive back to the hotel then. I can't handle looking at it."

"Deal," he said.

We found Sand, Sea and Sky right away. As soon as we walked through the door, I was in heaven. It was packed full of everything from vintage jewelry to Nantucket baskets and those Cape Cod bracelets everybody seemed to be wearing. I pointed to one in a case. "What are these called again?" I asked the woman behind the counter.

She looked up from a length of beads she was stringing. "Oddball bracelets," she said. "Actually, we're not allowed to call them that. The family who first started making them is trying to get them patented. They even put little tags on theirs that say 'the only authentic oddball.' So we're adding cobalt beads and Swarovski crystals to ours and calling them blueball bracelets."

"Cute," I said.

"It's dog-eat-dog down here," she said.

"Really?" I'd pictured this wonderful, utopian Cape Cod artists' community. I looked around to make sure Riley was okay. He was curled up in a chair by the front door, reading his joke book.

The woman put down her beads and adjusted the straps on her tank top. "Not always," she said. "There are some great people, some great shops. You just have to make sure you don't step on anybody's toes."

I was trying to casually look around for sea glass jewelry. I could see a few pieces, mostly pendants set in heavy sterling silver. "You don't happen to need any sea glass earrings, do you?" I reached up to touch my ears, but of course I hadn't remembered to wear any.

"Sure, they sell like crazy here. Bring in some samples.

By the way, I'm Marnie. My co-owner, Daria, is in the back working on some lampwork beads. Go introduce yourself before you leave."

"Thanks," I said. "I'm Ginger. I really love your store. You have some amazing things." I picked up a pin that seemed to be made entirely of old buttons.

"That one speaks to me, too," she said.

I ran my finger along the edge of the arched mother-of-pearl button in the center. "I've never quite thought of it that way," I said.

She picked up a pink and black ring that had an art deco look. "Oh, jewels are definitely a means of communication, and every single civilization has had them. They speak to us, and we wear them to tell each other who we are."

There was a tray of beads on top of the case. I reached in and picked up a tiny green bead shaped like a frog.

"That's Czech glass. It looks like malachite, doesn't it? I don't know about the Czechs, but the Chinese consider the frog a symbol of luck."

It couldn't hurt. I reached into my shoulder bag for my wallet.

⬥

RILEY AND I PUSHED ASIDE a tie-dyed curtain at the back of the store and introduced ourselves to Daria. She was sitting at a long plywood table and twisting what looked like a sparkler back and forth in the middle of a small propane flame.

"Wow," I said. "So that's how you make lampwork beads."

"It is indeed." Daria had a young, pretty face and gray hair that coiled around her head like a Brillo pad.

I could just make out a tiny bead at the end of the sparkler. I liked the little torchlike flame. It was so much more civilized than that great big gaping furnace Noah used.

She pulled the sparkler out of the flame and looked at it for a minute. Then she shoved it bead-first into a Crock-Pot.

"Is that a Crock-Pot?" I asked.

"Yeah, it's actually filled with vermiculite. I have a kiln in my studio at home, but this works fine for in here. The annealing process is the most important thing. You have to lower the temperature carefully, or the beads can break."

Riley pointed to one of the metal things sticking out of the Crock-Pot like an upside-down bouquet. "Is that a sparkler?" he asked.

"Sorry. It's just a metal rod. It's called a mandrel." Daria pointed to the contraption clamped to the table, with rubber hoses leading to the propane tank. "And this is called a minor bench burner."

Glass rods in all sorts of vibrant colors sat in clear Lucite boxes at one end of the table. I tried to imagine what it would be like to have my own inventory of glass rods, to order the colors I liked and arrange them any way I wanted to, to work in the back of my own little shop.

I had what I thought might be a brilliant idea. "I was just wondering," I said. "Has anybody ever tried to drizzle bits of colored glass onto sea glass?"

She smiled. "Let's try it."

There was no shortage of guinea pigs rolling around in the bottom of my shoulder bag. I let Riley pick out a small aquamarine piece. It had the weathered look of something that had been thrown around by the ocean for years and years.

Daria chose an orange glass rod. She nodded at some pliers. "Pick it up with those and hold it over here and let's give it a try. Put a pair of those goggles on first, though."

I held the sea glass in the flame and Daria heated the glass rod above it and then dotted it to the glass. "Okay," she said. "Take it out and let's see what we've got."

"How'd that happen?" Riley asked.

My beautiful piece of sea glass had turned into an ordinary piece of glass with orange polka dots.

"Yeah," Daria said. "Isn't that amazing? The etching just melts away. I really think the cosmetic people should know about this. Who knows, it might work on wrinkles."

Riley held his hands up to his cheeks and made a face like the kid in *Home Alone*. "Ouch," he mouthed.

I was thinking about how much I'd really liked that particular piece of sea glass. "I bet you could spend the rest of your life figuring this stuff out."

"That's my plan," Daria said. She picked up a mandrel. "Glass is really temperamental. Just when you think you know what you're doing, you get another curveball. But, it's all worth it because every once in a while you create something that's so beautiful you don't even know where it came from."

IT MUST HAVE BEEN all that glass, but now I was thinking about Noah again. I wondered if he'd ever done any glass beadwork. I wondered if he even knew I was gone. Riley and I pushed our way back through the tie-dyed curtain.

There was a knock at the big display window at the front of the store. When we turned to look, the twins were side by side, pressing their faces against the glass.

"Yikes," Riley yelled. "Run for your life!"

I saw at least one customer start to run. "Shh," I whispered to Riley. I tried to catch Marnie's eye to see if I'd blown my chances of ever selling her any earrings, but she didn't look up. Maybe she'd missed it.

The twins burst through the front door. Allison Flagg was right on their heels. "I take that back," I whispered to Riley. "It was actually excellent advice."

"Can I talk to you for a minute?" Allison Flagg asked.

I'd been around the block enough to know this was a question that never led anywhere good. As further evidence, it sure looked like she was glaring at Riley. The twins each took one of her hands. One of them looked angelically up at her mother while the other crossed her eyes at Riley.

I put my arm around Riley's shoulders. "Sure," I said. "Why don't we step outside? We can all snack on my car or something."

"Thanks anyway," Allison Flagg said. "But this isn't a social visit. I think you should know what your nephew has been saying. It's not the sort of thing I want my twins exposed to at this age. I'm very concerned. What did you mean by snack on your car?"

I really wanted to punch her out. I hated everything about Allison Flagg, the way she walked, the way she talked, the stupid crisp white preppie blouse she was wearing with those dorky capris with the sailboats on them, or whatever they were.

But I had Riley to think about. As a third child, and with

two busy parents, who must have been pretty tired by the time he came along, he probably never had this much individual attention. I was essentially a parent figure, and this time together was a huge opportunity for me to set a good example for him.

I looked Allison Flagg right in her nasty little eyes. "Your daughters vandalized our rental car with brownies, a crime punishable to the full extent of the law. And, we have witnesses."

The last part was a lie, but it worked great. The twins just hid behind her back and didn't even try to deny it. Allison Flagg glared some more at Riley. "Well, I'm sure your nephew provoked them."

I forced myself to smile. "Listen," I said. "How about if I take Riley and the girls to go buy a bucket and some sponges, and we'll meet you back at the hotel. The kids can wash the car off together in the parking lot."

Allison Flagg checked her watch. "Actually, I wouldn't mind getting a little shopping in before I head back to the hotel."

"I'll take that as a thank-you," I said.

Once we got rid of their evil real mother, I was sure I could help the twins change their nasty ways. First I was a kid, then my sister had kids, so I'd been around kids practically all my life. I knew how they operated, I knew how their minds worked. Sometimes I felt like I was still one of them.

It didn't take us long to find three sponges and a bucket. We even found a Wiffle ball and bat set for Manny. While Riley and the twins chatted, I stopped at a huge bulletin board with little slots for flyers. I took one for every store that might possibly be interested in my earrings.

I also grabbed a Childfree by Choice flyer, because it made me remember the first time I met Noah. Apparently the revolution had made it all the way across the bridge and onto the Cape. If the health club was the new singles bar, maybe Childfree by Choice was the new playgroup, just minus the kids. "Children Should Be Neither Seen Nor Heard at the Following Events," I read before I tucked it behind the other flyers.

"I thought you said I could drive," Riley said when we all climbed into the rental car.

"Talk to me in another eight years or so," I said.

The twins had started to giggle as soon as we came within sight of the car. I waited until they got themselves buckled into the backseat. "Okay," I said. "Enough of this twin stuff. It'll stunt your growth. I want names."

I looked at them in the rearview mirror. "Come on. We don't have all day."

"Mackayla," the one behind me said in a little voice.

"Mackenzie," the other one said, in pretty much the same voice.

"All right, Mack and Mack, listen up. We'll start with a simple apology, but I'm hoping for real redemption by the time this car is clean."

20

WHEN ALLISON FLAGG PULLED INTO THE HOTEL PARK-
ing lot, my rental car was looking a tiny bit better and the
kids were a whole lot wetter. For some crazy reason, the
two Macks couldn't wait to get back to their mother.

"Mom," one of the Macks yelled. "Save us!"

"Can Riley eat over?" the other Mack yelled.

Allison Flagg climbed out of her car and reached back
in for two pizza boxes. "Sure," she said. "I bought extra just
in case. We can have dinner down by the pool."

"Well," I said to give Riley an easy out. "It's been kind of
a long day. . . ."

Riley started jumping up and down. "Key, please. Key,
please," he chanted.

I pulled the room key card out of the pocket of my
jeans. "See," I said, "he's really tired. Maybe another time."

Riley was already running. "Bathing suit," he yelled. "Be
right back."

"Make sure he has his cell phone," Allison Flagg said.
"So he can call you when we're done. My twins need their
beauty sleep." She tilted her head. "And don't go too far. No
hot dates or anything."

It seemed to me that there was plenty of pizza for all of
us. "I don't have any plans at all," I said.

"I'll take that as a thank-you," she said.

AFTER RILEY GOT SETTLED in at the pool, I headed out to my rental car to get the gaffer's drill. It wasn't as if I wanted to have pizza with Allison Flagg anyway, but she should have at least invited me.

I was trying to decide whether to order room service for dinner, or go for a quick drive and pick something up. I clicked the car doors shut and headed back toward the hotel again. Maybe by the time I got the drill to my room, I'd be able to make up my mind.

I heard a car door slam. I kept walking. "Hey, where'd you get that drill?" someone yelled behind me.

I turned around. "Are you actually following me?" I yelled to Tim Kelly.

"Yeah, that drill you're carrying is implanted with a surveillance microchip. We call it the spy chip."

I looked at the drill, then turned around again and kept walking.

Tim Kelly caught up to me and put his arm around my shoulders. "No," he said. "Of course not. I'm staying here, too."

I stopped. "Really?"

"Yeah, pretty much everybody is. It's the only hotel they could get."

We looked at the back of the Fisherman's Lodge, where an ice machine was surrounded by logs to make it look like a woodshed. Or maybe an outhouse. "Can't imagine why this one was still available," I said.

"Got plans tonight?" the gaffer asked. His forehead wrinkled when he opened his hazel eyes wide, and there were streaks of blond and gray in his sandy curls.

I started walking again. His arm stayed attached to my shoulders. "Yup," I lied. "Planning to hang out with my nephew."

"Can't you get a babysitter?" he asked.

I started to slide out from under his arm, and he squeezed my shoulder with his hand.

I elbowed him and ducked. "I *am* the babysitter," I said.

"Ouch," he said. "Okay, truce. How about if you go get your nephew and I'll meet you both in the hotel café. My treat. I bet they have great buffalo here. Although we might have to shoot it ourselves."

I looked at the long brown paper bag he was carrying. "Is that a sub?"

"Yeah," he said. "But it's okay. I can save it for breakfast."

"What kind is it?"

It turned out Tim Kelly's turkey sub had cranberry sauce on it, just the way I liked it. We were sitting down by the stocked fishpond, dangling our feet off the bridge. We'd grabbed two bottled waters from the vending machine next to the ice cabin. I handed him a bottle of water. He handed me half of the sub.

"Thanks," we both said. The gaffer took a long drink, then broke off a piece of sub roll and dropped it into the water. A school of fish immediately circled and attacked.

"Geesh," I said. "Remind me never to swim here. They look like piranha."

He gave me a tiny push.

I grabbed his arm to keep from falling, then let go quick. "Cute," I said.

"Thanks. So tell me about this sorta boyfriend."

I threw the fish another piece of sub roll. "Not much to

tell. We had a big fight, and I don't really know where we stand. We both have lots of baggage, I guess."

Tim Kelly leaned back on his elbows. "Baggage? You want to talk baggage? Boy, have I got baggage."

"Well," I said. "Not to be competitive, but I have the carry-on, the garment bag, the weekender, and the sports bag." I counted them off on my fingers, then leaned back on my elbows. "The complete Louis Vuitton mono-grammed collection of baggage. Whatever that is."

"I have a daughter," he said quietly. "She's six. Her name is Hannah."

"You win," I said. I sat up and poured some water into the pond to see if it would attract the fish. They didn't fall for it for a second. "Did she come with a wife?"

"Ex." He sat up and took another long drink from his water bottle, then carefully screwed the top back on. "We had no business being together in the first place. She wants someone who will be home for dinner, and I spend most of the year traveling, unless I luck out and get a movie close to home like this one. But Hannah's amazing, and we're doing a pretty good job coparenting her. I just called her a little while ago and she said, 'Dad, I love you, but can I call you back later? I'm right in the middle of something.' She's *six*. Sorry, I didn't mean to ramble."

"That's really cute."

"Yeah, she's the best thing that ever happened to me." He finished off his last bite of sub, then crumpled up the white paper wrapping. "Okay, there's a woman I see, off and on. She has kids. It's complicated. Her husband has her two boys on the weekends, and weekends are when I spend time with Hannah . . . Never mind. Anyway, we're pretty much off, I think."

"Geesh," I said. "You're a really nice guy. Who knew?"

"Don't believe it for a second." He wiggled his eyebrows. "I can't wait for work tomorrow, so I can tell everybody I got you into bed."

"No way," I said. "But you could probably get away with kissing me."

⟫

TIM KELLY WAS a seriously good kisser. It was a lucky thing Riley called when he did, or we might have been headed into OLA territory. An OLK was hazardous enough.

"Be right there," I said to Riley. I grabbed the empty water bottles while Tim Kelly stuffed the sub wrapper into the paper bag.

"So," I said. "Guess I better go get my nephew."

"So," he said. "Guess I better go wait for my daughter to call back."

We looked at each other. "Take good care of my drill," Tim Kelly said.

As soon as Riley and I got back to our hotel room, I went into the bathroom to check the rock tumbler. The broken beer bottle was halfway to sea glass already. I managed to fish out a piece without cutting off my finger and showed it to Riley. "Do you think I should add some more sand to it, or just let it tumble for another day?"

He wrinkled up his nose. "I wouldn't mess with it. When the tumbler gets too heavy, it stops tumbling."

It seemed like there might be a message in there that I could apply to the rest of my life, but I couldn't quite put my finger on it. "Hey," I said. "Did everything go okay down at the pool?"

Riley nodded.

"Good," I said. "Let me know if you need me to knock any twins together or anything."

Riley jumped up on his bed and arranged his pillows, then reached for the remote and turned on the TV.

"Okay," I said. "I'm going to go drill for a while. Do you and your people have everything you need?"

Riley was already lost in his show. I went back to the bathroom and picked out a dark green piece of sea glass, thinking it would be easier to see when I was drilling than something more translucent. Then I rolled a little piece of clay into a snake and made the snake into a circle. I pressed it onto the glass and filled it with water to create a miniature pool right where I wanted the hole to be. I put on Tim Kelly's safety goggles. I plugged in his diamond bit drill. I turned his drill on.

Almost immediately, the drill bit skittered off the sea glass and landed on the sink countertop. I pushed the off button and inspected the gold-veined Formica for signs of damage. It was hard to tell.

There was a loud knock on the other side of the wall, over by the shower. I held the drill up in the air and turned it on again, just to see what would happen. The knock got louder.

Apparently I had two problems. At the very least. I repaired my tiny clay pool, but before I refilled it with water, I twisted the diamond drill bit back and forth by hand, just to get enough of a hole started so the bit would stay in place.

Then I unplugged the drill and headed out through the slider to our little cement balcony. "Excuse me," I said when I walked between Riley and the televison. He didn't even notice me.

There was more room to work out on the balcony, and luckily Tim Kelly had been kind enough to throw in an extension cord. I looked at the drill and took a moment to relive that kiss. It was a great kiss. I pushed it away again.

I plugged in the drill and turned it on.

"Hey, keep it down," a loud voice yelled. "Some of us are trying to have a vacation around here."

"Maintenance," I yelled in a low voice. "Emergency structural repairs."

"This place sucks," the voice yelled back. "When you finish out there, how about you do something to make our ceiling stop dripping. It's not like we haven't called the front desk three times about it."

"Will do," I yelled.

Eventually I managed to drill through a few pieces of sea glass, but it was work. I decided to save the rest for when I got back home. I'd found an old drill out in the garage, which was what I'd used the first time I tried drilling sea glass. Maybe I could buy a diamond drill bit for that. I hoped it only sounded expensive.

I brought the drill inside and locked the slider, just in case anybody came hunting for that noisy repair person. All the commotion didn't seem to have bothered Riley a bit. He was already asleep, curled up under the covers and hugging his stuffed shark. The remote was still in his hand. I peeled his fingers away and turned off the TV, and then I leaned down and gave him a kiss on his forehead. He made a funny face.

I put the freshly drilled sea glass pieces on my bedside

table. I found the frog bead and put that there, too, right next to the little greenish statue of St. Christopher.

Under the glow of my clock radio, it looked like a shrine. If I'd had a candle to light, I would have. "Okay, help me out, you guys," I whispered. "I'm looking for a little direction here."

My cell phone rang, and I opened it fast before it could wake Riley. "Hello," I whispered.

"Hey," Noah's voice said.

21

"I MISS YOU," NOAH'S VOICE SAID NEXT.

"Thanks," I whispered. I gave St. Christopher and the frog bead a little shrug, then tiptoed across the room and back out to the balcony. I slid the screen shut behind me and sat down on the little plastic chair.

"Did I get you at a bad time? You weren't asleep already, were you?"

I watched the lights twinkling in the parking lot. "No, I was just trying to wrap my head around the fact that you actually called me. Do you even have my cell phone number?"

"I got it from your dad. Those kittens are pretty cute."

"Mmm," I said. "They are."

"Anyway, I'm really sorry about what I said about not liking cats. You know that shredding thing the Boyster does with the newspapers? We turned a couple of them into collages. And they needed some color, so I gave him some acrylic paint in a cereal bowl and taught him how to dip his paws in. He took right to it. They're pretty amazing. A real Jackson Pollock vibe. I'm thinking he could even have a show in a year or two."

"You were in my apartment without me?"

"Your father was there."

"You went over to apologize to my cat?"

Noah didn't say anything, but I waited him out. "No, I went over to apologize to you, but you'd already taken off for Hollywood."

"I'm not in Hollywood. I'm on the Cape."

"You're kidding. I was going to fly out to find you. There's a glassblowers' colony in Laguna Beach I've always wanted to see. I figured we could check it out together."

I didn't say anything.

"God, I'm an idiot." He cleared his throat. "I don't give a rat's ass about your cat's talent or Laguna Beach. Okay, that's not true. Listen, what I really would have done was come out to see you. And Laguna Beach. In that order."

I couldn't stop myself. "Wow," I said, "I've never gotten a higher rating than Laguna Beach before. How do you feel about me in relation to Santa Monica?"

Now Noah wasn't saying anything.

I closed my eyes. "Sorry. I'm trying to let this go, but I still don't get that you'd give my cat art lessons when we're not speaking. And have this whole plan to come out to see me without even checking in with me."

"Isn't that what I'm doing now?"

I put my feet up on the split log railing and leaned my head back against the rough bark of the hotel.

"Okay," Noah said. "Here's the thing. The day after we had that stupid fight, it just hit me. Pretty much all I have to show for my entire life are some nice pieces of glass."

"Thanks," I said.

"No, that's not what I mean. I'm trying to apologize. Listen, please? I'm just trying to tell you that Seattle was bad. Really bad. I wasn't great before that maybe, but after, I think I just gave up."

"What do you mean?"

"Well, okay, I worked with a big glassblower out there for a few years, and then I went out on my own. And suddenly this guy is suing me for copyright infringement. I couldn't believe it. I mean, glassblowing is all about color and shape and movement. And nature. You spend days and days noticing that the yellow crocuses open first, and then the purple and then the white."

"I didn't know that."

"Well, yeah, and then you spend weeks trying to capture the exact feel of it and pull it into a vase you're working on, and suddenly this guy is trying to say he owns the whole concept of crocuses."

"That's crazy."

"Yeah, and what happens to art if da Vinci is the only one allowed to paint crooked smiles, you know? And only James Taylor can sing about fire or rain. Anyway, in court he tried to say I wasn't a real artist, that I wasn't capable of conceptualizing higher level art. That I was basically just a gaffer, and I was stealing his brilliant ideas."

Clearly I was hearing things. "Excuse me?" I said. "But isn't a gaffer an electrician?"

"Maybe. But it's also a glassblower who does the labor under another glassblower who has the vision, who's the real artist. Such a crock. Everything I did from the time I walked out that door was me—my vision, my style." Noah sighed. "I think what happens is that some of these guys start to believe their own press clippings."

"He lost, didn't he?"

"Yeah, eventually the case got thrown out. But I guess I was pretty obsessed by the whole thing, and well, I never saw the signs. My wife had already moved on to the next guy. I didn't even see it coming."

I rubbed the back of my hand across my mouth. "Wow," I said.

"Yeah, it was bad. Anyway, enough about me. I'm sorry about that stupid fight we had. And I'm sorry I haven't treated you better. Are you coming home for the weekend? Or can I come down and take you and Riley out to dinner or something?"

I closed my eyes. "I don't know yet. Can I get back to you when I figure out what's going on?"

"Sure. How's everything going down there with the movie? And how's your jewelry coming along?"

"Okay, I guess." A car pulled into the parking lot, and the headlights pointed right at me. I pulled my legs off the balcony and leaned forward in my chair. Some of my hair stuck to the bark wall and I had to reach back and pull it away. "I don't know. I always wanted to be one of those people everybody thought was talented. But from the time I was little, art seemed like a club I couldn't get into. Even with my first pasta necklace, I could tell nobody was that excited about it, and I could never weave those stupid pot holders right. I mean, how do you really know what color loop to use next?"

I thought Noah would laugh. I was probably even trying to make him laugh. "It takes courage to create," he said. "People are afraid of embarrassing themselves by not being good enough."

"Or maybe even by showing who they really are."

"That's a good point," Noah said. "I'm probably more afraid of embarrassing myself in life than in art, though.

Art gives you a little distance. It's you, but you're still a safe step removed."

"Hmm," I said.

"Don't worry about being brilliant, Ginger. If you work at anything seven days and a million hours a week, of course you're going to get good at it."

"That much, huh?" I said. "No, I'm only kidding. I really want to try. And you're a really good conversationalist. Who knew?"

Noah laughed. "Thanks. My jaw actually hurts. So, you'll call me later?"

"Tonight?"

"No, I meant later this week, when you know what's going on down there."

"Okay," I said. "I will."

∞

I TOSSED AND TURNED all night, and woke up with a bad case of kisser's remorse. As if I didn't have enough issues already, apparently I could add impulse control to the list. I stared at the popcorn ceiling over my bed, trying to figure out how I could get the drill back to the gaffer without actually running into the gaffer. Maybe he wouldn't even remember the kiss. Maybe he was on again with his girlfriend. It seemed timing, or lack thereof, really was everything.

Eventually my alarm went off. I rolled over and hit the button. Riley jumped right up and headed for the bathroom. "Hey," I yelled. "What do you want for breakfast?"

"Whatever," he said.

My eight-year-old nephew had turned into a teenager overnight. Or maybe he hadn't slept well either. I picked up the phone and called in chocolate chip pancakes for Riley and a veggie and egg white omelet for me. The décor might not be much, but at least breakfast was pretty good here, when it arrived hot.

I jumped in the shower when Riley got out, and then he read his joke book and I flipped through one of my jewelry books while we ate breakfast.

"So, you're in a good mood," I said finally.

"Shh," he said. "I'm trying to read."

"Whatever," I said.

We left our breakfast trays on the floor just outside the hotel room and headed for the elevator. I was carrying the gaffer's drill and goggles. Riley was still reading his joke book as we walked.

Riley looked up when we got out to the parking lot. "Is that my mother?" he asked.

Sure enough, a woman looking suspiciously like my sister was sitting behind the steering wheel of a huge SUV that looked suspiciously like her car. She was wearing big dark sunglasses and seemed to be staring straight ahead. I couldn't believe Geri thought she had to check up on me. And how nice of her to call first.

Perhaps belatedly, I looked at Riley to see if he was presentable. He looked pretty good, except for the fact that the stripes on his socks didn't quite match. I leaned over and wiped a smidgen of chocolate chip off his cheek.

"Mom!" Riley yelled. He started to run.

Geri's body jerked and she crashed her head into the window beside her.

"Were you sleeping?" I asked as soon as she opened the

door and climbed down from the heights of her ridiculously supersized vehicle.

She ignored me and gave Riley a big hug. "Oh, honey, I missed you."

Riley held on tight. "I missed you, too, Mom." It actually sounded like my laid-back little nephew was sobbing. "The twins mushed brownie all over the rental car and Aunt Ginger was really mean to them. It was only a *joke*."

Even with sunglasses, I could tell Geri was glaring at me. "What did Auntie Ginger do, honey?"

Riley let out a ragged little squeak. "She was really scary. She yelled at them and made us scrub it off, but we couldn't get it all off, and we got all wet. Can you stay here until the movie's over, Mom?"

I stared at the nasty little changeling before me and wondered what he had done with the real Riley. "I was only trying to help," I said. "I thought you wanted me on your side."

Geri held out her keys and clicked the lock on her SUV. "Okay, show me the rental car." She turned to watch a couple roll their suitcases past the log cabin ice machine. "And what kind of hotel is this anyway?"

The car still looked pretty bad. The largest deposit of brownie had thinned and spread out until it was roughly the shape of a boot, or maybe Italy, and then dried again. Smaller flecks of brownie dotted most of the windshield and the hood of the car. There was even a little bit on the hubcaps.

"What were you thinking?" Geri asked.

"I didn't *do* it," I said.

We climbed into the rental car. I drove. We followed the yellow signs to the beach parking lot in silence. I parked.

"I'll be right back," Geri said.

I picked up the drill and goggles. "Would you mind returning these to the electrical trailer while you're there?" I asked.

"Yes, I would," Geri said before she slammed the door and disappeared with Riley.

22

I POUTED ALL BY MYSELF IN THE RENTAL CAR. I LOOKED at the drill and the goggles. I looked at the car door. I imagined opening it, getting out, finding the gaffer. I couldn't do it. I leaned back against the headrest and closed my eyes.

Five minutes after she left, Geri was back.

"Why are you wearing sunglasses?" I asked. "You never wear sunglasses."

"Okay," she said. "It's all set. I apologized for you, and Allison Flagg is watching Riley while we go to the car wash. And Manny wants us to bring the bat and ball when we come back."

"We can't leave," I said. "The guardian has to be on the premises at all times."

"Allison has it under control."

"What do you mean, you apologized for me? I didn't *do* anything." I stared out through the windshield at the brownie poop. It was drying out and cracking into a road map of lines. I wanted to follow one of them right out of here. "Why does Riley hate me?" I asked. "I had no idea he was even upset."

Geri let out a puff of air. "Drive, will you? Kids always do that. They act like everything's okay, and then they fall apart as soon as they see their mothers."

"Really?" I had a sudden flashback to all the times I'd

barely made it home from school, only to burst into tears at the sight of my mother. I started up the rental car.

"Yeah. And watch what you say about the twins in front of Riley. He has a big crush on Mackenzie. At least he thinks it's Mackenzie."

"Well, we'd better nip that one in the bud right away. He's way too young for girls."

Geri twisted around to face me. *"We?"*

I put on the blinker and took a left toward the main drag. "Well, he is."

"I've got a news flash for you: You're not his mother. And, while we're at it, I've got another one: The whole world isn't only about you." Geri pushed her sunglasses farther up her nose. "Just drive, okay?"

"Fine," I said. "Just tell me if you see a car wash, *okay?"*

We found a Wash Me on our side of the road, tucked between a Seaside Sushi and a Cape Clam Shack. There was a surprisingly long line, especially given that everybody should have been vacationing, not washing their cars, but we pulled in anyway. Geri handed me some money, and I passed it over to a bored-looking college kid standing in a little booth. We reversed direction and I gave the change and receipt to Geri.

Of course, we managed to get ourselves into the slowest moving of the three car wash lines. I reached under the seat for the stack of flyers I'd left there last night.

"Want half?" I asked Geri.

Geri crossed her arms over her chest and puffed out some air. "Why would I want half?"

"Hey, it's not like I care. I was just being polite." I started flipping through them, then looked up again. Geri was just sitting there in those stupid sunglasses with her arms crossed. No cell phone, no BlackBerry. It was too much to ignore. "What is your problem today?" I asked. "And why did you take the day off anyway? I thought you and Seth were bringing the girls down this weekend."

Geri uncrossed her arms and held out her hand. "Okay, give me half."

I gave Geri a handful of brightly colored flyers and started dividing the rest into trash and save piles. Every time I had to inch the car forward, the piles got all messed up, so I'd probably have to do it all over again later.

"Oh, this is so true," Geri said.

"What?"

She cleared her throat. " 'Couples without children are invariably closer than those who produce offspring, as they are able to shower all their love and attention, not to mention their money, on each other. Once they breed, it is only a matter of time before couplehood takes second stage to parenthood.' "

"Is *couplehood* a word?" I asked.

"Seth and I used to celebrate our anniversary every month before we had kids," Geri said. "Now I'm lucky if he throws me a dozen roses once a year on the way out to soccer practice."

I put the car into drive again and rolled forward another few inches. "So," I said. "Any fun new ideas for your fiftieth?"

Geri tilted her head back and looked up at the ceiling of the rental car through her sunglasses. "One minute you think you have it all figured out . . ."

"Well," I said. "Will you look at that. We're next."

Geri kept looking at the ceiling, and eventually the car in front of us was finished, and the green light at the entrance to the car wash bay came on. I put the car back into drive and rolled slowly in until the exit light turned red and started flashing STOP.

Geri waited until the machine covered the car with suds and we lost sight of the brownie poop. The car was rocking a little to the rhythm of the wash. She took off her sunglasses and whispered something that almost sounded like, "I got fired."

"What?" I said. The HIGH POWERED RINSE sign had just started flashing, and it was really loud in the car.

"I said I got fired!" she yelled. I looked at her. She had really dark bags under her puffy red eyes. The sunglasses had been a good call.

"You?" I yelled. "I don't believe it. Why would they fire you?"

"Restructuring," she yelled. "Do you know how many people I got rid of by saying we were restructuring?"

"Why?"

"Why what?"

"Why did you get rid of them?"

"Because they weren't doing their jobs," she yelled. Then she lowered her voice. "Fifteen freakin' years," she said.

I was at a loss. My sister never used words like that. "Did you tell them it's almost your birthday?" I tried. "Maybe they'll reconsider."

"Do you know what the worst part of it was?" she yelled.

"What?" I yelled.

"They took my BlackBerry. And canceled the service. It was the only freakin' perk I ever freakin' had."

Geri started to scream, loud and long. She was scaring me, but I didn't know what else to do, so I joined in and we both just kept screaming and screaming and screaming.

When the light turned green again, we stopped. Geri fluffed up her hair and reached around in her bag for some lipstick. "Wow," she said. "That was great. I feel like a new person. I almost wish I smoked so I could have a cigarette."

I held out my hand for her lipstick. "You can't smoke. You're too perfect."

"Not anymore," she said. Her lower lip started to quiver.

I reached past the steering wheel to hug her. "Don't cry. You never cry."

She put her head on my shoulder. She was definitely crying. The car behind us beeped. "Sorry," I said to both the driver and my sister.

I put the car into drive long enough to pull into a parking lot next door. Geri was still crying. "Come on," I said. "Big deal. So you got fired. Everybody gets fired."

"Not me."

I sat. She sobbed. Occasionally, I reached over and patted her on the back. Twice I handed her a tissue. I wasn't very good at this, but I was doing the best I could. The thing was, as annoying as she could be, my sister had always been there for me. I was born into her safety net, and even though I'd been trying to climb out of it since I could crawl, it had always been a soft place to fall. Or borrow money. Or makeup. Or clothes. For more than forty-one years, she almost always let me be the baby and hadn't really asked for much in return. I owed her.

Finally, my sister blew her nose and took a long, ragged

breath. "And the day after tomorrow I turn fifty," she whispered. "That's why they fired me, you know."

"They can't do that. That's age discrimination. I think we should sue."

Geri blew out a puff of air and sounded almost like my sister again. "No, not because I was turning fifty." She shook her head. "Because I might have been a tiny bit obsessed with turning fifty."

It slipped out before I thought it through. "Ya think?"

She reached up and tilted the rearview mirror toward her. "Why didn't you tell me my eyes looked like this?"

I got my focus back. "You look fine," I lied.

She lifted her head to get another angle. "How did I get this old? You know, I can see it already. I'm going to get one of those saggy necks like a turtle. Who would hire someone with a turtle neck?"

"I think it's called a turkey neck. Grampa used to have one, remember?"

"Great." Geri started counting off on her fingers. "I'm about to turn fifty. I don't have a job. My husband never looks at me anymore. I have a pre-turkey neck." Geri sighed dramatically. "You don't know how lucky you are, your whole life stretched out in front of you."

When she buried her head in her hands, she looked a little bit like Manny, which probably meant she'd been wallowing long enough. I looked at my watch. "Wow, do you know how long we've been gone? Riley's going to wonder what happened to us."

Geri's lower lip started going again. "See," she sobbed, "I'm not even a good mother anymore."

"You're a great mom," I said. I patted her shoulder.

She found a tissue and blew her nose. "You're a great aunt. The best, really."

"Well," I said. "The good thing is, now I definitely know I'm never having kids. They really turn on you fast, don't they?"

"That was nothing," she said. "You've got the easy one. Try living with Rachel and Becca sometime. Especially now that Riley's here and they're not."

"COME WITH ME," I said after we checked on Riley. "I just have to return this." I was hoping I could tiptoe into the electrical trailer, drop off the drill and the goggles, and then fade into the background somewhere. Tim Kelly had a busy life. He probably wouldn't even notice I was gone.

We walked along the row of trailers in the parking lot until I found the right one. I tiptoed up the steps and put the drill and goggles down on the first shelf I came to. I thought about leaving a short note, but what would I say? *Dear Tim, Thanks for letting me borrow the drill. It worked great. P.S. About that kiss . . .*

I ran back down the trailer steps. Tim Kelly and Geri looked up. "So," Geri said. "It's about time I got to meet your gaffer."

"Your sister looks just like you," Tim Kelly said. "Does this mean you can go out tonight?"

"Oh, thanks," I said. "That's so nice of you. But my sister just got here."

"Don't be ridiculous," Geri said. "She'd love to."

"Great," Tim Kelly said. "How about an hour after we wrap for the day? I just need time for a quick shower."

"Perfect," Geri said.

"Okay," he said. "I'll meet you in the lobby, Ginger." Tim Kelly held out his hand to my sister. "Nice meeting you, Geri."

23

I WAITED UNTIL TIM KELLY WAS OUT OF EARSHOT. "I can't believe you did that," I said. "And you accused me of acting like I was Riley's mother? News flash: You're not *my* mother. Or my pimp, for that matter."

"Oh, please. Like I'll ever make any money on you."

We left the parking lot and stepped onto the sand. "I can't believe you interfered in my personal life like that. It's not your business."

"You should go out with him. He's a nice guy."

"Oh, right. You know him so well. What did you talk to him for, thirty seconds?"

"He's really cute. Great eyes."

I bent down and picked up a piece of sea glass. "So, why don't you go out with him then? Maybe Noah and I can double with you or something."

"Oh, sure. Like Noah would go on a real date."

I stood up again and started walking. Fast.

Geri caught up with me and grabbed my arm. "Guess what? I decided what I want to do for my birthday."

I hoped it wasn't going to involve any more crying. This nurturing stuff was really exhausting. "What?"

She slid her sunglasses down her nose and looked over them. "Do you think they'd let me be an extra if you tell them it's almost my birthday?"

"Geri, over here," Allison Flagg yelled. She patted the picnic table she and her groupies had taken over. "Sit with us."

She'd been here for mere minutes and already my sister was Miss Popularity.

"Come on," Geri said. She put her arm around me and brought me into the group the way she sometimes used to when her high school friends were over and I didn't have anybody to play with.

We sat down and everybody who hadn't bothered introducing themselves to me earlier introduced themselves. Geri was twiddling her thumbs, I noticed. It seemed like a clear case of CrackBerry withdrawal. Maybe I'd have to get her a pair of knitting needles and some yarn for her birthday.

"So," Geri said. "Ginger's going to try to get me on as an extra for my fiftieth birthday."

"Good luck," one of the women said.

"What do you mean?" Geri asked.

"Everybody wants to be an extra," she said.

Allison Flagg reached down and plucked a stray piece of beach grass. "Little sister might be able to make it happen. That gaffer can't get enough of her."

"I know what I'll do," I said, just to get out of there. "I'll go ask Manny. I bet he'd do anything for Riley's mom."

"Shh," Allison Flagg said. "They're starting."

"Quiet," somebody was saying as I sat on the sand and casually started to slide my way down to Manny. I passed the high tide line, where there was a pretty good assortment of sea glass tucked in with the patches of broken shells and seaweed. I picked up some really teeny pieces, so small I hoped they wouldn't get lost in my pocket.

Maybe I could find a way to collage them all together and make a pin, kind of like the button pin I'd seen at Sand, Sea and Sky, but beachy.

Manny pushed himself out of his chair and adjusted his baseball cap. "Okay," he yelled down to Riley, "when I say action, you're going to look down and see what's left of your arm for the first time."

Riley nodded. "What am I feeling?" he asked.

"Goddamn method actors," one of the people in the chairs whispered, and the people in the other chairs laughed quietly.

Manny ignored them and took a couple of steps toward Riley. "Shock, horror, revulsion, and then maybe it deepens to just a touch of morbid fascination."

"Cool," Riley said.

"Marker," somebody said.

"Rolling," somebody else said.

"Action," Manny Muscadel said.

Everybody watched in silence as Riley looked down at his fake arm and his eyes widened in horror. "Cut," Manny said. "Print. Let's do one more just to be sure we've got it."

Manny walked back and stood next to me. "He's amazing," he said. "You just see the kid. You don't see the actor at all."

I looked up at Manny from my seat on the sand. I wasn't sure what to say. "Do you think it's because he's not an actor?"

Manny looked down at me for a long moment. "That's a really good point," he finally said.

This was my opportunity. I widened my own eyes, going for pleading and hard-to-say-no-to. "Sorry to bother you, but Riley would really like it if his mother could be an extra. For her fiftieth birthday. You know, he hasn't had a lot of time to shop, what with the movie and everything. It could be sort of like a birthday present?"

"Fine," he said. "Tell the background guy I said it was okay."

I couldn't stop myself. "Me, too?" I asked.

"It never ends," he said. I waited for him to bury his head in his hands, but he resisted. "All right. Just keep an eye out for my mother while you're at it, will you? Make sure she doesn't get trampled or anything."

"Will do," I said. I looked over at my sister and gave her a big thumbs-up.

∞

WE FOUND THE EXTRAS GUY after lunch. He wasn't overly receptive. "Isn't that just dandy," he said as he walked back and forth with his clipboard at breakneck speed. "Good thing I always save a few slots so nobody gets left out on their birthday. Jesus. I gotta tell you, Manny Muscadel is going to be shooting wedding videos when this is over."

"Throw in a cake and some pony rides and you could probably have a sweet little side business," I suggested. It was actually not a bad idea. I had to remind myself to stay focused on my sea glass. And my sister.

The extras guy unhooked his walkie-talkie from his belt loop. "Don't start," he said. "And don't make me regret this. We've got the background holding set up over there. Act like you know what you're doing."

"Now?" Allison Flagg asked. She was standing beside

my sister, practically holding her hand. "Don't we get to go to makeup first?"

"What are *you* doing here?" I whispered.

"Geri said I could come," she whispered back. "It's *her* birthday present."

"I don't have to wear a bathing suit, do I?" Geri asked the extras guy.

He conked himself on the head with the clipboard. "Of course not, honey. Wear your favorite snowsuit. You'll fit right in." He turned and race-walked off.

Fortunately we got to keep on our shorts and T-shirts, though lots of people were wearing bathing suits. A tiny part of me still wanted to be discovered, but not necessarily in my bathing suit. It seemed that the plan was for the crowd to surge forward on the beach when Riley started to scream. Apparently the movie was in no danger of acquiring a plot. It also seemed like it might take the rest of the year to set up the shot, since it involved a camera backing uphill over a dolly track in the sand.

As we walked over to the holding tent, Geri pointed to a section of beach that was marked with caution tape and surrounded by lots of people. "Is that where the shark is?" she whispered.

I looked. "I'm not sure. If it has any brains at all, it's already taken off again to try to find a better movie."

The extras looked just like normal people, which I supposed was the point. Everybody was sitting around in folding chairs under the tent, drinking bottled water and fanning themselves.

"Well, this is fun," Allison Flagg said about five minutes later.

I was just about to say, *Well, who invited you?*, when Geri's cell phone rang. She pulled it out of her bag and said hello. I knew it wasn't a BlackBerry, but I was glad she still had something.

Geri walked to the edge of the tent to take her call, and Allison Flagg and I ignored each other. I wished I'd planned ahead and brought some earring-making supplies, but I had to settle for turning my chair sideways so I could see and digging in the sand with my toe. I found a big fat piece of light green sea glass and bent over to pick it up. Tim Kelly walked by and I pretended not to notice.

"That was Seth," Geri said when she came back. "He wanted to know where I'd like to have my birthday dinner when he and the girls get here Friday."

"That's all you're going to do?" Allison Flagg said. "Isn't this your fiftieth?" It might have been my imagination, but it seemed like she was sending some accusatory energy my way. I kept digging for sea glass.

"It's fine, really," Geri said. "Being an extra is plenty. I'll be immortalized on celluloid at fifty." She ran her hand up and down her neck. "Do you think all this flabby stuff will show?"

Allison Flagg leaned forward. "What flabby stuff? I don't see anything. You look great. Nobody would ever guess you were almost fifty."

"Thanks," Geri said.

I kept digging. When we were kids, we used to try to dig all the way to China. It would be nice to still believe it was possible.

The extras guy clapped his hands. "Okay, background. In your places, everybody. And turn those cell phones off and keep them off."

"THEY'RE KILLING ME HERE," Manny said. "I can't believe the studio took away my crane shot."

"It's not what you got, it's how you make it work for you," Riley said.

"Thanks, kiddo," Manny said. "I don't know what I'd do without you."

Riley turned and rolled his eyes at the twins, and they both started to giggle.

Some people came over to sweep the sand off the dolly track again. Riley went back into the water, and the extras guy yelled, "Places," even though we'd already been in our places for what felt like a couple of centuries.

"Picture's up and clear."

"Rolling."

"Marker."

"Action."

My heart started beating like crazy and my legs wobbled a little as I pretended to talk with Geri and Allison Flagg. Being an actor was much harder than I had thought it would be. I was waiting for Riley's scream, but it still took me by surprise. My heart actually skipped a beat, and then started racing. I don't know whose side of the family he got it from, but he sure had one bloodcurdling scream.

We all turned and started surging toward the water.

"Cut!" Manny yelled from the top of the beach.

We did it again. And again. And again. Over and over, with the hot afternoon sun beating down on us. The extras were like a big flock of sheep, and the extras guy was the shepherd, nipping at our heels to keep us in place until

Manny finished getting his shots. I only hoped it would happen in this lifetime.

In between takes one zillion and one zillion and one or so, Geri leaned over and whispered, "I am so over this. Do you think anybody would notice if we left?"

The extras guy had good ears for a shepherd. "Don't you dare," he said. "I've already signed your vouchers." He clapped his hands together and yelled, "Places, everybody."

"By the way," I asked him, "which one is Manny's mother? I'm supposed to keep an eye on her."

"Let me see," he said. "It's hard to keep the family members separate from the birthday parties." He put his hands on his hips and looked around. He pointed to a woman in a bikini. "That one," he said before he walked off again.

"Ohmigod," Geri said. "That's Manny's *mother*? I am seriously depressed. How old do you think she is?"

We all watched Manny's mother for the next eight or ten takes, weighing good genes against probable surgeries, until Manny finally yelled, "Cut! Print!"

I licked my parched lips to make it easier to speak. "Well, Sis, happy birthday."

Geri shook her head. "You know, I don't think that was quite it. Your fiftieth is supposed to be memorable, and all I'm going to remember is Manny's mother in that bathing suit."

"I've got just the thing out in my car," Allison Flagg said. "I'll be right back."

24

AS SOON AS I TURNED MY CELL PHONE BACK ON, IT started to ring. "Hi, Dad," I said.

"Have you seen him?" my mother asked.

"Who?" I asked. For some strange reason, I thought she might have been talking about Noah.

"Your father."

"Oh. Have you tried my apartment?"

"I'm there now."

"Gee, just make yourself at home," I said. I kicked the sand with my toe and reached down to pick up a sand dollar. I wondered if it would shatter if I tried to drill a hole in it.

"Thanks," my mother said. "Listen, those kittens are making a real mess over here. They're awful cute, though, I'll give them that." I waited while my mother talked baby talk to the kittens. "What is our old rumpus room table doing over here anyway?"

"Ask Dad," I said.

"I'll have to find him first."

Try the dump, I almost said, but I caught myself just in time. My mother would connect the dots soon enough. I waited while she talked some more baby talk to the kittens. I wondered if my father had given them names yet, or if he'd wait and let me help him decide. What would you name black and white kittens? Vanilla and Chocolate?

Salt and Pepper? Ebony and Ivory? Opal and Onyx? Knock Knock and Who's There?

"How's your sister holding up?" my mother finally asked.

I tiptoed a few steps away from Geri. We were waiting for Riley to come out of special effects, where he was having his stump removed. She was twiddling her thumbs again, and her lower lip looked like it might start quivering at any moment. "One minute she's up, the next she's down," I whispered.

"She'll be fine," my mother said. "And it will turn out to be an opportunity in disguise. Keep reminding her she can be anything she wants to be."

"I don't think I have to, Mom. She pretty much has it down by now."

"Well, good. And don't tell your sister, but we'll be coming down with Seth and the girls to celebrate her birthday. Listen, your phone is ringing. I'd better get it in case it's your father."

I flipped my cell phone closed as soon as I heard the dial tone. "Who was that?" Geri asked.

"Just Mom," I said. "She was looking for Dad."

Geri raised her eyebrows.

"Okay, okay," I said. "And she wanted to know how you were doing."

Geri looked down at her twiddling thumbs as if they belonged to someone else. "What did you tell her?"

"That you could be anything you want to be?"

We were still laughing when Allison Flagg came running over. She handed Geri an oversize paperback book. "Here, you can borrow this for the night. You'll definitely find something for your fiftieth in it. It's got everything. Luxury, adventure, insider tips by location, great florists."

"Florists?" I said. "Sounds exciting."

She gave me a dirty look. "It is *the* guide to be listed in. It can change your life. I'm on a committee to try to get the town of Marshbury included."

"Wow," I said. "You're really selling this."

"*User's Guide,*" Geri read out loud, "*to the Fun, Feisty, and Fabulous.*" She held it out to Allison Flagg. "Thanks so much for thinking of me, but I've been researching for months. I probably could have written this."

Allison Flagg stroked the cover reverently and gave the book a little push back in Geri's direction. "No, really, you won't be able to put it down."

Now I was curious. I grabbed the book from Geri.

Allison Flagg grabbed it from me.

I grabbed it back from Allison Flagg. I felt like we were in a *Three Stooges* episode, and my next move would be to try to poke her in the eyes with two fingers, and she'd hold the book up to block me.

Geri held out her hand, and I gave her the book. "Grow up, you two," she said. She turned to Allison Flagg. "Thanks, I appreciate it. I'll read it tonight."

"Good idea," I said. "It'll probably put you right to sleep."

Allison Flagg glared at me and took the book back from Geri. "Okay, let me find a good one. Here, just listen to this."

I yawned.

Allison Flagg cleared her throat. Then she paused, as if she were expecting a drumroll. "*Italian Monks. Every day at four-thirty in the winter and five-thirty in the summer on this street corner in Florence you can hear them singing Gregorian chants.* There's a phone number, too."

"I didn't know monks had phones," I said. I wondered if Noah had happened to stop by Florence while he was in Italy. Maybe he'd heard these very same monks. I could ask him later. I'd have a quick bite to eat with the gaffer, since there didn't seem to be an easy way out of it, and then I'd call Noah.

"Very cool," Geri said.

"Oh, I already know about this one," Allison Flagg said. *"Custom makeup blended just for you by fashion chemists in Paris. Ten thousand dollars and up, depending on skin tones."*

"I heard Nicole did that," Geri said. "And Elton."

"Not to be cheap," I said, "but is there a sale page?"

"I don't think so," Allison Flagg said. "But how about a solar-powered milk frother? It comes in six colors, and it's only nineteen ninety-five."

"Yeah," I said. "But then you have to put in the skylight to make it work."

"Not necessarily," Geri said. "You could use it outside."

"SO, DO YOU THINK we'll actually find something in that book we can do for your birthday?" I asked my sister as we walked across the parking lot while Riley ran ahead.

"I doubt it," Geri said. "I was just being polite. It's a skill you might want to consider cultivating."

I pretended her comment was too subtle for me to catch. She sighed. "I mean, it's not like I can afford to go to Florence, now that I'm not working."

Her lower lip looked like it was ready to start again. "Oh, come on," I said. "You couldn't afford to go to Florence even when you were working."

"Thanks," Geri said.

Most of the cars had cleared out of the parking lot, and a few stray seagulls were dive-bombing a garbage can. "So," I said. "What do you think you'll do for work next?"

Geri's lower lip started to quiver again.

"What's the rush?" I said. "Take some time off. Enjoy yourself for a few months."

Geri stopped walking. "Are you crazy? Do you have any idea how much our mortgage payment is?"

"You can always move in with me," I said. My sister shook her head and stomped off to catch up with Riley.

We picked up takeout for Geri and Riley so they could eat it out by the pool at the Fisherman's Lodge. When we got to the hotel, we stopped at the front desk so Geri could ask the same pierced, pink-haired girl wearing the same GONE FISHING T-shirt to send a cot up to our room. This was a detail I would only have thought of after I'd changed into my pajamas. We waited for the pink-haired girl to acknowledge us, and Riley grabbed the key card so he could run up to the room and change into his bathing suit.

When we got to the pool, we saw Allison Flagg and the twins eating takeout at one of the round tables. They all looked up and waved.

"Great," Geri said. "Civilized company for dinner."

"Where?" I asked. Riley came back wearing a suit and carrying a towel, and ran right by us.

"Walk," Geri said. She shifted her arms under the takeout bag. "Ouch," she said. "This is hot. Okay, I'll see you later. Have a good date."

"It's not a date," I said. "You know, maybe I'll go take a walk or something first. It'll only take me a minute to change."

My sister looked me up and down. "Make it two," she said.

"Action!" Riley yelled from the top of the slide. Then he let go and started sliding.

My sister and I looked at each other. Geri shook her head. "Last time we called home, he said 'Ciao, baby' when he hung up."

"I wouldn't worry about it," I said.

"Of course not," she said. "You're not his mother."

⁂

I TIPTOED PAST the pool area, since I was wearing my sister's new summer-weight jacket from Chico's. It was a great jacket, funky and sophisticated at the same time, and a perfect fit. I'd talked her into buying it because it was more my style than her usual Ann Taylor look, and I was hoping I'd be able to borrow it down the road. Since she was the one who had said yes to the gaffer, it seemed only fair that tonight was the night. It looked better on me anyway, because I had the good sense to wear it with jeans and leather flip-flops instead of something dressier. I certainly didn't want to look like I was trying too hard.

Tim Kelly was waiting in the lobby. He was wearing jeans and a long-sleeve button-down shirt. The shirt was white, crisp but untucked, and the sleeves were rolled up, exposing his tanned forearms. His hair was still wet. Maybe it was just the white shirt, but I didn't remember him being quite so handsome.

"Wow," he said. "You look great. So, where would you like to go for our second date? Think we can find another bridge?"

"It's not really a date," I said. I stopped a safe distance away from him.

He shook his head. "Relax, will you? There's almost no chance that I'm going to propose . . . tonight. So, what kind of food do you feel like? Mexican? I know a place down the road that makes great margaritas. It's really close. We can walk, if you don't trust yourself to be alone in a car with me."

"I'll try to control myself," I said.

We ended up walking anyway. Bacalao de Capa had tall dark booths. The walls were painted a mix of deep blue, terra-cotta, and gold, and a candle flickered on the forged iron wall sconce next to us. A waiter placed a basket of tortilla chips on the table. "Can I start you off with a drink?" he asked.

Tim Kelly looked at me. "Two margaritas?" he asked.

I looked at the waiter. "I'll have a seltzer," I said. "With extra lime."

"Okay," the gaffer said. "I'll have the Cadillac Margarita Cuervo Gold special with Cointreau and Grand Marnier, please. With salt."

"Don't hold back on my account," I said.

"And two straws," he said. "In case my date comes to her senses."

"I'm not really his date," I said.

The waiter dropped off our drinks. Tim Kelly ordered the Steak Fajita Supreme and I finally decided on the Tortilla Shrimp Salad.

I held up my seltzer. "Cheers," I said.

"Give me your cell phone," the gaffer said.

"What?"

He held out his hand. I gave him my cell phone. He punched in some numbers and gave it back to me. "Okay," he said. "I'm on your speed dial. When and if you decide to move beyond that sorta boyfriend of yours, give me a call. And in the meantime, let's just relax and have a nice meal, okay?"

"Okay," I said.

I put my phone away and leaned over and tried a tiny sip of Tim Kelly's margarita.

"So," he said. "Tell me everything there is to tell about Ginger Walsh. Don't leave anything out."

I leaned back and got comfortable. "Well," I said. "I was a really cute baby. . . ."

"Oh, speaking of cute babies," Tim Kelly said. He leaned to one side, so he could pull his wallet out of his jeans. He opened the wallet and pulled out a little clear accordion file of photos. He stretched it across the table between us.

I took another sip of his drink, bigger this time.

"Okay, this was Hannah's first smile, at least pretty close to the first one."

"She's beautiful," I said.

"And this is her at soccer practice this year. She's unbelievable at defense. Most of the other kids her age just follow the ball wherever it goes, but Hannah has a real sense of the big picture. It kills me to miss so many of her games, but her mother videos them and sends me a copy, and Hannah and I watch them over the phone together and take turns doing the play-by-play."

I nodded.

"Sorry," Tim Kelly said. "I'm boring you."

"No, no," I said. "Not at all." I pointed to a picture. "What's this one?"

"Oh, that's her first ballet recital. She was a cuddly duckie. Except she forgot she was onstage and kept turning around to try to see her tail feathers. . . ."

I nodded and smiled through the cuddly duckie story. It was a long story, so I found myself imagining what my daughter would be like if I'd happened to have one. By the time our food arrived, I'd decided she'd look a lot like Riley, but with pigtails. She'd hate ballet, but she'd be highly verbal and pretty good at soccer.

Tim Kelly folded up the pictures to make room for our plates. "Sorry," he said. "I didn't mean to monopolize the conversation."

"No, it was great. Really." I sawed through a shrimp and popped half of it into my mouth.

By the time we finished eating, we were entertaining each other with our worst job stories and laughing a lot. He insisted on paying the check, so we fought about that for a while, and eventually I agreed just to leave the tip.

On the walk back to the hotel, we talked as if we'd known each other for a long time. The stars were out and there was a nice cool breeze. Tim Kelly liked to walk at a fast pace the way I did. We stopped just outside the back door of the hotel.

"Thanks," I said. "I had fun."

"Me, too," he said. "I know it wasn't really a date, but do you think I can kiss you anyway?"

I leaned forward and gave him a quick kiss on the lips. I turned away fast, grabbed the door handle, and pulled.

It was locked.

"Damn," I said. "I hate when that happens."

Tim Kelly laughed. When I turned back around, he was waiting. It was a long kiss, and even better than our first one. Eventually, I found my key card and unlocked the door. We walked across the lobby together and headed for the elevator.

"No way," I said when the elevator opened. "You take this one and I'll get the next."

Tim Kelly looked at me. I looked at him. "Are you sure?" he asked.

It wasn't easy, but I nodded. I held up my cell phone. "I've got your number," I said.

25

"HOW DID IT GO?" GERI ASKED THE SECOND SHE OPENED the door to let me in.

"Fine," I said.

"Is that my jacket?"

I pulled the door shut behind me and looked down. "Well, what do you know. It's pretty dark in that closet."

"Give it to me right now, before you ruin it. I knew you only talked me into buying it so you could borrow it." I peeled off the jacket and handed it over to my sister. "So," she said. "Did he kiss you good night?"

"I'm going to pretend you didn't really ask that."

Geri put the jacket on a hanger and hung it up in the closet. "On the cheek or on the lips?"

"Listen," I said. "Just because you're married doesn't mean I have to provide you with your vicarious thrills. Go rent some porn or something."

"Shh," Geri said. We both looked over at Riley. He was sitting on the edge of one of the beds, completely lost in a video game.

The cot had arrived. It didn't look too healthy. The springs were kind of sticking out at the sides along with the sheets, which I wasn't feeling completely confident were fresh, since they were pretty wrinkly. I unhooked the metal latch at the top, and the cot sprang open until it was taking up most of the available floor space in our junior suite. I leaned over and delicately sniffed the sheets. Inconclusive.

I gave the mattress a push. Instead of pushing back, it just surrendered and flattened itself against the springs. "Well," I said. "I'm certainly not sleeping on this."

Riley looked up. "It's my room," he said.

Geri and I both looked at him.

He rubbed his eyes. "Well, it is. *Techlickly*. So I shouldn't have to sleep on it. Plus I have to work tomorrow. Nobody else has to work tomorrow."

I wondered if Geri had told him about losing her job. Do you tell an eight-year-old you got fired, or do you just say something like, *Mommy decided she wants to spend more time with you and your sisters?*

Geri sighed. "Well, I'm not sleeping there. It's almost my birthday. . . ."

"Okay," I said. "I'll sleep on it tonight. But you have to sleep there tomorrow night, Riley, because the next day is your mom's birthday, and when she turns fifty, she'll be too old to sleep on a cot."

I thought it would make her laugh, or maybe even volunteer to sleep on the cot just to prove me wrong, but her lower lip actually started to quiver again. I was too tired for this. I threw one of the pillows from my former bed onto the cot and went in to check on my sea glass.

The rock tumbler was still tumbling around, but the motor was sounding almost as tired as the mattress looked and I felt. I pulled the plug, and the bathroom was suddenly quiet. I pried off the red plastic cap and carefully poured off the water. Then I closed the drain and sprinkled the sand-caked glass onto the bottom of the sink.

I picked up a piece of glass, and turned on the water just enough to rinse off some of the sand. When I dried it with a corner of my T-shirt, lo and behold, an amazingly perfect piece of blue sea glass appeared right before my very eyes. It felt like magic. I wondered if Noah felt like this when he made his first bong.

I rinsed off the rest of the pieces and set them to dry on a towel on the edge of the sink. Most of them were from the dark green beer bottle Riley and I had broken in the parking lot, but even these had rounded edges and were frosted to perfection.

My sister knocked on the bathroom door. "Can you hurry up? Riley needs to brush his teeth before he goes to bed."

"Just a minute," I said. I towel-dried the sea glass and scooped it all up in my hand, so it wouldn't accidentally get washed down the drain. Then I opened the door with the other hand.

Riley headed into the bathroom, and I added the sea glass to my bedside shrine. The shrine seemed awfully far from my new home on the cot, so I relocated it, piece by piece, to the dresser on the other side of the room.

My sister was sitting on my former bed, checking out Allison Flagg's book. The room was starting to close in like a sardine can, so I grabbed one of my jewelry books and headed out to the balcony.

It wasn't dark yet, but you could see the moon as well as the sun, kind of like a double feature. It was a new moon, which always made me a little bit sad that it was so fresh and full of potential, and I was still, well, me. The Fisherman's Lodge parking lot was quiet, but I could hear cars driving around out on the road, and some loud music was playing down the street somewhere.

By the time Geri came out to the balcony, holding Allison Flagg's book in one hand and St. Christopher in the other, it was getting dark enough that I was starting to have trouble reading. "What did you do with those rosary beads you took, anyway?" she asked.

"Nothing yet," I said. "That's funny, I was just reading about prayer beads. Did you know that beads have been used for prayer throughout history? And in just about every culture of the world. Buddhist prayer beads were originally made from the wood of the holy bodhi tree, because Buddha became enlightened under it."

"You don't say," Geri said.

"Yup. It says here that rosary beads are made in a circle, with a hanging crucifix to divide the beads, so you know when you reach the end. It's strange to see the Catholic stuff lumped in with everything else, like it's just another culture. Remember when we were growing up, it was a mortal sin to go into a church that wasn't Catholic? At least I think it was mortal. I was always mixing up mortal and venial sins."

"That's why you were always grounded."

"Good point," I said.

The empty white plastic chair made a screeching sound when my sister pulled it forward. She sat down and stretched out her legs so that her bare feet were resting on the railing, and she put the book and St. Christopher on her lap.

"Greek prayer beads are called *komboloi*, and the religious ones sometimes have a medal of St. Christopher attached."

Geri held up St. Christopher like he was a Barbie doll. "Did you hear that, big guy?" she asked him.

I closed my book and hugged it to my chest. "I don't remember seeing ones like that, but I remember coming in for a landing in Greece, and the guy next to me on the plane had a big amber string of them, and he was fidgeting away like crazy and sweat was dripping off his forehead. I was sure he knew something I didn't, and we were all going to die."

Geri was making St. Christopher dance back and forth along the railing now. "How did you ever get the nerve to do all that traveling? Especially when you went by yourself? I'd be so afraid I'd get lost before I even got out of the airport."

I shrugged and put my feet up next to Geri's. "Any airport in the world, you just follow the signs to the baggage claim. And, anyway, some of the best times happen when you get lost." I looked over at the little sliver of moon. "Traveling's so much easier than staying in one place."

Geri put St. Christopher down for a nap in her lap. "I don't know," she said. "Maybe I should have been more adventurous. I'll never get anywhere now."

"Sure you will. The kids will grow up, and you and Seth will have plenty of time to travel."

"Yeah, right. You know, those Childfree people have a point."

Even though I knew Riley was safely inside the hotel room, I still looked over my shoulder. "Don't say that. I mean, you're a *mother*." She didn't say anything, so I added, "Come on, Gerr, you're scaring me."

She smiled. "Don't worry. Of course I love the kids. And Seth. They're the best things that ever happened to me.

It's just that I think turning fifty means you want to keep everything you already have, but you also want everything you haven't managed to get yet, too. Before it's too late."

Geri pushed her feet against the balcony until the front legs of the chair lifted off the ground. It was one of the more daring moves I'd ever seen her make. "God," she said. "I never had any idea how selfish I'd been until I had kids. All that time to think about whether I felt like going out or staying in, or spending hours in the bathroom without anyone banging on the door."

"Yeah, it's great," I said. "Especially at holidays, when you're forty-one and they still put you at the kids' table."

My sister shook her head. "Oh, puh-lease, nobody puts you at the children's table."

I pushed my own chair back, much farther than Geri's. "I was speaking metaphorically."

"So what's going on with Riley's rock tumbler?" she asked.

"I'm making homegrown sea glass."

"Is there a market for that?"

I plopped my chair back down. "What's that supposed to mean?"

Geri plopped her chair down, too. "Nothing. I'm just trying to figure out what to do next, that's all. And a thought just crossed my mind."

"Not a long journey," I said.

"Very funny," she said. "I was thinking maybe we could go into business together or something. I'm going to need a new job, and you could certainly use some help getting your jewelry act together."

"Are you serious?"

"Yeah. I've already done some research. We definitely need an online presence so we can sell directly to customers, and I was thinking we could also do home jewelry parties. We can keep the sea glass earrings. . . ."

"Gee, thanks," I said.

"But we need something that will brand us. Something unique and fresh that nobody else is doing."

An idea that had been rattling around in the back of my head finally stepped forward. "Hey," I said. "You know those bottles of sand Mom and Dad collected? What if we found tiny bottles with corks and made them into necklaces? We could add sand, or leave them empty, or maybe put a message inside. You know, something cute that explains that you're supposed to fill them with sand from your favorite beach. Or wishes or fairy dust, or even samples of blood. Didn't Angelina Jolie and Billy Bob Thornton do that when they were married?"

"See," Geri said. "That's why you need me. You start with a good idea, but then you don't know when to stop. Okay, I'll go online first thing in the morning and find out where we can buy the bottles. I think the necklace part might be a little tacky, but the sand bottle idea is great. If we can find the right bottles. Maybe we should think about multiples, like those rows of test tube vases."

"I still like the necklace idea," I said. "It wouldn't have to be tacky."

"We'll see. And we'll have to get going right away, because we'll need to sell about a zillion of them so I don't have to get another job. Our mortgage payment was killing us even when I was working."

Amazingly, I had another brilliant idea. "What would it do to your payments if you bought Mom and Dad's house?"

"Probably cut them in half. You know, that's not a half bad idea."

"I could pay you rent, and we could run the business right out of the garage. . . ."

"Seth would never go for it without a garage for his car."

"Fine," I said. "We wouldn't want Seth's Beamer to get wet. We could run the business out of my apartment. But we'll have to renegotiate the rent."

"Wait, just let me think about it." We both sat quietly for a minute, and I resisted the urge to push too hard, because that always backfired with Geri.

Finally, she took a deep breath. "Okay, let me talk to Seth and see what he thinks. Dad's right, you know. New houses have no soul. Great closet space, though."

26

"SO," I SAID. "WHEN ARE YOU GOING TO CALL SETH?"

"Not tonight. I have to plan my strategy first. It's a big decision. And I think he'll be a little bit worried about whether Mom and Dad will actually move out."

I smiled. "Well, at least you know Mom will. Maybe you should call them first, just to get the ball rolling."

"No. It's way too soon for that."

"Okay," I said. "I guess I can wait till tomorrow." I picked Allison Flagg's book up off the balcony floor and handed it to her. "Come on, let's find something good to do for your birthday."

Geri leaned over the balcony so she could catch the light from the parking lot. *"One of Last Call's intoxicatingly handsome employees will deliver himself to your place of inebriation by way of motorcycle. Once there, the custom Italian cycle folds up and stows neatly in your trunk, and said handsome employee drives you home again in your car.* God, that sounds so sexy."

"It sounds okay," I said. "But we'd have to get drunk first. And then we'd probably puke all over the handsome employee. And, most likely, they don't have a Last Call franchise on the Cape anyway."

"We could start one," my sister said.

"Yeah, but then we'd have to go all the way to Italy for the motorcycles."

"And the handsome employees."

"And what would we feed them? Where would they sleep?"

Geri sighed. "You're right. It's a lot of work."

"It always is." I pushed myself out of the chair and tiptoed into the hotel room. I opened the minibar and took out two minibottles.

I tiptoed back out and handed one to Geri. "Here you go. We'll just stay right here and pretend."

"Is Baileys Irish Cream from Italy?" she asked.

"I'm pretty sure," I said.

"Where's my glass?"

"Don't you know anything? You have to drink from the bottle or it's not an authentic minibar experience. Plus, I don't want to sound like Mom, but we have no idea who's been drinking from those glasses."

We put our feet back up on the balcony, and Geri got St. Christopher up from his nap to do some more dancing on the railing. He looked bored, so I borrowed him from her and started teaching him a gymnastics routine. It was almost completely dark now, and he was starting to glow.

"Careful," Geri said when I had to move fast to catch him after an aborted tumbling pass. "It's a long way down."

"Relax," I said. "It's only two stories, and we're not even sure he's breakable. Plus, he's St. Christopher, for God's sake. He can protect himself."

Geri took a tiny sip from her tiny bottle. "You know, guys like Noah make me nervous. I feel like they're looking right through me."

I wasn't exactly sure where that came from, but there was a guilty pleasure in sitting in the almost dark and getting to talk about Noah without having to be the one to bring him up. I took my own tiny sip and almost dropped St. Christopher again. "You mean like they have X-ray vision?"

Geri grabbed St. Christopher from me and put him back in her lap. "No, it's more like I'm transparent. Like there's not enough there to see. Or something. Never mind. This is too heavy for me."

"Guys like Seth are so boring," I said.

Geri laughed. "He loves you, too. Hey, what's the longest you've ever been without a boyfriend?"

"Let's see. I don't know. Maybe two or three months. I've always been pretty magnetic, in case you haven't noticed."

"Yeah, right."

"How about you? What's the longest you've ever been without a husband?"

"Ha." Geri took another sip of her Baileys and pretended to feed some to St. Christopher. He seemed to like it.

"Did you ever date anyone before Seth? One of the Cro-Magnon men or George Washington or something? I can't even remember."

"I can't either."

I reached over and put my little twist-off cap on St. Christopher's head. It tilted to one side, which I thought gave him kind of a jaunty look. "Say you did date back in prehistoric times," I said, "and you had to pick between two cavemen. How would you have done it?"

"Oh, that's so easy. You just make lists of each of their good and bad points, and whoever has the best list wins. It's in all the magazines and on all the websites."

St. Christopher and I looked at each other. At least one of us rolled our eyes.

Geri took another tiny sip of her Baileys. "Okay, I'll do

it. Tim Kelly is cute, funny, he has great eyes, he has a trade so he can always find work, and he seems to be completely normal."

"We hardly know him, he travels constantly, and he has a six-year-old daughter."

"So," Geri said. "You like kids." She took another sip and put the bottle on the floor beside her. "Okay, now Noah. He doesn't call you, he doesn't need you, he's completely self-absorbed, he's talented, and he has a great bod."

"Was that the good list or the bad list?" I asked.

"I decided to combine them."

"He is kind of like his own planet," I said. "You know, completely self-sufficient, an entire world of his own. But I'm a lot like that, too. Even if I am living in an apartment on my parents' property and planning to go into business with my sister. So, maybe that's why Noah and I make sense, because neither of us really needs anyone else."

Geri held St. Christopher up to her mouth like a microphone. "'Everybody needs somebody la-la,'" she sang, possibly channeling both Dean Martin and Jewel at the same time.

"I don't know," I said. "He did call me, though. He said he wants things to be different."

"Of course he does," Geri said. "That's because he can feel the gaffer breaking through the force field. Guys can always tell when someone else is interested."

"You are so bizarre," I said.

"It's true. How else can you explain the fact that you can go months without dating, and as soon as one guy asks you out, they're suddenly coming out of the woodwork?"

"I thought you said you couldn't remember dating?" I

drained the last of my Baileys and pushed myself up from the chair. "What country shall we go to next?"

"What are my choices?"

"France or Scotland."

"Surprise me."

When I came back out, Geri was hanging over the balcony and flipping through the *Fun, Feisty, and Fabulous* book again. "Is Riley asleep yet?" she asked.

"Yup. Snoozing away with his stuffed shark."

"You don't happen to have a flashlight with you, do you?"

"Sorry," I said.

"I'm not sure I'll be able to handle giving this back to Allison tomorrow unless I get my own copy. Maybe you can watch Riley tomorrow while I find a bookstore." She turned it over. "It's only twenty bucks."

"But you could buy a solar-powered milk frother for that."

She gave up on trying to read in the dark and came back to her plastic seat again. I handed her a nip of Grand Marnier. "France it is," I said. "The Scotch bottle was the wrong color. This way we can tumble a brown batch after we break them."

"We're not really going to break them, are we?"

I ignored her and held up my tiny bottle. "Here's to minibars," I said. "May the road rise up to meet them."

"May the wind always be at their backs," Geri said, holding her bottle up.

We clanked our minibottles. "May the roof above them never fall in," we said together.

"Which might well happen here," I added.

"By the way," Geri said, "two's my limit."

"Don't worry," I said. "It's all we can fit into the tumbler anyway."

⬥

"REMIND ME NEVER TO GO to Ireland and France on the same night," Geri said the next morning while we waited for Riley to get out of the shower. She popped two Advil into her mouth and washed them down with a large swig of water.

I held out my hand for some Advil. "Don't be ridiculous. They're both European. You can't get a hangover unless you mix continents. Plus, I think it takes more than two bottles each containing three drops of alcohol."

Geri poured two Advil into my palm. I tapped the bottle and got another one. "So, why are you overdosing on Advil then?" she asked.

"My foot is killing me. I had no idea little bottles were so hard to break."

"I told you not to jump on them. You put them in a bag and crack them on the edge of the balcony."

I swallowed the Advil and chased them with a gulp of my sister's water. "Who made you the bottle-breaking expert?" I asked.

"Hey, my feet feel fine."

Riley came out of the bathroom and handed his mother the hair gel. "Can you do this? It gets my hands all sticky."

It hadn't seemed to bother him before his mother got here. I probably would have done a great job on his hair gel if he'd asked. "Meet you in the car," I said.

We got to the set in time to have breakfast, and as soon

as we finished, Geri and Riley headed over to get his stump attached. I'd brought my earring supplies with me, and I decided I'd take advantage of the fact that the movie people had roped off such a large area. It was prime real estate and probably more square footage of Cape Cod beach than I'd ever have to myself in season for the rest of my natural life.

I'd find a nice quiet place at the top of the beach and spend most of the day wrapping wire around my new pieces of sea glass. As soon as I had enough earrings, I'd stop by Sand, Sea and Sky again. I'd tell them about the new idea for the sand-holding bottles, too, though I should probably think of a better name for them first.

Just as I was getting comfortable, Allison Flagg sat down beside me, which pretty much ruined everything. "Ooh, what's that?" she asked.

"Nothing," I said. I wrapped another loop of wire around a piece of dark green sea glass.

"Well, you don't have to be so nasty." She picked up a small rock and moved it to a more aesthetically pleasing position in the sand. "Anyway, since I knew you weren't going to do it, I have a surprise party all planned for Geri."

"What? How did you know I wasn't going to do it?"

She moved the rock back to where it had started. "Oh, puh-lease. Anyway, it's all set for tonight. As soon as we wrap for the day, everybody will meet over at the hotel pool."

I pulled tight, and the sea glass popped right out of the wire and landed on the sand. Allison Flagg was seriously bad for my art. "Today? It's not even her birthday until to-morrow."

"Exactly. She'll be completely surprised this way. Anyway, Manny is sending stuff over from craft services, and I ordered the cake, so all you have to do is take your time getting back to the hotel and then deliver the birthday girl. Think you can handle it?"

I couldn't imagine anything I'd rather do less. But I knew how happy it would make Geri, so I caved. "Yeah, okay." I took a deep breath. "And thanks."

Allison Flagg almost smiled. She moved the rock again, then hugged her knees to her chest and wrapped her arms around them. "So," she said. "I went to the party supply store and bought a whole bunch of pink balloons, and I rented a helium tank."

"Thank goodness you thought of that," I said. "Whatever would we do without a helium tank?"

"I know. It just isn't the same if the balloons don't soar. And I got pink paper garlands. Oh, and those puffy paper birds. You know, the kind you buy folded shut, and when you lift the metal tabs and open them up, they make those wonderful honeycombed shapes."

"You mean those lovebirds they use at weddings?"

As soon as I said it, Allison Flagg's potential smile disappeared. "They can be for anything you want to use them for." She pushed herself up to a standing position and brushed her hands back and forth to get the sand off. "I can't imagine why you're still single," she said.

27

I PICKED UP MY CELL PHONE AND CALLED MY APART-
ment, just to see who might happen to be there this time.

My father answered on the first ring. "Keep your eyes
peeled," he said. "If they come back for me, I might have
to make a break for it. They have no idea how sorry
they're gonna be. I know my constitutional rights."

"Dad?" I said.

"Oh, Toots, I thought you were the other Toots. Wait a
minute, let me tell Champ and the babies you're on the
line. Here, say hello to them yourself."

"What's going on, Dad?" He didn't say anything, so I
talked some baby talk to Boyfriend. I wrapped it up with
"I'll be home soon, honey, now go get Dad for me," hoping
it might get my father back on the phone.

"Okay, Dollface, I better keep the lines open. I've got
big plans to make. Those coppers will never get away with
this. Over and out."

I replayed my father's side, which was basically the
only side, of our phone conversation a few times. Then I
called my mother. The answering machine picked up. "Hi,
Mom," I said. "Dad is acting really strange. Even for him.
He's at my apartment now if you're still looking for him.
Love you. Bye."

One of the nice things about having a mother was that

once you passed something off to her, you could pretty much stop worrying about it.

∞

RILEY, GERI, AND I were killing time before the party. They didn't know it, so the pressure was all on me again. Fortunately, Geri hadn't managed to sneak out to get her own copy of Allison Flagg's book because she was too busy watching Riley, so our first stop was to go buy one for her. Riley picked out another joke book while we were at it, and I finally managed to choose one jewelry-making book, even though I wanted them all. One thing about Cape Cod, you could always find a great bookstore.

"You know," I said, once we got out to the car again, "we really need a name for those sand bottles. And we also need a name for our company."

"Life's a Beach," Geri said.

"Isn't that the truth. Is that for the bottles or the company?"

"Both. It's called branding."

"Don't you think we should discuss it for a while? What about Sisters by the Sea? Or Sisters of Synchronicity?"

"Ha," Geri said.

"Or Ginger's Gewelry, or even Gingerly, though I suppose those two are a little bit more about me than you. You know, I think we should take some time right now, and each come up with a list of ten names. Maybe twenty."

"Come on," Geri said. "Let's go back to the hotel. This is my last day to hang out at the pool as a younger woman. And Riley's probably dying to go swimming."

"He's been on the beach all day," I said. "Water's probably the last thing on his mind." I looked in the rearview mirror and tried to catch his eye. Maybe I could send him a signal.

"The beach and the pool are two entirely different things," my nephew said from the backseat. "That's a yes," he added.

I drove down the road and pulled into the parking lot of CVS. Geri was flipping through her new book. "How about 'Botox, Beverly Hills' for my birthday? It says if you can teach yourself not to overexpress, it actually lasts longer."

"We'll never make it back in time for dinner. And anyway, you probably need an appointment."

"Okay, how about 'Blow Dry, Boston'? That's not very far."

"Boring. And it'll be gone the minute you wash your hair. I thought you wanted something that's more of a memorial."

"Thank you so much for making me sound dead." Geri looked up. "What are we doing here?"

"I'm just concentrating on your birthday possibilities. Okay, give me something else."

Geri nodded. "Ooh, listen to this. *Polymer Hair Extensions. In four to six hours, 100 percent European hair will be bonded with strands of your existing hair very close to the scalp, resulting in much improved volume, length, and flexibility over traditional hair extension techniques.* You know, I think I read somewhere that polymer hair extensions are the new Botox."

"Even so, you lost me at four to six hours." I twisted the steering wheel back and forth a few times. "I couldn't sit still that long for a full body transplant. How do they get all those Europeans to give up their hair, I wonder."

"Oh, wow, there's even a listing for tiaras."

"Perfect. You could wear it to a PTA meeting."

Riley leaned over between the two front seats with his book. "Okay, my turn," he said. "Which fish is the most musical?"

"I don't know," Geri and I said together. "Which fish *is* the most musical?"

Riley giggled. "A tune-afish."

"That's a good one," Geri said. She flipped through a few more pages. "How about 'Teeth Whitening, New York City'? That would be faster. And it must last for a while."

"You know," I said, "I've always wanted to do that. Okay, it'll be my treat for your birthday." I opened my car door. "Wait right here. I'll make the arrangements."

I walked slowly up and down the aisles of CVS just to kill some more time before the party.

Eventually, I opened the car door and threw Geri a package of Crest Whitestrips. "Here you go. Happy fifty. We can split the box. I even sprang for the Supreme."

It's hard to laugh and wear Whitestrips at the same time. They kept slipping, and we had to nudge them back over our teeth with our fingernails.

"It seems," Geri mumbled, "that the trick is not to over-express while you're wearing them." This cracked us both up again.

"Shh," I mumbled. "You're not supposed to talk." That made us laugh even harder.

"Can I try some?" Riley asked.

"Why not?" Geri mumbled. "Just don't tell your sisters.

Or your father. Not that you should ever keep secrets from your family . . ."

"I get it, Mom. Rachel and Becca would want some, too, and Dad's just not a Whitestrips kind of guy."

While Geri was getting Riley's strips all set up, I looked at my watch. I still had at least half an hour to kill. I gave my lower Whitestrip a little tug and pretended to look for my keys.

"Uh-oh," I said carefully. "Did anybody see where I put the car keys?"

The three of us split up and wandered the aisles of CVS. Twenty-five minutes later, I took the keys out of my shoulder bag and kicked them under a counter. "Oh, look," I yelled. "I found them!"

I could feel Geri wanting to strangle me all the way from the other side of the store. "The good news is," I said when we'd climbed back into the car, "our thirty minutes are up. We can take off our Whitestrips now."

"WHY DID WE PARK in the front?" Geri asked as we walked up to the main entrance of the Fisherman's Lodge. "And I still don't understand why you wouldn't stop for takeout."

"Thanks," she added when the lumberjack held the door open for us. Today he had a fishing pole over his shoulder instead of a rifle, which reminded me I still hadn't asked about those fishing swivels so I could try making bracelets with them. Maybe I could sneak back out here later.

I cut in front of my sister and started across the lobby in

the direction of the pool. "I told you, I'll go back out for food. It's my fault I lost the keys. Riley shouldn't have to wait any longer to get into the pool. Your teeth look great, by the way."

Geri took a couple of long steps to catch up with me. "Don't try to change the subject. We were already in the car. It's completely inefficient to do it this way."

I ignored her. "Hey, Riley, let's go see how crowded the pool is, then we can go upstairs and you can throw on your suit."

We rounded the corner to the pool entrance, and a great big white cardboard sign sitting on a rough timber stand blocked our way. PRIVATE PARTY, it said in pink letters. A flock of white puffy paper lovebirds perched on top of the sign. They were anchored to the stand with criss-crosses of clear tape.

"Wouldn't you know it," Geri said. "There's a wedding here tonight." She shook her head. "If you hadn't lost the keys, we could have been in and out of the pool by now." She turned and started to walk away.

"That's okay, Aunt Ginger," Riley said.

"Thanks," I said. "Wait," I yelled to my sister.

She turned around.

"I know," I said. "Let's peek inside. I love weddings."

"You hate weddings," she said.

"Well, maybe they're not using the whole pool area," I said. "Come on, Riley, let's go check it out." I grabbed his hand and pulled him past the sign.

"You can't go in there," my sister yelled. "It's a private party."

I pulled Riley around the corner and put my fingers to my lips. "She's coming," I whispered.

Allison Flagg started waving her arms around like an air traffic controller.

"I'll meet you upstairs," we heard my sister yell.

"Do something," Allison Flagg hissed.

Riley and I looked at each other. I shrugged. He screamed. It was a brilliant and bloodcurdling scream, guaranteed to bring a mother running.

"Surprise!" everybody shouted when my sister rounded the corner.

Geri stood there with her mouth open for a moment or two, then gave me a big hug. "Thank you. I can't believe you did this for me," she whispered.

"Well, Allison Flagg helped a little," I whispered back.

There was a long table set up at one end of the pool area. It was covered with things like shrimp cocktail and roll-up sandwiches, and sitting in the center of the table was a big pink cake with just the right understated number of candles.

Riley ran off to join the other kids. Geri was completely surrounded by people, so I looked around for someone to talk to. A bartender wearing a GONE FISHING T-shirt stood behind the outcropping of rocks that formed the bar. She was pouring some champagne for the gaffer.

He turned around and saw me before I could look away. I smiled. He smiled back. He picked up the glasses and started walking in my direction.

He walked right past me and handed a glass of champagne to my sister. "There you go, birthday girl," he said. "By the way, what are you doing for the next fifty years?"

My sister giggled and flipped her hair around. "Oh, thank you, Timmy. Find a date for my husband and a babysitter who drives, and I'm all yours, big guy."

"Cheers," he said as he clicked his champagne glass to hers.

"Timmy?" I said to no one in particular. When had my sister learned to flirt like that, and why hadn't I been taking notes? The gaffer was actually being kind of sweet. What a nice birthday present to give to a fifty-year-old married mother of three. You almost couldn't tell it was basically a sympathy flirt.

I turned around to go get my own drink.

Since it was my sister, I figured I really had to stay around for the cake, but I couldn't wait to get back to my room. I hung out with the bartender for a few minutes, and talked her into saving me some of the interesting bottles. They were serving sparkling water in these great cobalt blue bottles, and I was dying to get my hands on some.

"There you are," Geri said. She stood beside me at the bar, and the gaffer walked around to stand on her other side. "I can't believe Manny sent all this stuff over. That was so nice of him."

I ignored the gaffer, not that he seemed to notice. "Where's your friend Allison?" I asked Geri.

"Oh, she's got some more balloons to blow up. And she wants to wait on the cake so everyone has enough time to enjoy looking at it before we cut into it."

I yawned.

"More champagne, gorgeous?" the gaffer asked.

I held up my full glass before I realized he was talking to my sister. I put it down fast, but possibly not fast enough. He smirked.

"Thanks, handsome," she said. "But I think I'll switch to water. Ginger's probably dying to get her hands on some of those blue bottles."

28

"IS IT ALMOST TIME FOR THE CAKE?" I ASKED.

Allison Flagg looked at her watch. "Let's just give it a few more minutes." She slid the cake a quarter of an inch to the right and straightened one of the candles. "I think the dance people are here. I told them to bring a boom box and some party music. Is there anything you want me to request?"

I looked over at the gaffer and smiled. " 'Just a Gigolo'?" I suggested.

He smiled back. "How about 'Hey Jealousy'?"

"Oh, I know, how about 'YMCA'?" Geri said. "It's Riley's favorite."

"Just shoot me now," I said.

Allison Flagg took off to find the dance people, and I tried to think of an exit line. "So," Geri said. "Isn't this the best party?"

"Mmm," I said. "I'm really happy for you."

"Which one of you is older anyway?" the gaffer asked.

"Oh, you," Geri said. She gave her hair another flip.

"Dad!" Riley yelled from across the room.

"Ohmigod!" Geri said. "Seth! And the girls! And Mom and Dad!" She detached herself from the gaffer and handed me her empty blue water bottle.

"Sorry about your girlfriend," I said to the gaffer, even though I knew it was childish. The first notes of "YMCA" blasted out.

✺

MY MOTHER AND FATHER were dancing up a storm. Rachel and Rebecca tried to resist. "This is so dorky," Rachel said.

"Totally," Becca said.

"Okay, just this one song," Rachel said.

Seth and Geri were dancing away, too, and even though Seth kept messing up the letters on "YMCA" and he really should have changed out of his suit and into something more casual, I could almost imagine living next door to him.

"Wanna dance?" the gaffer asked.

"I don't think so," I answered.

He smiled.

I walked into the middle of the dance floor, which was actually the patio area next to the pool. Riley and the two Macks had a pretty good conga line going, so I jumped onto the end of that, right behind Manny's mother. Every time we'd hear the four beats that signaled the YMCA part was coming, we'd all drop our arms and face the middle.

As soon as the song was over, I found my parents. They were holding hands and actually swinging them back and forth.

"Toots!" my father said when he saw me.

"Hey," I said. I gave them each a hug, then pulled back to read my mother's T-shirt. BODY PIERCING SAVED MY LIFE it said in discreet purple glitter letters.

"You're kidding, right?" I asked.

My mother held the hem of her T-shirt and stretched it

down so I could get a better look. "Like I always say, keep 'em guessing." She winked at my father and wiggled her hips a little.

My father grabbed her and they tangoed a few steps, even though Kool & the Gang was singing "Celebration" now. When he dipped her, her head almost touched the ground. She was amazingly flexible for a woman her age. All that yoga was really paying off.

"Hey, Dollface," he said, after they remembered me and tangoed back. "What about mine? I made it all by myself." My father let go of my mother and stretched out the fabric on his worn white T-shirt. In wobbly black marker, he'd written, I KNOW MY RIGHTS.

"Your father," my mother said, "got himself into a little pickle." She leaned over and gave my father a kiss on the lips.

"It was a big pickle, Toots," my father said. "They arrested me and everything. I loved every minute of it. Do you know they don't have handles in the backseat of those copper cars? You're in there till they get good and ready to let you out, I kid you not."

"It was like being back in the sixties," my mother said. She leaned over and kissed him again.

"Excuse me," I said. "But do you think you could stop being disgusting long enough to tell me what happened? Either that, or you might want to consider getting a room."

My mother and father actually giggled. "We already have a room," my mother said.

"For the whole night," my father added. "Hot diggitty."

I couldn't believe it. "What about Boyfriend and the kittens? You said you'd watch them."

"Relax," my mother said. "One of our friends is stopping by to give them fresh food and water."

"She's not my friend," my father said. "Not until she starts keeping her hands to herself, anyway."

"Oh, you," my mother said. She kissed him again.

"I hate to interrupt," I said. "But you still haven't told me what happened."

My parents tore themselves away from each other. "Okay," my mother said. "The way it happened was that there's a thirty-minute antiloitering rule in the Take It or Leave It section of the dump."

"No, Toots, it's more than a rule. It's a genuine Town of Marshbury law I broke. But I know my constitutional rights. I can gather in a public place anytime I damn well feel like it."

"My hero," my mother said. "So, to make a long story short, they kept giving him tickets for staying too long, and he ignored them."

My father wiggled his bushy white eyebrows. "I mean, I was already at the dump, so how hard could it be to dispose of the evidence?"

"And then, the other day," my mother said, "they decided to give him a police escort home."

"And we're taking this all the way to the Supreme Court if we have to," my father said. "You can bet on it, Toots." He put his arm around my mother's shoulders. "Your mother and Champ and the babies and I have been all holed up at your place, planning our strategy."

My mother put her arm around my father's waist. "It's more than a little bit romantic," she said. "It reminds me of our first apartment, right after we got married. We've even been talking about selling the house to Geri and Seth and moving in there for good."

"Excuse me?" I said. "What about the townhouse? What about *me*?"

"After you get yourself settled, of course, Dollface," my father said.

"Sure, not a problem," I said. "I'll just go sleep on the street."

My father elbowed my mother and pointed to Manny's mother. "Don't look now, but I think I see that Ann-Margret over there. Not that I'm interested or anything, but I know you're a big fan of hers, Toots."

WE ALL GATHERED AROUND the cake while Allison Flagg lit the candles. She started at one end and worked her way slowly from left to right, stopping after every second candle to blow out the match and carefully add it to the fan shape she was creating on a pink napkin with the other blown-out matches.

"Holy crap," I said mostly to myself. "If she keeps this up, we'll be here all night."

"Now, now," the gaffer said. I looked over at him. He smiled. I took a big step away.

Finally, the candles were lit and everybody sang "Happy Birthday."

"Thank you all so much," Geri said when they finished. Tears were streaming down her face, which made my own eyes tear up, despite my best intentions. "This is the most wonderful birthday party I've ever had." She pointed to a pile of presents, most of them brought in by Seth and the kids and my parents. "Can I save these for tomorrow so I'll have something to look forward to?"

"It's all ahead of you, Toots," my father yelled. "Just you wait and see."

I didn't even stick around for a piece of cake. As soon as the Beatles started singing their song about saying it's your birthday, I figured it was safe to head out to the lobby to check on those fishing swivels. If I could get my hands on some, maybe I could try making a sample bracelet tonight.

"So, where are we going next?" I heard the gaffer say behind me. He caught up to me in the middle of the lobby and matched his steps to mine. Out of the corner of my eye, I saw him start to put his arm around me, then change his mind and put it back down again.

I stopped walking and crossed my arms over my chest. "What is your problem?" I asked.

He crossed his arms over his chest and grinned. "You give a whole new meaning to the word *jealousy*," he said.

I glared at him. "Jealous?" I said. "Me? Oh, puh-lease. Of what?"

He squinted and tilted his head back and forth. "So, which one of you is older anyway?" He uncrossed his arms and hooked his thumbs in the belt loops of his jeans. He grinned.

"And to think I used to have a crush on you."

He laughed. "You should have seen your face the minute I started paying attention to your sister. I have three sisters, so I know how it goes. Wait, you really did have a crush on me?"

"Maybe a little," I said. "But I'm over it now, thank you

so much. Now, if you'll excuse me, I have some fishing swivels to hunt down."

He burst out laughing. "Come on, just sit for a minute. Please? I was only trying to make you see that you're really crazy about me."

"You wish," I said.

"Yeah," Tim Kelly said. "I do." He pointed to an oversize bark-covered love seat sitting next to the fountain in the middle of the lobby.

"You know, we've already been though all this," I said. "I thought we decided we were just going to be friends."

"Where did you get that? We decided you were going to call me as soon as you were ready. I was just trying to push up the timetable."

The bark-covered love seat was surprisingly comfortable. Tim Kelly put his arm around me. I picked up his hand and handed it back to him.

"Sorry," he said. He sat on his hands. I laughed.

"Made you laugh," he said. "Oh, by the way . . ." He stopped and looked over the back of our love seat. He leaned a little closer, until his head was practically touching mine. "I overheard two of the producers talking while I was in the men's room," he whispered. "The head honcho at the studio just got fired. Looks like they'll probably cut what they have and send this movie right to video."

"Oh, no," I said. "Does Manny know?"

Tim Kelly shrugged. "I don't think so. Poor guy."

"At least his mother's here," I said. Riley would probably be just as excited about having a video, but I really felt bad for Manny.

Our bark-covered love seat was facing the mammoth rough-hewn wooden front door, and the lumberjack doorman had been leaning back against the wall next to it, with his fishing pole leaning back beside him. He stood up straight now and swung the fishing pole over his shoulder and reached for the door.

Tim Kelly's head was still inches from mine, which meant his lips weren't much farther away. Maybe just one more kiss wouldn't be the worst thing that could happen.

The doorman held the door open and Noah walked into the lobby.

I jumped up. "Noah!" I yelled.

He stood right where he was. He was wearing a new long-sleeve denim shirt and dark cargo pants, and he had even shaved.

I stood right where I was, too. I could feel myself blushing. If I were a magician, I would have made Tim Kelly disappear right before everyone's eyes. Instead, he stood up and cleared his throat. He took a few steps toward Noah, so I did, too.

"Noah, Tim. Tim, Noah," I said, for lack of a better idea. Noah held out his hand.

The gaffer shook it. "Ah," he said. "The monk."

29

"HOW LONG HAS THAT BEEN GOING ON?" NOAH ASKED. "God, I'm such an idiot."

I'd followed Noah to the parking lot. Out of the corner of my eye, I saw the doorman open the door. The gaffer came out, pushing the helium tank for Allison Flagg, who was laughing and flipping her hair around. Riley and the Macks were right behind them. "Hey, Noah," Riley yelled as he ran past us.

"Hey, Riley," Noah said. His eyes never left mine.

"It's nothing," I said, though I wasn't completely sure it was true.

"I thought you were going to call me," Noah said.

"I was," I said. "I've just been really busy."

"I can see that," he said. He put his hands in his pockets. "That monk thing that guy said? You shouldn't have repeated that to him. That was private."

"I didn't say you were a monk. I said I was a monk. I wasn't betraying you. I was copying you. There's a huge difference."

We looked at each other. "Your parents invited me," Noah said. "I thought it would be all right."

"Of course it's all right," I said.

Noah shrugged. "I drove down here to tell you I love you, you know. How's that for lousy timing?"

I hesitated. I wasn't sure what to say. Or even what to

feel. Maybe I did love Noah, but hadn't I also been ready to kiss the gaffer about three minutes ago?

Noah shook his head. "Listen, I don't think coming here was such a hot idea. I'll see you, okay?"

"Okay," I whispered as he walked away.

⟪⟫

I PUSHED THE BUTTON for the elevator. The back door to the Fisherman's Lodge opened, and my father wheeled his suitcase inside.

"Aloha, Toots," he said.

"Hi, Dad," I said.

He stopped and opened his wallet and put the key card back inside, then tucked his wallet into his shorts pocket. He reached down to pull up his matching maroon socks. "I'm just bringing up the suitcase," he said. "The old broad's already up there, fluffing the pillows." He winked. "We just wanted to get the room set up, then we're heading back down again for some more dancing. The night's still young."

"Dad," I said. "Don't call her an old broad."

"Listen, Dollface," he said. "That's between your mother and me." He grinned. "The old battle-ax is crazy about me, what can I say?"

The elevator landed with a thunk and opened, and we stepped inside. "What floor can I get you, Toots?" my father asked.

"Second, please," I said.

"Your mother and I are on the fourth. It's practically the penthouse, for chrissakes."

I leaned back against the cool, vinyl elevator wall. "That's great, Dad."

"Whoops, I almost forgot." He bent over and started un-zipping the outside compartment on his suitcase. He stood up straight again and handed me a slightly squished green stuffed frog. "Here, I brought you a present. Re-member when you were just a little whippersnapper, and every time it was your sister's birthday, you got so jealous I had to go out and find something just for you?"

The elevator stopped at the second floor. I held the door open. "Oh, Dad," I said. "Thank you."

"Take good care of that now. It's an authentic Jazzy J Frog. They're not easy to find, you know."

I took a closer look. The frog was about a foot tall and it was holding a sparkling Styrofoam globe in one arm.

"Squeeze its foot," my father said.

I did, and the globe lit up and began changing colors, and Jazzy J started singing a bluesy version of "What a Wonderful World."

"Howsabout that?" my father said. "Look. His lips move and everything. You don't see that every day, now do you, Toots?"

❦

I MANAGED TO FIT all my stuff into my suitcase, even the rock tumbler. I rolled the suitcase over to the door and did a final check for anything I might have missed. I found Ri-ley's socks in one of the drawers. I took a few minutes to separate them and sort them by color. Matching red stripes with red stripes, and green with green, I rolled them into pairs again.

My earring supplies were still in my shoulder bag from this morning. I pulled out all the sea glass. I chose the two closest matching cobalt pieces, both shaped almost like triangles and the exact color of Noxzema jars. Then I went out to the balcony. I took my time and made the best pair of earrings I was capable of making at this point in my life.

I put them on the coffee table with a note. *Happy fiftieth birthday. I love you. Thanks for being my sister.* I left her the rosary beads, too, all in one piece. I just didn't feel right about taking them apart.

I tucked Jazzy J under my arm and rolled on out the back door of the Fisherman's Lodge. Nobody noticed me leaving, not even the gaffer. I bumped my suitcase down from the sidewalk to the parking lot.

The two Macks screamed as soon as they saw me. Riley looked up from taping a puffy paper bird to my rental car. "Oops," he said.

"Ohmigod," I said. "You're one of them."

"Run!" one of the Macks yelled. They did.

Pink frosting hearts decorated my windshield, and puffy paper birds were taped to the roof of the car, and to the outside mirrors, too. Their honeycombed wings looked like they couldn't wait for a good breeze to start flapping. I reached out with one finger and sampled the frosting. Not bad.

I threw my suitcase into the trunk and rearranged my shrine on the passenger seat. I let St. Christopher ride shotgun. Jazzy J sat next to him on the seat, and I made a circle with the sea glass and the frog bead around them both.

I was basically okay until I started driving. Embarrassing as it was to admit, those puffy paper lovebirds always sort of got to me. When my eyes started to tear up, I figured if I was going down this road, I might as well go all the way. I squeezed Jazzy J's foot, and his globe started flashing again.

For five exits Jazzy J sang "What a Wonderful World" over and over and over again while I alternated between singing along with him and sobbing away. I had a little trouble seeing through my tears, but the centers of the frosting hearts on the windshield were well placed and crystal clear. Riley and the Macks had done a great job in the tape department, too, so I didn't lose a single lovebird.

I wanted to drive forever. I could start all over again. New apartment, new job, new boyfriend. Or maybe I'd head to Logan Airport and jump on the next plane going anywhere. Maybe this cycle I'd actually make it all the way to a full life.

I wasn't sure if it was fear of success or fear of failure, or if I was just one of those people who knew how to start things but not what to do next.

My whole life began to flash before my eyes. I remembered my first pixie haircut, when I came out of the hairdresser's looking like a boy, and everybody at school called me Johnny until it grew back. I remembered running for secretary of my Brownie troop and losing. I remembered the chorus teacher in fourth grade asking me not to sing so loud, so the other kids could have a chance. I remembered my first spin-the-bottle game in sixth grade, when the bottle didn't point at me once, and the boy I had a crush on asked another girl to go steady. Clearly the writing had been on the wall a long time ago.

There was a new arched steel suicide fence at the Sagamore Bridge. Or maybe it wasn't really new, but I just hadn't noticed it the last time I'd driven down to the Cape.

DESPERATE? the same old sign that had been there for as long as I could remember said. CALL THE SAMARITANS.

I drove off the bridge and onto the rotary. It was slated for replacement by a straightaway everyone was calling the *flyover*, so I circled around a couple times just because I still could. I was on my third loop around before I realized I had absolutely no idea where I was going. I could go back to the hotel and start fresh with the gaffer. I could try to work out the mess with Noah. I could go home. I could keep driving around the rotary.

There was no sense causing an accident, so I waited until I was off the rotary and heading north on Route 3 before I called the Samaritans' number.

"Hi, this is Doug," a mellow voice said.

Jazzy J was still singing, so I turned him facedown to muffle the sound. "I bet you hear from a lot of lonely people," I said.

"Yeah, we do," Doug said. "That's why we're here."

I wiped some tears away and tried not to sniff too loudly. "Do any of them ever, you know, get less lonely?"

"Sure, lots of them," he said. He had a very reassuring tone, which I supposed was the idea.

"So you don't think it's like a set point? You know, that you'll just keep screwing up your life to make sure you end up back at the same old level of lonely?"

"Nah," he said. "That's just an old wives' tale."

"Okay, thanks. I'll call you back if things work out," I said.

"Thanks," Doug said. "It's always nice to hear good news."

The tires of my rental car made a crunching sound on

Noah's mussel shell driveway. The lights were out in his studio, so I knocked on the side door of the house.

Sage started to bark. "Come in," Noah said in a flat voice.

I pushed the door open. Sage jumped up and I squatted down so she could lick the salt off my face. "Hey," Noah said. I looked up, and my heart did a little dance in my chest when I saw him.

"Okay, here's the thing," I said. "I get that you're ready to be in a relationship now, but I think you should make sure that it's really me you want, and that I just don't happen to be in the right place at the right time. And maybe I should have called you, but do you have any idea how much time I spent sitting around pretending I wasn't waiting for you to call? Oh, and, by the way, I love you, too."

I realized I was still squatting, so I stood up. We were still standing about ten feet apart. I started to laugh. "God, we're both horrible at this."

"Hey, speak for yourself," Noah said. He closed the gap between us.

Eventually, we stopped kissing. "This really is the thing, you know," Noah said. "It's definitely you I want, and I'm sorry it took so long for me to figure it out. I love you. And I really do want to spend my life with you."

We kissed some more and then Noah reached past me to shut the door.

He stopped and looked out at my car. "Was there a wedding I should know about?"

"Long story," I said.

He pulled the door closed. "About that other guy, the one who was just about to kiss you?"

"The truth?"

He nodded. I could feel him start to take a step away.

I put my arms around him and held him tight. "I'm not sure I realized this before I was driving up here, but my whole life, whenever a relationship got complicated, it just seemed easier to start moving on to the next guy rather than stay around and work things out. I don't want to do that anymore."

"I don't want you to do that anymore either," Noah said.

Noah insisted on going out for a real dinner date to celebrate. It was late, so we got a table overlooking the water at Wave.

"To us," Noah said, touching his champagne glass to mine.

"To us," I said.

Noah took a sip of his champagne, then put his glass down and reached over to hold both my hands. "You know, it's funny how life goes. I would have thought by this point I'd be married with a house full of kids."

"Me, too," I completely surprised myself by saying.

"Really?" he said. "I thought you didn't want kids."

I took a deep breath. "I don't know," I said. "Maybe I made myself pretend I didn't want the things I didn't think I was going to get."

We looked at each other. "You're scaring me," I said.

"No pressure," he said. "We can always try another pet first."

"Dog or cat?" I asked.

"You don't really think I'm going to answer that, do you?"

30

I COULDN'T BELIEVE MY SISTER WAS GETTING ANOTHER birthday cake. I thought the party Allison Flagg and I had thrown for her the night before should have been more than enough, even for a fiftieth. But no, while Noah, Seth, and my father fired up the grill on my parents' side patio, the kids were in the kitchen, frosting the cake they'd secretly baked, and my mother and I were supposed to keep Geri outside so she wouldn't see it. Not that any of us could exactly miss the unmistakable smell of just-baked cake, even out in the yard.

"Guess what Seth gave me for my birthday?" Geri asked.

"I give up," my mother said.

"A new BlackBerry."

"Pretty romantic," I said.

The birthday girl looked over her shoulder to make sure the coast was clear. "Follow me," she whispered.

My mother and I trailed her into the garage. Geri grabbed a shovel, and we headed back outside and over to the saint hole.

That old boyfriend of mine, the one who couldn't stop quoting Yogi Berra, would have called this déjà vu all over again. "We really need to find a new hobby," I said. "This saint thing is getting old."

"I'm still angling, but Seth hasn't quite caved yet," Geri

said. "I just don't want to take any chances on the house selling before he comes around."

"Good thinking, dear," my mother said. "Your father is just about there. I'd like to think, figuratively speaking, he has one foot in our new townhouse already."

Geri handed me the shovel, and I flipped the little green circle of grass off the top of the hole with one expert flick of the wrist. I scooped out some dirt, then reached down and pulled St. Joseph out by his little plastic feet.

"There you go, big guy," I said as I brushed him off.

Geri held out her hand.

I put him behind my back. "I don't think so," I said.

"But it's my birthday," Geri whined. "And, besides, you already have St. Christopher."

"Exactly," I said. "St. Joseph wants to play with St. Christopher."

"The Church is frowning on that these days," my mother said.

We both turned to look at her. "Good line, Mom," Geri and I said at the same time. "Owe me a Coke," we both said as fast as we could.

My mother gave a little curtsy, then held out her hand for St. Joseph. "I'll take him to the townhouse with us for good luck," she said.

I handed him over. "All right," I said. "I guess they can visit each other."

I gave Geri the shovel, and she started filling in the hole again. "So, what's the scoop on you bringing Noah today?" she asked. "Must be love, it's not even dark out."

"Cute," I said. She was making a mess of things, so I grabbed the shovel away from her and started doing it the right way myself.

"Too bad," she said. "I was kind of rooting for the gaffer."

"What *is* a gaffer anyway?" my mother asked.

"An electrician," Geri said. "Everybody knows that."

"Don't talk like that to your mother," my mother said. "Even if it is your birthday."

"Sorry, Mom," Geri said.

I put the circle of grass back and leaned on the shovel. "I don't know," I said. "I think it just hit me that I could spend the rest of my life leapfrogging from guy to guy, or I could stick around long enough to try to make it work with Noah."

"Good girl," my mother said.

"Well, just make sure you hang on to the gaffer's contact info," Geri said. "It never hurts to have a backup plan."

"Thank you so much for your optimism," I said.

A part of me was a little bit sad that I couldn't have Noah *and* the gaffer, but most of me was ready to press delete. I fished my cell phone out of my pocket and found the gaffer on my speed dial.

I held up the phone. "Say good-bye to the gaffer," I said to Geri.

"Don't do it," she yelled.

I had to. We gave the gaffer a moment of silence after he was gone, then Geri clapped her hands together. "You know, this reminds me of a joke I used to tell in fourth grade."

"You are so bizarre," I said. I started walking back to the garage with the shovel.

They caught up to me. "Okay," Geri said. "What's green and hops from bed to bed?"

"I don't know, what?" my mother and I said.

"A prostifrog!" Geri said.

We looked at her blankly.

"I think you mean prosti*toad*, dear," my mother finally said.

Geri let out a puff of air. "So that's why nobody ever laughed."

I put the shovel back in the garage and pulled the door shut. "You so didn't get the joke gene," I said. "And by the way, just because I haven't been with the same guy since 1752 doesn't mean I have a single promiscuous bone in my whole body."

"Oh, puh-lease," Geri said. "It's not like I haven't read your college diary."

"Mom!" I said. "Did you hear that?"

The stereo blasted out from the house, and Eva Cassidy started singing "What a Wonderful World." I thought about running up to my apartment to get Jazzy J so they could make it a duet, but I couldn't seem to move. Her voice gave me shivers, like it always did. There was something about her singing that was so pure, so heartfelt, so simple. Maybe that was art. I wondered if a piece of jewelry I made would ever make anyone feel this way.

Geri had already ordered the Life's a Beach bottles online, so I just might find out soon enough. One thing about going into business with my sister, she was pretty productive once she stopped obsessing about turning fifty.

The door opened, and Noah and Sage and the kids came running out of the house. Noah squatted down so Becca could climb onto his back, and Riley jumped up on Rachel's. They piggyback raced across the yard with Sage chasing after them.

My father came out next. He stopped and pulled up his matching tan socks, then put one hand behind his ear and tilted his head. "I knew there was nothing wrong with those speakers, Toots," he yelled over the music. "Can you believe someone left them at the Take It or Leave It? Good thing I already had them in the trunk before those coppers caught me."

My mother sprinted across the yard to meet my father, and they started to dance. Seth came out and started walking over to Geri. "Five more minutes on those coals," he yelled.

I turned around, and Noah and the kids were right behind me. Riley looked down from Rachel's back. "Sorry about your car, Aunt Ginger," he said.

"That's okay," I said. "Sorry about your movie."

"It's okay. Manny said he'd send me a video."

Rachel galloped off with Riley. Becca jumped down from Noah's back and ran after them. Sage waited until Noah gave her a pat, then she was right behind them.

"Hey," Noah said. He leaned over and gave me a kiss in broad daylight. He smelled like charcoal and dog, which was sexier than it should have been.

"Hey," I said.

We smiled at each other for a moment or two, then he handed me something wrapped in newspaper. "Here, I made this for you. Your father told me how you get jealous when Geri gets presents and you don't."

"Don't ever forget that," I said. I unwrapped the crinkled newsprint. "It's gorgeous," I said. "What is it?"

"It's a frog palace. Basically, it's a variation on the toad abode. I'm not sure how functional it is, and I don't know if essentially you're ever going to improve on the lily pad, but that was the vibe I was going for."

I turned it around in my hands so I could get a better

look. The swoop of the green glass roof was so graceful I wanted to shrink myself down so I could walk through the front door. "Wow," I said. "You're amazing. I'd love to live in one of these. It doesn't come in a larger size, does it?"

"Of course it does," Noah said. "Move in with me, and I'll whip us up a bigger one."

"Just like that?" I asked.

"Just like that," Noah said.

When we stopped kissing, Eva Cassidy was still singing, though she'd moved on to "Blue Skies" now. My parents were still dancing, and Geri and Seth were dancing now, too. Rachel was pushing Boyfriend and the kittens around in the new double cat stroller my father had found for them, and Becca and Riley each held one of Sage's front paws while they circled around together.

"Hey," I said. "You don't want to dance, do you?"

"Sure, I do," Noah said. "I thought you'd never ask."

USER'S GUIDE TO THE

Fun, Feisty, & Fabulous

ALL NEW & EVEN
FABBIER EDITION

TAKE TWO

Wedding videos by a real pro. Capture the scope, the enormity, the epic impact of your special day.

www.manuelmuscadel.com

THE MORE THE MERRIER

You can be massaged by five people at once at the Energy Bank in London. Conveniently located near the Shoreditch stop on the London Underground. 132 Commercial Street, London, E1 6NG. 020 7650 0718.

LIFE'S A BEACH

Cutting-edge sea glass jewelry plus our signature Life's a Beach bottles to fill with sand on your next romantic trip to your favorite beach. Call Ginger or Geri at 781-555-LIFE to schedule a Life's a Beach home party.

www.lifesabeachboutique.com

COSMONAUT FOR A DAY

Experience Moscow and true weightlessness at the same time. Each exotic zero-gravity maneuver provides a major twenty-six-second adrenaline rush. Breakfast included.

www.incredible-adventures.com

YO, MUTT'S UP?

Pooch parties, mutt mingles, and the very best in luxury dog and cat items, including pup pastries and cattitude T-shirts. A utopia for parents and their four-legged substitute children.

www.muttropolis.com

SPARKS WILL FLY

Very experienced gaffer will head up the electrical department on your next film. Also available for house calls between movies.

www.timkelly.com

WHEN YOU REALLY NEED IT

These actors will pretend to be your own personal fan club and scream, faint, and beg for your autograph. Entertainment Express. 1-800-939-7737.

www.entertainmentexpress.us

ART AFFAIR

Join the hundreds of artists and master craftspeople who gather every summer in Laguna Beach for Art-A-Fair, Southern California's fastest growing arts festival.

www.art-a-fair.com

MAKE IT TO MARSHBURY

Like Mayberry RFD, but with better beaches. Don't miss the Marshbury Beautification Committee's annual house and garden tour.

www.marshburymassachusetts.org

FIND YOUR INNER GUTSY WOMAN

Gutsy Women Travel was created to celebrate the indomitable spirit within every woman to experience the world. Amalfi? Amsterdam? Start packing. Call 866-IMGUTSY.

www.gutsywomentravel.com

RED HAT REVOLUTION

Fun after fifty for women of all walks of life. You must attend functions in full regalia—red hat and purple outfit.

www.redhatsociety.com

DIP ME IN CHOCOLATE

At the Spa at The Hotel Hershey, you'll experience the Whipped Cocoa Bath and the Chocolate Bean Polish, and luxuriate in the Chocolate Fondue Wrap. 100 Hotel Road, Hershey, Pennsylvania.

www.hersheypa.com

NOAH THE GLASSBLOAH

Award-winning hand-blown glass art. Witches' Balls a specialty. For open studio schedule and portfolio photo gallery, go to the website.

www.noahtheglassbloah.com

BACON OF THE MONTH CLUB
One pound of the best artisan bacon delivered one day a month for a year, whether you need it or not. Pig pen (ballpoint) and T-shirt included with membership. Call 888-472-5283. www.gratefulpalate.com

DIVINE INTERVENTION FOR YOUR HOME
Make sure your house is the first on the block to sell with this genuine plastic St. Joseph statue, sealed in clear wrapping to protect it from the dirt. Instruction booklet included. www.stjosephtradition.com

MALAYSIA MAY I?
Hoo boy, how long has it been since you've been to Malaysia? One hundred traditionally crafted bungalows and suites re-create seventeenth-century Malay dwellings. Pristine five-mile beach. Tanjong Jara Resort. Call 011-60-9-845-1100.

GORGEOUS GUMBALLS
Triple-head vending machine with chrome stand combines three full-size vending machine heads into one machine, tripling your options—and your pleasure. Every family should have one. www.gumballs.com

LLAMA DRAMA
Trekless too long? A three-hour trip from Northern Vermont Llama Company costs a mere $45 and will be the high point of your trip to Waterville, Vermont. Call 802-644-2257 before your friends beat you to it.

FIGGIN' UNBELIEVABLE
Fruits of the Shore signature treatment inspired by lakeshore fig trees. Gentle exfoliating fig scrub, aromatic fig milk soak, followed by a fantastic full body fig lotion massage. Lake House Spa, Austin, Texas. www.lakehousespa.com

OH, THOSE PUFFY PAPER BIRDS

Honeycombed decorations, artfully arranged by party planner with extensive beautification experience. Call Allison Flagg. 1-781-555-LOVE.

CANYON RANCH ROUNDUP

Round up five, six, or seven of your friends and head for Tucson, Arizona, or experience the ultimate healthy vacation in the gorgeous wooded hills of Lenox, Massachusetts. Fitness classes, outdoor sports, spa treatments, and life enhancement. No extra charge for spiritual awakenings.
www.canyonranch.com

YOUR PERFECT MATCH

Is your personal life a bit of a beach these days? Whether Noah the glassbloah or Tim Kelly the gaffer is your type, he just might be online waiting for you now.
www.perfectmatch.com

GIRLFRIENDS SPA-AHHH THERAPY

Catch up on everything but sleep in a luxurious suite with up to five of your old or new best friends. Aromatherapy fifty-minute massage, plus breakfast, dinner, and a signature pedicure (for up to fifty of your favorite toes). Sundara Spa, Wisconsin Dells, Wisconsin. Call 1-888-735-8181.
www.sundaraspa.com

ALL ABOARD!

Spend a decadent three hours traveling by trolley to three of Boston's culinary landmarks and enjoying scrumptious chocolate desserts from the city's best chefs. Chocolate trivia included.
www.trolleytours.com/ChocolateTour

MY BIG BREAK

Experienced eight-year-old actor/comic seeks growth opportunity. Head shot available upon request.
www.freeriley.com

If you enjoyed

LIFE'S A BEACH,

be sure to catch Claire Cook's new novel,

SUMMER BLOWOUT,

coming in June 2008 from Voice.

An excerpt follows.

LIPSTICK IS MY DRUG OF CHOICE. I GRABBED A TUBE OF Nars Catfight, a rich, semi-matte nude mauve, on my way out of the salon. Easy access to beauty products is one of the perks of the business.

There were lots of cars in the parking lot, but I saw him almost as soon as I pushed the door open. He was sitting in the driver's seat, leaning back with his eyes closed. I was surprised I couldn't hear that big fat snore of his all the way from here.

I was across the parking lot before I knew it. I had a large chocolate brown shoulder bag with me, and I swung it sideways to gain some momentum. Then I picked up speed and hurled it at the windshield as hard as I could.

My ex-husband jumped like he'd been shot and crashed his head into the window beside him. In that instant I understood every wronged woman who had ever run over her husband. Or cut off his penis. I could have killed him. Easily. And then gone back for seconds.

Craig was looking at me with real fear in his eyes. I liked it. He looked down at the ignition, maybe calculating his chances for escape. He reached for the button and lowered the window about two inches. "What the hell was that?" he asked through the crack.

"What the hell was *that*? What the hell are you doing here?"

"Sophia's car's in the shop," he actually said. "She needed a ride."

If there was a gene for getting it, my former husband had clearly been born without it. "You're pond scum," I said. "No, you're lower than pond scum. If there's anything lower than pond scum, you're it." I stretched forward and started picking up the contents of my shoulder bag, which were scattered all over the hood of Craig's stupid Lexus. He didn't even own it. It was leased. I hoped he got completely screwed when it was time to pay for the scratches.

My Nars Catfight, which had somehow ended up on the hood, too, twinkled up at me. I reached for it and covered my lips in slow, soothing strokes. A round hairbrush rolled to the pavement. I bent down and picked it up, then stood and pointed the sharp end at him. "Get off my father's property. Now."

Craig shook his head, like I was the one with the problem. "Bella, it's Sophia's father's property, too."

"Great," I said. "Let me go find him for you. Then he can be the one to kill you."

That did it. Even before he'd left one of my father's daughters for another one of his daughters, my father hadn't been too crazy about Craig, and he knew it. He started up the car. "Just tell Sophia I'm waiting down the street for her, okay?"

"Sure," I said. "I'm all over it."

Up until then, he'd been looking over my head or off to the side of my face. Now he looked me right in the eyes, just for a second. Despite myself, I felt a little jolt of something, possibly insanity. Embarrassing as it would be to admit it, I had this sudden crazy urge to keep him from driving away.

I rested one hand on the hood of the car. Craig flinched. "How're the kids?" I asked.

He put the car into drive. "They're not your kids, Bella," he said. "Forget about them."

✑

I MADE IT TO MY FIRST GIG in record time, possibly propelled by the smoke coming out of my ears. Then I waited. And waited.

I couldn't take it anymore. I fumbled in my makeup kit so I could sneak another quick fix. After some consideration, I decided Revlon Super Lustrous in Pink Afterglow was a good choice for a recently divorced brunette with green eyes and ivory skin who'd just attacked her ex-husband's car and had lips that were a lot dryer than they used to be.

The housekeeper came in again. "He's on the telephone right now," she said.

I rolled down my lipstick fast. I popped the top back on and tossed it into my makeup kit.

"Thanks," I said. I tried to be discreet, but I couldn't resist running my tongue along my lower lip, savoring the rush as the emollients kicked in. The thing about lipstick is that, unlike the rest of life, it never lets you down. At least for the first five minutes. And even when it wears off, there's still the never-ending quest for a better, longer-lasting shade to keep you going.

"Can I get you anything?" she asked.

I knew it wouldn't be polite to say, *Yeah, my client,* so I just shook my head. When the housekeeper turned to walk away, I could see that the seam in her panty hose was crooked beneath her tight khaki skirt. A black skirt might have been more forgiving, but with khaki it really ruined the whole effect. Who even wore panty hose anymore, and the extra points she should have gained for the effort were more than canceled out by the appearance of a crooked crack. Or a possible buttocks imbalance. Apparently she didn't have any friends working in the house. A good friend tells you when your crack looks crooked.

I looked at my watch again. If the governor-running-for-senator actually showed his face during the next five minutes or so, I'd just about make it to my next job. No wonder they'd pawned him off on me. Sophia, who was his regular makeup artist, was also the regular makeup artist for the senator running for reelection against him. Since they were having a pre-season televised brunch debate at Faneuil Hall at eleven, they both needed makeup at the same time. I would have picked the other guy, too.

I grabbed a round black Studio Tech foundation compact and opened it. Yup, it was still MAC NW25. Partly to kill time, and partly just in case he turned out to be lighter or darker than he looked in the newspapers and on television, I reached into my kit and pulled out NW23 and NW30. I should have checked in with Sophia, but we weren't exactly speaking.

I'd commandeered one of the bay windows in the library to arrange my makeup, and then I'd pulled a wing chair over in front of it. It was my best shot at getting some decent light in this mausoleum. The gold and maroon velvet drapes appeared to have been there since the Boston Tea Party. The dark, leathery books on the floor-to-ceiling shelves didn't look much newer either.

My cell phone vibrated and danced around inside my

purse. I wouldn't normally answer it while I was on a job, but because the client wasn't there yet, I reached in and picked it up. "Hello," I whispered.

"He's off the phone now," the housekeeper's voice whispered back.

I held out my cell phone and looked at it, then put it back to my ear. "Great," I said.

"Can I get you some coffee?"

"Nope," I said. "But thanks for asking."

My stomach growled. Mario had brought in breakfast sandwiches for everybody this morning, but I'd forgotten to grab one on my way out of the salon. Craig's Lexus would probably have ended up wearing it anyway, so I supposed it didn't really matter.

Off and on for the last hour, I'd been eyeing a huge library ladder on rollers that hooked over a brass track way up near the ceiling. I walked over to it. I put one foot up on the second rung, gave a little push, and lifted my other foot off the floor. It was kind of like riding a very tall scooter. Maybe I could at least find a decent book to flip through while I waited. I wondered if Governor What's His Name had actually read any of these, or if a decorator had found them for him. Massachusetts didn't have a governor's mansion, so this was probably just an over-priced rental.

I was halfway down one wall and picking up speed, when the housekeeper cleared her throat behind me. I figured it would be undignified to say *Oops,* so I just braked with my free foot and climbed off. I pulled my periwinkle tank top down to meet my chocolate brown capris. "Nice to see you again," I said. Not for the first time I noticed that her upper lip could use a good waxing.

"He's almost here," the housekeeper said. "He said to tell you it only takes him four minutes."

I wasn't sure that was something he should be calling attention to in an election year, but I knew my place, so I didn't say anything.

"He's eating his eggs, then he'll brush. Then he'll have me call for the car. And then he'll be in." She looked over at the window where my stuff had been camped out almost as long as the dust in the drapes. "Are you sure you're all set for him?"

A man poked his head through the heavy wooden doorway. He took a minute to look me up and down, in that creepy way at least one teacher in every high school in America has been checking out his students since the beginning of time. I glared at him. He was shorter and paler than the governor, or at least the way I imagined the governor, probably only an NW 15. His lips were chapped, and his skin looked a little flaky, too. Moisture starts from the inside, so upping his water intake and adding some fish oil capsules would be his best bet. Of course, class starts from the inside, too, and as far as I could see, he didn't have a prayer in that department.

He finally finished ogling me and put his hands in his pockets. "And what are you pretty gals up to in here?" he asked.

The housekeeper tugged at the waistband of her khaki skirt in a fruitless attempt to realign things behind her. "We're just waiting to give the governor a little touch of makeup before his interview," she said.

The man shook his head. "Makeup," he said. "Better him than me, I guess." He leaned back into the hallway. "Gals," he yelled. "Free makeup in the library. Any takers?"

The look I gave him should have curled his eyelashes, but he didn't appear to notice. An anorexic blond with the wrong shade of hair for her complexion strolled in, gave me a bored look, then walked back out. The man followed her. The housekeeper followed the man.

I stood alone.

Sometimes the makeup artist is like a rock star. She's the guru you've been searching for. She can help you change your looks and maybe even your life. Other times, the makeup artist is like a maid. The toughest part is that you never know which one it's going to be when you walk through the door. Clearly, I was not having a rock star kind of day so far.

I walked over to a shelf, closed my eyes, and grabbed a book. I was hoping for a good one, but it turned out to be something boring about torts. Whatever they are. For lack of a better idea, I balanced the book on top of my head and took a couple of long, gliding steps. In health class back in sixth grade, we'd actually had to practice this to improve our posture. In hindsight, it wasn't a bad idea. It's not makeup, but good posture can go a long way toward creating the illusion of beauty.

And not to be depressing, but aren't some of the best parts of life really just an illusion?

IN BESTSELLING AUTHOR CLAIRE COOK'S LATEST ROMANTIC comedy, we follow Ginger Walsh as she navigates her life after moving back home into her parents' FROG (Finished Room Over Garage) to hilarious and poignant results. The bonds of sisterhood, the meaning of success, the highs and lows of singlehood, dealing with families and their many quirks—*Life's a Beach* is full of interesting and fun themes to discuss, and the questions below are intended to assist your reading group's conversation about this book.

Discussion Questions

1. Are you a Ginger? Do you have a sister just like Geri? Do you think most women you know fall into one category or the other?

2. Have you ever met an Allison Flagg in real life? Was she dead-heading a beach rose?

3. Do you think Ginger ended up with the person she was meant to be with? If you could date either Noah or the gaffer, which one would you pick and why? Do you think their characters are based on real men, and if so, do you think Claire Cook has their phone numbers?

4. The father in *Life's a Beach* is a bit of a dump picker. Do you have a family member who can't stay away from the dump? Is there a Take It or Leave It, a Put'n'Take, or a Swap Shop in your town? (Or a great dumpster in your city?) What's the best thing you ever found there?

5. Ginger Walsh, the heroine of *Life's a Beach*, is transitioning from a life in sales to what she hopes will be a more fulfilling life as a sea glass artist. Claire Cook always wanted to be a novelist, yet didn't go after her dream until she was in her forties. If you decided to quit your current job, what dream would you pursue?

6. Who is your favorite minor character in *Life's a Beach*? Why?

7. Would you ever let one of your own children become a child actor? Why or why not?

8. Ginger's older sister, Geri, is struggling with how to celebrate her fiftieth birthday. What will/did you do for yours? Of all the ideas listed in the "User's Guide to the Fun, Feisty, and Fabulous" at the back of the book, which one would you most like to try?

9. When book groups met to discuss *Must Love Dogs*, they often served Sarah's Winey Macaroni and Cheese, made without butter, with white wine instead of milk, and in wineglasses for best effect. What will your book group serve when discussing *Life's a Beach*? (Don't forget to post your great ideas on EveryWomansVoice.com!)

10. Which scene in *Life's a Beach* made you laugh the hardest? Which one brought a tear to your eye? Which one gave you the biggest jolt of recognition?

Q. LIFE'S A BEACH *is the story of two sisters finding themselves, and each other, in midlife. What made you decide to write a novel about sisters?*

A. I'm always the last to know what my novels are really about, so it wasn't until readers started telling me they couldn't wait to send a copy to their sisters, or reading it made them want to call their sisters, or even wish they had a sister, that I realized *Life's a Beach* is about two sisters. Nobody loves you like a sister, or drives you crazier.

Q. *Their interaction is hilarious, and it feels so true to life. Do you have a sister?*

A. Oh, yeah. Actually I have four of them, plus three brothers. We're scattered all over the country now, but we're still very much, in order of birth, DannyClaireCathyMary-SusieJimmyTriciaandKevin.

Q. *Could you pick out a Ginger and a Geri in the group?*

A. I'm sure there are little bits of my sisters in both Ginger and Geri. Still, my fiction never feels particularly autobiographical to me. It's as if I take all the things that are real, and all the stories I've heard, plus everything I imagine, and put them into a paper bag, shake them up, and then take them out in a completely new configuration. I guess that's my Shake 'n' Bake theory of writing a novel.

I relate to all the characters, both two- and four-legged, in my novels. I think you have to, at least to some degree, in order to write the characters. It's all about being a good eavesdropper, and it's all grist for the mill. I've always been that person at the restaurant listening to the conversation at the next table, at *your* table. It's nice to finally have found a career where that becomes nondeviant behavior.

Q. *How did having your second novel,* MUST LOVE DOGS, *made into a major motion picture starring Diane Lane and John Cusack inspire the movie scenes in* LIFE'S A BEACH?

A. I loved everything about hanging around during the filming of the *Must Love Dogs* movie and really wanted to share some of that experience with readers when I wrote *Life's a Beach*. So I took lots of notes on the movie set, and in the first draft of the novel, the fictional movie took place in Hollywood. But the Hollywood parts didn't seem as fresh as they might be, so in the next draft of the novel, I moved the movie to Cape Cod, where it really came alive!

Q. *When did you first know you were a writer?*

A. When I was three. My mother entered me in a contest to name the Fizzies whale, and I won in my age group. It's quite possible that mine was the only entry in my age group since "Cutie Fizz" was enough to win my family a six-month supply of Fizzies tablets (root beer was the best flavor) and a half dozen turquoise plastic mugs with removable handles. I majored in film and creative writing in college and fully expected that the day after graduation, I would go into labor and a brilliant novel would emerge, fully formed, like giving birth.

Q. *So what happened?*

A. In a word: nothing. I guess I knew how to write, but not *what* to write. Looking back, I can see that I had to live my life so I'd have something to write about, and if I could give my younger self some good advice, it would be not to beat myself up for the next couple of decades. When I was in my forties and sitting in my minivan outside my daughter's swim practice at 5 A.M. it hit me that I might live my whole life without ever once going after my dream of writing a novel. So, for the next six months I wrote a rough draft in the pool parking lot, and it sold to the first publisher who asked to read it.

So many women have written to say that my story has been an inspiration to them, and I hope that's true. My first novel was published when I was forty-five, and at fifty I walked the red carpet at the Hollywood premiere of the movie version of my second novel.

Q. *Do you think you'll ever write a sad book?*
A. In one of the many gifts of midlife, I've learned that I don't have to write everybody's books, just mine. I read voraciously and widely, but I think my gift as a novelist is to make people laugh. And also to recognize themselves and their quirky families and maybe feel a little bit better about them.

Q. *Philosophically speaking, do you think life really is a beach?*
A. I guess I'd have to say yes, in both senses. Life really can be a bitch sometimes. Just when you start to think you have it all together—bam! And yet, there are certainly so many days that are just a walk on the beach, and I think we have to be ready to enjoy each and every one of them.

CLAIRE COOK is the bestselling author of *Must Love Dogs*, *Multiple Choice*, and *Ready to Fall*, as well as the upcoming *Summer Blowout*. She teaches workshops for aspiring writers and women coming into their own at midlife, and has had previous stints as a fitness teacher and dance and aerobics choreographer. She lives on the South Shore of Massachusetts, often called the Irish Riviera, with her husband, where they are occasionally visited by their borderline adult children and their laundry.